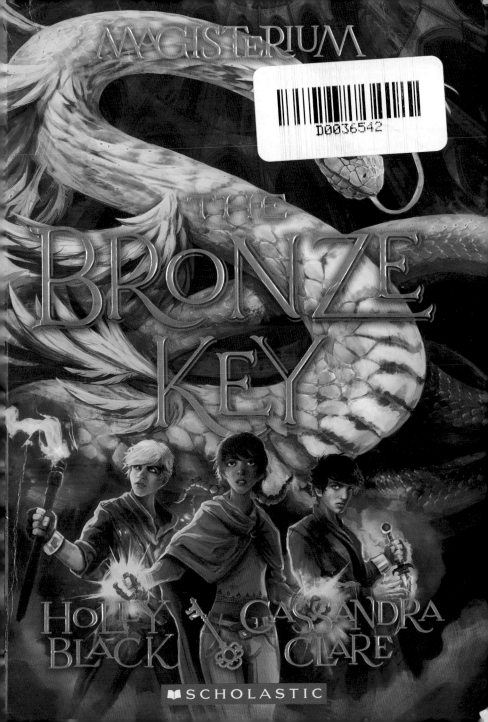

MAGISTERIUM

THE

BRONZE
KEY

HOLLY
BLACK

CASSANDRA
CLARE

SCHOLASTIC

Also by
HOLLY BLACK *and*
CASSANDRA CLARE

THE IRON TRIAL

THE COPPER GAUNTLET

FOR JONAH LOWELL CHURCHILL,
WHO MAY BE THE EVIL TWIN

↑≈△○@

MAGISTERIUM

BOOK THREE

THE BRONZE KEY

HOLLY BLACK *and* CASSANDRA CLARE

WITH ILLUSTRATIONS BY
SCOTT FISCHER

SCHOLASTIC INC.

Copyright © 2016 by Holly Black and Cassandra Claire LLC
Illustrations © 2016 by Scott Fischer

This book was originally published in hardcover by Scholastic Press in 2016.

All rights reserved. Published by Scholastic Inc., *Publishers since 1920*. SCHOLASTIC and associated logos are trademarks and/or registered trademarks of Scholastic Inc.

The publisher does not have any control over and does not assume any responsibility for author or third-party websites or their content.

No part of this publication may be reproduced, stored in a retrieval system, or transmitted in any form or by any means, electronic, mechanical, photocopying, recording, or otherwise, without written permission of the publisher. For information regarding permission, write to Scholastic Inc., Attention: Permissions Department, 557 Broadway, New York, NY 10012.

This book is a work of fiction. Names, characters, places, and incidents are either the product of the author's imagination or are used fictitiously, and any resemblance to actual persons, living or dead, business establishments, events, or locales is entirely coincidental.

ISBN 978-0-545-52232-8

10 9 8 7 6 5 4 3 2 1   17 18 19 20 21

Printed in the U.S.A.   40
First printing 2017

Book design by Christopher Stengel

CHAPTER ONE

CALL MADE A few final tweaks to his robot right before sending him into the "ring" — a section of garage floor outlined in blue chalk. He considered it the fighting zone for the robots he and Aaron had painstakingly built out of car parts, metal magic, and a lot of duct tape. On that gasoline-soaked floor, one of their robots would be tragically rent to pieces and the other would emerge victorious. One would rise and the other would fall. One would —

Aaron's robot chugged forward. One of its little arms shot out, wobbled, and beheaded Call's robot. Sparks fizzed in the air.

"No fair!" Call yelled.

Aaron snorted. He had a smudge of dirt on his cheek and some of his hair was sticking straight up after he'd run his hands through it in frustration. The relentless North Carolina heat had left him with a sunburned nose and freckling on his cheeks. He didn't look at all like the polished Makar who'd spent the previous summer at garden parties, chatting with dull, important grown-ups.

"I guess I'm just better at building robots than you," Aaron said carelessly.

"Oh, yeah?" Call replied, concentrating. His robot began to move, slowly at first, then faster as metal magic reanimated its headless body. "Take *that*."

Call's robot lifted an arm, and fire shot out like water from a hose, spraying Aaron's robot, whose whole body began to smoke. Aaron tried to summon water magic to douse it, but it was too late — the duct tape was burning. His robot collapsed in a pile of smoking parts.

"Woo-hoo!" Call cried out — he'd never taken any of his dad's advice about being a gracious winner to heart. Havoc, Call's Chaos-ridden wolf, woke suddenly when a spark landed on his fur. He began to bark.

"Hey!" Call's father, Alastair, yelled, running out of the house and looking around with slightly wild eyes. "Not so close to my car! I just fixed that thing."

Despite the scolding, Call felt relaxed. He'd felt pretty relaxed all summer. He'd even stopped assigning himself Evil Overlord Points. As far as the world knew, the Enemy of Death, Constantine Madden, was dead, defeated by Alastair. Only Aaron and Tamara, frenemy Jasper deWinter, and Call's father knew the truth — that Call *was* Constantine Madden reborn, but without any of his memories and, hopefully, without his penchant for evil.

Since the world thought Constantine was dead and Call's friends didn't care, Call was off the hook. Aaron, despite being a Makar, could go back to goofing around with Call. They'd be heading back to the Magisterium soon, and this time they'd be Bronze Year students, which meant they'd be getting into some really awesome magic — fighting spells and flying spells.

Everything was better. Everything was great.

Also, Aaron's robot was a smoking wreck.

Really, it was hard for Call to imagine how things could get better.

"I hope you guys remembered," said Alastair. "Tonight is the party at the Collegium. You know — the one in our honor."

Aaron and Call looked at each other in horror. They had forgotten, of course. The days had gone by in a blur of skateboarding and ice cream and movies and video games, and both of them had completely blanked out on the fact that the Assembly of Mages was throwing a victory party at the Collegium, in recognition of the fact that the Enemy of Death had been defeated after thirteen long years of cold war.

The Assembly had chosen five people to honor: Call, Aaron, Tamara, Jasper, and Alastair. Call had been surprised that Alastair had agreed to go — Alastair had hated magic, the Magisterium, and everything to do with mages for as long as Call could remember. Call suspected Alastair had agreed because he wanted to see the Assembly clap for Call and for everyone to agree that Call was on the side of good. That he was a hero.

Call swallowed, suddenly nervous. "I don't have anything to wear," he protested.

"Neither do I." Aaron looked startled.

"But Tamara and her family bought you all those fancy

clothes last year," Call pointed out. Tamara's parents had been so excited at the thought that their daughter was friends with a Makar, one of the rare mages who could control chaos magic, that they had practically adopted Aaron, bringing him into their house and spending money on expensive haircuts and clothes and parties.

Call still couldn't quite understand why Aaron had decided to spend this summer with him and not the Rajavis, but Aaron had been very firm about it.

"I grew out of those," Aaron replied. "All I have are jeans and T-shirts."

"That's why we're going to the mall," said Alastair, holding up his car keys. "Come on, boys."

"Tamara's parents took me to Brooks Brothers," Aaron said as they headed toward Alastair's collection of refurbished cars. "It was kind of weird."

Call thought of their tiny local mall and grinned. "Well, get ready for a different kind of weird," he said. "We're going to travel backward in time without magic."

↑ ≈ △ ○ @

"I think I might be allergic to this material," said Aaron, standing in front of a full-length mirror in the back of JL Dimes. They sold everything — tractors, clothes, cheap dishwashers. Alastair always bought his work overalls there. Call hated it.

"It looks fine," said Alastair, who had collected a vacuum cleaner somewhere along their travels through the store and was examining it, probably for parts. He'd also picked up a jacket for himself but had failed to try it on.

Aaron took another look at the alarmingly shiny gray suit. The legs bagged around his ankles and the lapels reminded Call of shark fins.

"Okay," Aaron said meekly. He was always very conscious that everything bought for him was a favor. He knew he didn't have money or parents to get him things. He was always grateful.

Aaron and Call had both lost their mothers. Aaron's father was alive, but in prison, which Aaron didn't like for people to know. To Call, it didn't seem that big of a deal, but that was probably because Call's secret was so much bigger.

"I don't know, Dad," Call said, squinting into the mirror. He was wearing dark blue polyester that was too tight underneath his arms. "These might not be our sizes."

Alastair sighed. "A suit's a suit. Aaron will grow into his. And yours, well — maybe you should try something else. No use getting something that's only good for tonight."

"I'm taking a picture," Call said, pulling out his phone. "Tamara can give us advice. She knows what you're supposed to wear to stuffy mage events."

There was a whoosh as Call texted Tamara the photograph. A few seconds later she texted back: *Aaron looks like a con man who got hit with a shrink ray and you look like you're going to Catholic school.*

Aaron looked over Call's padded shoulder and winced at the message.

"Well?" Alastair asked. "We could duct-tape the legs. Make them look shorter."

"Or," Call said, "we could go to a different store and not embarrass ourselves in front of the Assembly."

Alastair looked from Call to Aaron and gave in with a sigh, putting back his vacuum cleaner. "Okay. Let's go."

It was a relief to get out of the airless, overheated mall. A short car ride later Call and Aaron were standing in front of a thrift shop that dealt in vintage stuff of all kinds, from doilies to dressers to sewing machines. Call had been here before with his dad and remembered that the proprietor, Miranda Keyes, loved vintage clothes. She wore them constantly, without much respect for matching colors or styles, which meant she was often seen wandering around their town in a poodle skirt, go-go boots, and a sequined tank top with a pattern of angry cats.

But Aaron didn't know that. He was looking around, smiling hesitantly, and Call's heart sank. This was going to be even worse than JL Dimes. What had started out kind of funny was starting to make Call feel a little sick inside. He knew his dad was "eccentric" — which was a nice way of saying "weird" — and he'd never really minded, but it wasn't fair that Aaron had to look "eccentric," too. What if all Miranda had was red velvet tuxedoes or something even worse?

It was bad enough that Aaron had spent the summer drinking lemonade from a powder mix, instead of from fresh lemons the way they made it at Tamara's house; sleeping on a military cot that Alastair had set up in Call's room; running through a sprinkler made from knife holes in a garden hose; and eating regular old cereal for breakfast instead of eggs cooked to order by a chef. If Aaron showed up at this party looking stupid, it might be the final straw. Call might lose the Best Friend War for good.

Alastair got out of the car. Call followed his dad and Aaron inside with a sense of foreboding.

The suits were in the back of the room, behind the tables of odd brass musical instruments and the jadeite bowl of rusty keys. It was a lot like Alastair's own shop, Now and Again, except that the ceiling was hung with fur-collared coats and silk scarves, while Alastair specialized in the more industrial end of antiques. Miranda came out of the back and talked to Alastair for a few minutes about what she'd brought back from Brimfield — a huge antiques show up north — and who she'd seen there. Call's dread grew.

Finally, Alastair found his way to telling her what they needed. She gave each of the boys a sharp evaluating look, as though she were looking through them and seeing something else. She did the same thing to Alastair, her eyes narrowing before she disappeared into the back.

Aaron and Call amused themselves by wandering around the store, each one of them trying to find the weirdest object. Aaron had discovered a Batman-shaped alarm clock that said "WAKE UP, BOY WONDER" when he pressed the top, and Call had unearthed a sweater made out of taped-together lollipops, when Miranda reemerged, humming, with a pile of clothes that she stacked on the counter.

The first thing she pulled out was a dressing jacket for Alastair. It looked like it was made from satin with a subtle, deep green pattern to it and a bright silk lining. It was definitely old and weird, but in a not-embarrassing way.

"Now," she said, pointing at Call and Aaron, "your turn."

She handed each one of them a folded linen suit. Aaron's was the color of cream and Call's was dove gray.

"Same as your eyes, Call," said Miranda, looking pleased with herself, as Call and Aaron threw the suits on over their shorts and T-shirts. She clapped her hands and gestured for them to look in the mirror.

Call stared at his reflection. He didn't know much about clothes, but the suit fit him, and he didn't look bizarre. He actually looked kind of grown up. So did Aaron. The light colors made them both look tan.

"Is this for a special occasion?" asked Miranda.

"You could say that." Alastair sounded pleased. "They're both getting awards."

"For, um, community service," said Aaron. He met Call's eyes in the mirror. Call guessed it was only sort of a lie, though most community service didn't involve severed heads.

"Fantastic!" said Miranda. "They both look so handsome."

Handsome. Call had never thought of himself as handsome. *Aaron* was the handsome one. Call was the one who was short, limped, and was too intense and sharp-featured. But he guessed that people selling stuff had to tell you that you looked good. On a whim, Call pulled out his phone, took a picture of his and Aaron's reflections in the mirror, and sent it to Tamara.

A minute later the reply came back. *Nice.* Attached to the message was a short video of someone falling off a chair in surprise. Call couldn't help laughing.

"Do they need anything else?" Alastair asked. "Shoes, cuff links . . . anything?"

"Well, shirts, obviously," Miranda said. "I have a lot of nice ties —"

"I don't need you to buy me anything else, Mr. Hunt," said Aaron, looking anxious. "Really."

"Oh, don't worry about that," Alastair said with a surprising lightness in his voice. "Miranda and I are in the business. We'll work out a trade."

Call looked over at Miranda, to find her smiling. "There was a little Victorian brooch at your store I had my eye on."

At that, Alastair's expression stiffened a little, then relaxed almost immediately into a laugh. "Well, for that, we're definitely taking the cuff links. Shoes, too, if you've got them."

By the time they left, they had huge bags filled with clothes and Call was feeling pretty good. They drove back to the house with barely enough time to take showers and comb their hair. Alastair came out of his bedroom reeking of some ancient cologne and looking snappy in his new jacket and a pair of black trousers he must have unearthed in the back of his closet. Muttering, he immediately started hunting around for his car keys. He barely looked recognizable to Call as the dad who worked around the house in tweed and denim overalls, the dad who'd spent all summer helping them make robots out of spare parts.

He looked like a stranger, which meant Call started to actually think about what was soon to happen.

All summer he'd been feeling pretty smug over the Enemy of Death's demise. Constantine Madden had been dead for years, preserved in a creepy tomb, waiting to have his soul returned to his body. But since no one had known that, the whole mage world had been waiting for Constantine to start up the Third Mage War again. When Callum had brought the Enemy's severed head back to the Magisterium, proof that he was incontrovertibly dead, the whole mage world had breathed a sigh of relief.

What they didn't know was that Constantine's soul lived on — in Call. Tonight the world of mages was going to be honoring the actual Enemy of Death.

Even though Call had no desire to hurt anyone, the threat

of a Third Mage War was far from over. Constantine's second-in-command, Master Joseph, had control of Constantine's Chaos-ridden army. He had the powerful Alkahest, which could destroy chaos wielders like Aaron — and Call. If he got tired waiting for Call to come over to his side, then he might attack all on his own.

Call slumped down at the kitchen table. Havoc, who'd been sleeping under the table, looked up with his disturbing coruscating eyes, as if sensing Call's distress. Although it should have made Call feel better, it actually made him feel a little worse.

He could almost hear Master Joseph's voice: *Good job getting the whole mage world to lower their guard, Call. You can't escape your nature.*

He pushed the thought back firmly. All summer he'd worked on not constantly checking himself to see if he was showing signs of maybe turning out evil. All summer he'd been telling himself that he was Callum Hunt, who had been raised by Alastair Hunt, and he wasn't going to make the same mistakes Constantine Madden had made. He was a different person. He *was*.

A few minutes later, Aaron came out of Call's room, looking dapper in his cream-colored suit. His blond hair was brushed back and even his cuff links shone. He looked just as happy as he ever had in the designer suits that Tamara's family had given him.

Or at least he looked happy until he saw Call and did a double take.

"You okay?" Aaron asked. "You look a little green around the gills. You don't have stage fright, do you?"

"Maybe," Call said. "I'm not used to people looking at me a lot. I mean, people look at me because of my leg sometimes, but it's not a *good* kind of looking."

"Try to think of it as the end scene in *Star Wars* where everyone cheers and Princess Leia puts medals on Han and Luke."

Call raised an eyebrow. "Who's Princess Leia in this visual? Master Rufus?"

Master Rufus was the teacher of their apprentice group at the Magisterium. He was craggy, gruff, and wise, and had a lot more gray hairs than Princess Leia.

"Later," said Aaron solemnly, "he will wear the gold bikini."

Havoc barked. Alastair held up his car keys, triumphant. "Would it help you boys if I promised that tonight is going to be boring and uneventful? The party is supposed to honor us, but I guarantee that it's mostly for the Assembly to congratulate itself."

"You sound like you've been to one of these before," said Call, standing up from the table. He smoothed his suit anxiously — linen wrinkled fast. Already he couldn't wait to get back into jeans and a T-shirt.

"You've seen the wristband Constantine wore when he was a student with me at the Magisterium," said Alastair. "He won a lot of awards and prizes. Our whole apprentice group did."

It was true that Call had seen the wristband. Alastair had sent it to Master Rufus the first year Call had been at the Magisterium. All students were issued wristbands of leather and metal: The metal changed whenever the student entered a new year at the school, and the wristband was also studded with stones, each one representing an accomplishment or talent. Constantine's had more stones than Call had ever seen before.

Call reached to touch his own wristband. It still showed the metal of a second-year Copper student. Like Aaron's, Call's gleamed with the black stone of the Makar. Call's eyes met Aaron's as he dropped his hand, and he could tell Aaron knew what he was thinking — here he was, getting an award, being honored for doing good, and it was still something that made him just like Constantine Madden.

Alastair shook his car keys, jangling Call out of his reverie. "Come on," Alastair said. "The Assembly doesn't like it when its honorees are late."

Havoc tailed them to the door, then sat with a thump and a thin whine. "Can he come?" Call asked his father as they walked out the door. "He'll be good. And he deserves an award, too."

"Absolutely not," said Alastair.

"Is it because you don't trust him around the Assembly?" Call asked, though once he did, he wasn't sure he wanted the answer.

"It's because I don't trust the Assembly around him," Alastair replied with a stern look. Then he headed out the door, leaving Call no choice but to follow.

CHAPTER TWO

THE COLLEGIUM, LIKE the Magisterium, was built in such a way that it was concealed from non-mages. It rested beneath the Virginia coastline, its corridors spiraling deep below the water. Call had heard of its location, but still wasn't prepared for Alastair to stop them as they were walking along a jetty and indicate a grate at their feet, partially concealed under leaves and dirt.

"If you put your ear close to that, you can usually hear an incredibly dull lecture. But tonight, you might actually be able to hear music." Although Alastair's words weren't particularly complimentary to the Collegium, he spoke in a wistful way.

"You never went here, though, right?" Call asked.

"Not as a student," Alastair said. "There was a whole generation of us that mostly didn't go. We were too busy dying in the war."

Sometimes Call thought, uncharitably, that everyone

should have left Constantine Madden alone. Sure, he'd done terrible experiments, putting chaos into the souls of animals and creating the Chaos-ridden. Sure, he'd reanimated the dead, looking for a way to cure death itself and bring back his brother. Sure, he was breaking mage law. But maybe if everyone had left him alone, so many people would still be alive. Call's mother would still be alive.

The real Call would still be alive, too, he couldn't help thinking.

But Call couldn't say any of that, so he said nothing at all. Aaron was looking out over the waves at the setting sun. All summer, having Aaron at the house had felt like having a brother, someone to joke around with, someone who was always there to watch movies or destroy robots. As the drive to the Collegium had gone on, though, Aaron had become quieter. By the time Alastair had parked his silver 1937 Rolls-Royce Phantom near the boardwalk and they had passed a giant weird statue of Poseidon, Aaron had pretty much stopped talking entirely.

"You okay?" Call asked as they walked on.

Aaron shrugged. "I don't know. It's just that I was prepared to be the Makar. I knew it was dangerous and I was scared, but I understood what I had to do. And when people gave me stuff, I understood why. I understood what I owed them in return. But now I don't know what it means to be a Makar. I mean, if there's no war against the Enemy, that's great, but then what do I —"

"We're here," Alastair said, coming to a stop. Waves crashed on the black rocks around them, kicking up salty spray and frothing in little tide pools. Call felt the light rain of it, like a cool breath across his face.

He wanted to say something to reassure Aaron, but Aaron wasn't looking at him anymore. He was frowning at a scuttling crab. It crossed a braid of seaweed, tangled with a piece of old rope, the threadbare ends floating in the water like someone's unbound hair.

"Is this safe?" Call asked instead.

"As safe as anything connected with the mages," Alastair said, tapping his foot on the ground in a quick, repetitive rhythm. For a moment, nothing happened — then there was a grating sound and a square of rock slid aside to reveal a long spiraling staircase. It wound down and down, like the one in the library of the Magisterium, except there weren't rows of books here, only the curving staircase and, at the very bottom, a glimpse of a square of marble floor.

Call swallowed hard. It would have been a long walk for anyone, but for him, it seemed impossible. His leg would be cramping by the time they got halfway down. If he stumbled, it would be a very scary fall.

"Um," said Call, "I don't think I can . . ."

"Levitate yourself," Aaron said quietly.

"What?"

"Levitation is air magic. We're surrounded by rock — dirt and stone. Push down on it and it'll lift you. You don't have to fly, just float a few inches off the ground."

Call glanced toward Alastair. Even now, he was a little wary of doing magic around his father, after all the years Alastair had spent telling him that magic was evil, that mages were evil and wanted to kill him. But Alastair, glancing down at the long stairway, just nodded curtly.

"I'll go down first," Aaron said. "If you fall, I'll catch you."

"At least we'll go down together." Call started to back down the stairs, putting one foot carefully in front of the other. Call could hear the noise of voices and clinking silverware far below. He took a deep breath and reached out to touch the force of the earth — to reach into it and draw it into himself, then push off, as if he were pushing off from the side of a swimming pool into the water.

He felt the drag on his muscles and then a lightness as his body rose into the air. As Aaron had instructed, he didn't try to lift himself more than a few inches. With just enough space to clear the steps, he drifted downward. Though he wanted to tell Aaron he wasn't going to fall, it was kind of nice knowing that if he did, someone was poised to catch him.

Alastair's steady footsteps were also reassuring. Carefully, they made their way down, Alastair and Aaron walking, Call hovering just above the stairs. A few steps from the bottom, he let himself drift gently down. He hit the stairs and stumbled.

It was Alastair who reached out to grab his shoulder. "Steady on," he said.

"I'm fine," Call said gruffly, and limped quickly down the last few steps. His muscles ached a little, but nothing like the pain he would have been in if he'd walked. Aaron was already on the ground and gave him a big grin.

"Check it out," he said. "The Collegium."

"Whoa." Call had never seen anything like it. The spaces of the Magisterium were often magnificent, and some were enormous, but they were always clearly underground caverns carved from natural rock. This was different.

A huge hall opened in front of them. The walls, the floor, and the columns that held up the roof were all gold-flecked white marble. A tapestry map of the Collegium decorated one wall. There was a huge dais that ran along one side of the room, and multicolored banners hung behind it. Sayings from the works of Paracelsus and other famous alchemists were printed across them in gold. *All is interrelated*, said one. *Fire and earth, air and water. All are but one thing, not four, not two, and not three, but one. Where they are not together is only an incomplete piece.*

A huge chandelier hung from the ceiling. Fat crystals dangled from it like teardrops, scattering light in all directions over the large crowd of people — members of the Assembly in golden robes, Masters of the Magisterium in black, and everyone else in elegant suits and dresses.

"Fancy," said Alastair, grimly. "Too fancy."

"Yeah," said Call. "The Magisterium is a real dump. I had no idea."

"There aren't any windows," Aaron said, looking around. "Why aren't there windows?"

"Probably because we're underwater," Call answered. "Wouldn't the pressure break the glass?"

Before they could continue their speculation, Master North, head of the Magisterium, came toward them out of the crowd. "Alastair. Aaron. Call. You're late."

"Underwater traffic," said Call.

Aaron elbowed him.

Master North gave him a stern look. "Anyway, you're here. The others are waiting with the Assembly."

"Master North," said Alastair with a curt nod. "My apologies for our lateness, but we are the honorees. You could hardly start without us, could you?"

Master North gave a thin smile. Both he and Alastair appeared as though they might become quickly exhausted by the strain of being civil. "Come with me."

Aaron and Call shared a look before following the adults through the room. As the crowd grew more tightly packed, people started to press in at them, staring at Aaron — and at Call, too. One middle-aged man with a paunch caught Call's arm.

"Thank you," the man whispered before letting him go. "Thank you for killing Constantine."

I didn't. Call stumbled on as hands reached out of the crowd. He shook some, avoided others, gave one a high five and then felt stupid.

"Is this what it's like for you all the time?" he asked Aaron.

"Not before last summer," Aaron said. "Anyway, I thought you wanted to be a hero."

I guess it's better than being a villain, Call thought, but let the words die on his tongue.

Finally they came to where the Assembly was waiting, separated from the rest of the room by floating silver ropes. Anastasia Tarquin, one of the most powerful members of the Assembly, was talking to Tamara's mother. Tarquin was an extremely tall, older woman with masses of upswept, bright silver hair, and Tamara's mother had to crane her neck to look at her.

Tamara was standing with Celia and Jasper, all three of them laughing about something. It was the first time Call had seen Tamara since the start of summer. She was wearing a bright yellow dress that made her brown skin glow. Her hair fell in heavy, dark waves around her face and down her back.

Celia had done something weird and elegant and complicated with her blond hair. She was in a seafoam-green gauzy thing that seemed to waft around her.

Both the girls turned toward Call and Aaron. Tamara's face lit up and Celia smiled. Call felt a little bit like someone had kicked him in the chest. Weirdly, it wasn't an unpleasant feeling.

Tamara ran over to Aaron, giving him a quick hug. Celia hung back as though struck with sudden shyness. It was Jasper who came up to Call, clapping him on the shoulder, which was a relief, as nothing about Jasper made Call feel as if his world was tilting. Jasper just looked like his usual smug self, his dark hair sticking up with hair gel.

"So, how's the ole E-o-D, himself?" Jasper whispered, making Call flinch. "You're the star of the show."

Call hated that Jasper knew the truth about him. Even if he was fairly sure Jasper would never reveal his secret, it didn't stop Jasper from making comments and needling him every chance he got.

"Come," Master Rufus said. "Time is wasting. We have a ceremony to attend, whether we want to or not."

With that, Call, Aaron, Tamara, Jasper, Master Rufus, Master Milagros, and Alastair were herded up onto a raised dais. Celia waved good-bye as they went.

Call knew they were in trouble when he saw there were chairs up on the dais. Chairs meant a long ceremony. He wasn't wrong. The ceremony went by in a blur, but it was an extended and boring blur. Various Assembly members made speeches about how integral they personally had been to the mission. "They couldn't have done it without me," said a blond Assembly member Call had never seen before. Master Rufus and Master Milagros were praised for having such fine apprentices. The Rajavis were praised for having raised such a brave daughter. Alastair was praised for his diligence in leading their expedition. The kids themselves were credited with being the greatest heroes of their time.

They were applauded and kissed on their cheeks and patted on their backs. Alastair was given a heavy medal that swung on his neck. He began to look a little wild-eyed after they stood up for the sixth round of applause.

No one mentioned severed heads or the whole misunderstanding where they had thought Alastair was in league with the Enemy or how no one at the Magisterium had even known that the kids were going on the mission. Everyone acted like this had been the plan all along.

They were all given their Bronze Year wristbands and stones of glimmering red beryl to show the worth of their accomplishment. Call wondered what the red stone meant exactly — every stone color had a meaning: yellow for healing, orange for bravery, and so on.

Call stepped up to have Master Rufus place the stone in his wristband. The red beryl went in with a click, like a lock being shut. "Callum Hunt, Makar!" someone in the room shouted. Someone else stood up and cried out Aaron's name. Call let the shouts wash over him like a bewildering tide. "Call and Aaron! Makaris, Makaris, Makaris!"

Call felt a hand brush his shoulder. It was Anastasia Tarquin. "In Europe," she said, "when they discover someone is a chaos mage, they don't celebrate them. They kill them."

Call turned to stare at her in shock, but she was already

moving away through the crowd of Assembly members. Master Rufus, who clearly hadn't heard her — no one had but Call — came forward toward Aaron and Call. "Makars," he said. "This isn't just a celebration. We have something to discuss."

"Right here?" Aaron asked, clearly startled.

Rufus shook his head. "It's time for you to see something very few apprentices ever see. The War Room. Come with me."

Tamara looked after Aaron and Call worriedly as they were led away through the crowd. "The War Room?" Aaron muttered. "What's that?"

"I don't know," Call whispered back. "I thought the war was over."

Master Rufus led them expertly behind the floating ropes, avoiding the eyes of the crowd, until they reached a door set into the far wall. It was a bronze door, carved with the shapes of tall ships sailing, cannons, and explosions over the sea.

Rufus pushed the door open, and they entered the War Room. Call's words about why there were no windows echoed in his own head — because there were plenty of windows here. There was a marble floor, but every other surface was glass, and the glass glowed with enchanted light. Beyond the glass Call could see sea creatures swimming by: fish with brightly colored stripes, sharks with coal-black eyes, graceful flapping rays.

"Whoa," said Aaron, craning his neck. "Look up."

Call did and saw the water above them, glowing with the light of the surface. A school of silvery fish shot by and then pivoted according to some unseen signal, all of them racing off in the new direction.

"Sit," Assemblyman Graves — old, grumpy, and mean — said. "We realize this is a celebration, but there are things we must discuss. Master Rufus, you and your two apprentices should sit here." He indicated chairs beside him.

Call and Aaron exchanged a reluctant glance before shuffling over to take their seats. The rest of the Assembly members were arranging themselves around the table, making small talk. Above them, visible beyond the glass, an eel ribboned its way through the sea and snapped up a slow-moving fish. Call wondered if it was an ominous sign.

Once the room had quieted down, Graves resumed speaking. "Thanks to the efforts of our honorees this evening, we are having a very different discussion than we could have anticipated having. Constantine Madden is dead." He looked around the room as if waiting for that information to sink in. Call couldn't help feeling that if it hadn't sunk in yet, it never would, given how many times *The Enemy of Death is dead!* had been repeated during the honoring ceremony. "And yet" — Graves slammed his hand down on the table, making Call jump — "we *cannot* rest! Constantine Madden might be defeated, but his army is still out there. We must strike now and root out the Chaos-ridden and all of Constantine's allies."

A murmur went around the room. "No one has been able to detect any sign of the Chaos-ridden since Madden's death," said Master North. "It's as if they disappeared when he died."

Several mages looked hopeful at this, but Graves only shook his head grimly. "They are out there somewhere. We must assemble teams to hunt them down and destroy them."

Call felt a little queasy. The Chaos-ridden were basically mindless zombies, all their humanity pushed out to make room for chaos. But he'd heard them speak. Seen them move, even kneel to him. The idea of a pyre of their burning bodies made his stomach turn.

"What about Chaos-ridden animals?" asked Anastasia Tarquin. "Most of them never served the Enemy of Death; they're the descendants of the unfortunate creatures that did. Unlike the Chaos-ridden people, they're alive, not reanimated bodies."

"Still, they're dangerous. I move that we exterminate them all," Graves said.

"Not Havoc!" Call yelled before anyone could stop him.

The members of the Assembly turned in his direction. Anastasia had a small smile on her face, as though she'd enjoyed his outburst. She seemed like someone who didn't mind when things didn't go the way everyone else expected. Her gaze slid to Aaron, gauging his reaction.

"The pet of the Makaris," she said, looking back at Call. "Surely Havoc can be exempted."

"And the Order of Disorder has been studying other Chaos-ridden beasts. Keeping some alive for their research has value," added Rufus.

The Order of Disorder was a small group of rebellious mages who lived in the woods just outside the Magisterium, studying chaos magic. Call wasn't sure what he thought of them. They'd tried to force Aaron to stay and help with their chaos experiments. They hadn't been nice about it, either.

"Yes, yes," said Graves dismissively. "Perhaps a small number can be saved, although I have never much cared for the Order of Disorder, as you well know. We need to keep an eye on them, to be sure that none of Constantine's conspirators are hiding out among them. And we need to find Master Joseph. We cannot forget that he's still dangerous and will almost certainly attempt to use the Alkahest against us."

Anastasia Tarquin made a small note on a paper. Several other mages murmured among themselves; quite a few were sitting up straight, trying to make themselves look important. Master Rufus was nodding, but Call suspected he didn't much like Graves, either.

"Lastly, we must make sure that Callum Hunt and Aaron Stewart use their Makar abilities in the service of the Assembly and the larger mage community. Master Rufus, it is going to be integral that you report regularly on their teaching as they move into their Bronze, Silver, and Gold Years, readying themselves to go to the Collegium."

"They are *my* apprentices." Master Rufus raised a single brow. "I need to have independence to teach them as I see fit."

"We can discuss that later," said Graves. "They are Makars before they are students of the Magisterium. It would be well for both you and them to remember that."

Aaron shot Call a worried glance. Master Rufus looked grim.

Graves went on. "Due to the Magisterium's proximity to the largest number of Chaos-ridden animals, we're going to expect the school to take point on their destruction."

"You can't possibly expect the students of the Magisterium to spend their school time murdering animals," protested Master Rufus, rising to his feet. "I object strongly to this suggestion. Master North?"

"I agree with Rufus," said Master North, after a pause.

"They're not animals. They're monsters," Graves argued. "The woods around the Magisterium have been full of them for years, and we haven't treated the situation with the serious-ness that we could, because the Enemy could always have made more. But now — now we have a chance to extermi-nate them."

"They may be monsters," said Rufus, "but they look like animals. And there are those, like Havoc, who give us all pause and reason to wonder if they might be saved rather than destroyed. Surely it is in the interests of the whole mage world for our students to learn mercy. Constantine Madden," he added, in a low voice, "never did."

Graves shot him a look of something very close to hatred. "Fine," he said in a clipped voice. "The removal of the Chaos-ridden animals will be dealt with by a team headed up by myself and other members of the Assembly. Please don't expect me to entertain any complaining about how we'll be cluttering up the woods where your students practice. This is more important than your school."

"Of course," Master Rufus said, still in the same low voice. Call tried to catch his eye, but Rufus was imperturbable.

"That leaves us with one last point of business," said Graves. "The spy."

This time the murmur that ran around the table was very loud indeed.

"We have reason to believe there is a spy in the Magisterium," Graves pronounced. "Someone freed the elemental monster Automotones and sent him to kill the Makar Aaron Stewart."

Everyone looked at Call and Aaron.

"Yep," Call said. "That did happen."

Graves nodded. "We will be placing various spy traps in the school, and Anastasia will be guarding the tunnels where the great elementals are kept. The spy will be caught and dealt with appropriately."

Spy traps? Aaron mouthed to Call. Call tried not to laugh, because what he was picturing was a big pit in the ground hidden with important papers or something. But since, for once, it seemed like the Assembly and the Magisterium had an actual plan to take care of a real danger, maybe Call could spend his Bronze Year just learning stuff and getting into the regular, fun kind of trouble instead of the world-ruining kind.

So long as he kept Havoc out of the woods and away from the animal murderers.

So long as Master Joseph didn't come back.

So long as there really was nothing wrong with his soul.

Call,
I need to talk
to you alone.
Meet me in
the trophy room.
— Celia

CHAPTER THREE

A**FTER THE ASSEMBLY** meeting, Call and Aaron were free to return to the party. Hors d'oeuvres were being passed around, but Call didn't feel hungry. He was thinking about Havoc's Chaos-ridden family and all the other Chaos-ridden animals out in the forest. Call didn't remember *being* Constantine Madden, but that didn't mean that he didn't owe something to the innocent creatures Constantine had changed. There had to be something he could do.

"So how was the secret meeting?" Jasper asked, walking up with Celia and Tamara. All three of them looked bright-eyed and relaxed, like they'd been laughing a lot. Or maybe dancing. Some dancing had started on the other side of the party. Call eyed it with suspicion and alarm.

"Weird," Aaron said, oblivious to Call's mood. He grabbed a cheese puff off a passing waiter's plate and stuffed it into his mouth. Then he made a muffled sound, appearing as though he'd planned to say more before hunger had taken over.

Call filled them in. "It was all about Chaos-ridden people and animals. Getting rid of them, basically."

"Not Havoc!" Tamara said, dark eyes horrified. Call was pleased with her for having the same reaction he'd had. It was nice to be reminded that Havoc was also important to his two best friends.

Two more waiters came by with plates and snacks. Call took three shrimp toasts from one and a chicken skewer from the other. He should probably try to eat something, he thought, though his stomach felt knotted. Jasper piled an enormous amount of food onto his plate and began shoveling his way through it with the determination of a shark.

"Havoc got a pass," Call said. "But basically Graves is in cleanup mode. Everything that's left over from the time of the Enemy of Death, he wants erased."

Tamara was clearly bubbling over with questions. "Did you —" she began, but then looked over at Celia and seemed to think better of it. Celia hadn't been with them when they'd left the school to try to find Alastair. She didn't know Call's secret. "Never mind. We should just have fun tonight. Aaron, come on, dance with me."

Aaron managed to grab another cheese puff before he was seized by Tamara. He handed his empty plate to Jasper and disappeared into the mass of dancing people in a swirl of Tamara's yellow skirts.

Celia gave Call a hopeful look he pretended not to see. With his leg, he had no hope of doing anything but embarrassing himself on a dance floor. Call smiled at her but said nothing. After the awkward moment had stretched out as long as an awkward moment possibly could, Celia sighed.

"I'm going to get a drink," she said, and headed off toward an enormous punch bowl.

"Smooth," said Jasper. "I guess everything they say about Constantine having deadly charisma was maybe not so accurate."

Out of all of them, Jasper was the only one who Call sometimes caught looking at him with suspicion or worry, as if maybe he didn't know him at all.

"I'm not the Enemy," Call said under his breath.

"Let's test that," said Jasper, glancing at Call's plate. "The Enemy of Death would never give me his last chicken skewer."

Call handed it over without comment. He wasn't that hungry, anyway.

"The Enemy of Death would also never introduce me to that hot girl who just waved at you."

Call looked over in surprise to see that the hot girl Jasper was talking about was actually a girl he'd met before, a friend of Tamara's older sister, Kimiya. She had long black hair and elegant cheekbones. She waved when she saw him looking in her direction.

Call gave Jasper his most evil look. "You're right," he said, and walked off to find Alastair. He thought he'd seen him talking to Anastasia Tarquin, her silver hair bobbing above the crowd. Call was pushing through a knot of people by the drinks table when someone tapped him on the shoulder.

It was the girl Jasper had mentioned, Jennifer Matsui. She was a Gold Year, like Kimiya, and up close she was a head taller than Call.

"Callum!" she said brightly. "Congratulations on the award."

"Thanks," Call said, craning his neck to see Jasper staring at him from across the room, as if he couldn't believe what was happening. "It was a very good . . . award."

That hadn't been what he'd meant to say at all.

"I have something for you," she said, dropping her voice to a low, conspiratorial whisper. "A pretty blond girl gave it to me."

She held out a folded piece of paper with Call's name scribbled on it. Puzzled, he took it. Jennifer blew him a kiss and bounced off through the crowd, back toward Kimiya and the small knot of older students who were giggling together. Call saw a familiar face — Alex Strike, one of the few older students he was friends with. Alex and Kimiya had broken up last year, but from the way they were standing and laughing together, either they'd gotten back together or at least they were friends again.

Call unfolded the note.

Call, I need to talk to you alone. Meet me in the trophy room. — Celia.

For a long moment, he just stared at it, heartbeat accelerating. He tried to tell himself that he shouldn't be worried, that Celia was his friend and that they'd taken lots of walks with Havoc outside the Magisterium. This wasn't much different from that. But in his experience, when someone "needed to talk to you," it was usually about something bad.

Or it could be the other thing, a *dating* thing. He'd seen the Bronze Year students hold hands and share drinks and giggle a lot in the Gallery. He really hoped she didn't want to do that. But what if she did? And what if he wasn't any good at it?

Besides, he didn't even know where the Trophy Room was.

His palms had started to sweat.

Call gritted his teeth and wiped his hands on his pants. Hadn't Jasper just been testing his Evil Overlordliness? That was what Call needed to focus on. Evil Overlords, even ones who might not remember Evil Overlording, shouldn't be scared of meeting up with their friends who just happened to be girls. Call was going to be fine. He had this.

With renewed and slightly desperate optimism, he headed toward the tapestry map. He could see Tamara and Aaron, still dancing out on the floor with the others. He wondered if it had occurred to Tamara to ask him to dance, but he knew she would always choose Aaron first. He'd accepted it a long time ago. He didn't even really mind.

Anyway, Celia had said to come alone. Which he should definitely do if this was going to be about dating. Which he really hoped it wasn't.

According to the map, the Trophy Room wasn't far. He headed away from the crowd, through a set of doors and down a marble corridor with small alcoves set into the walls, holding old manuscripts and artifacts. Call liked the clicking sounds his shoes made on the floor as he went. He stopped to peer at an old wristband that must have been the prototype for the one he wore. The leather had been worn thin and several of the stones were missing from their setting. He didn't recognize the name of the mage who was on the plaque behind it, but the date of his death was 1609, which seemed like a very long time ago.

A few more steps and Call came to the Trophy Room. Over the door, a sign read AWARDS AND HONORS. The door was propped open, so he slipped noiselessly inside.

It was a dim, solemn room, smaller than the main hall. Like the hall, the space was illuminated by an enormous chandelier, this one with blown-glass arms in the shape of octopus tentacles, each sucker dripping with crystals, as though droplets of water clung to them. The walls were covered with a collection of plaques and medallions that must have been given to students at the Collegium.

Call was entirely alone.

He took a turn around the room, glancing at the pictures of mages on the walls, wishing for a window where he could look at a fish or something to pass the time. He was sure Celia would be along in a minute.

After several minutes passed, he took out the note again and reread it. Maybe he'd misunderstood. Maybe she'd written that she'd meet him in fifteen minutes or an hour. But no, the note didn't specify any time.

After a few more minutes, he decided she wasn't coming.

He felt unexpectedly glum. If this was his first date, it was a bust. Celia had probably written the note and then forgotten all about him and found someone else to dance with — someone who actually could dance. Maybe she was dancing with Jasper. Or she was waltzing around with an impressive Gold Year student who could tell her all about his achievements, and she was so mesmerized that she'd stood Call up. Later he'd meet her outside the Magisterium to walk Havoc and she'd wave it off. *I was going to meet you,* she'd say, *but you know how it is when you meet someone who's actually interesting! Time just flies.*

Call looked at his reflection in the glass of a trophy case. His hair was sticking up. Probably Call would be alone forever, and die alone, and Alastair would bury him in a car graveyard.

The door opened; there were footsteps. Call whirled, but it wasn't Celia standing there. It was Tamara and Aaron.

"What are you doing in the Trophy Room?" Tamara asked, frowning. "Are you okay?"

Aaron looked around, puzzled. "Are you hiding in here?"

Call was entirely sure that nothing like this — being stood up and humiliated — had ever happened to Aaron. He was doubly sure nothing like this had happened to Tamara.

Come to think of it, what were Tamara and Aaron doing here together? What if they'd been going off to do some kind of hand-holding dating thing together? It was bad enough that Call was sure Tamara would always choose Aaron first, but if they were dating, then Aaron would always choose Tamara, too.

"Are you okay?" Aaron asked, frowning in confusion at Call's silence. "Your dad told us he saw you come this way."

Relief washed over Call that they hadn't come here to be alone, but to find him. Now all he had to do was figure out how to explain what he'd been doing. "Well," he said, taking a step toward them, "you see —"

He was cut off by a grind and screech, a terrible metallic sound. Call looked up to see the chandelier hurtling toward him, octopus arms and dazzling crystals and all.

"*Call!*" Tamara screamed. The chandelier tumbled brilliantly down toward Call. Something hit him hard from the side. Pain shot up his leg as he struck the floor and skidded, someone's fingers digging into the back of his jacket.

It was Tamara. He saw a blur of her dark hair and yellow

dress, and then the chandelier hit the floor beside them. It was like a bomb going off. There was a horrible musical shattering. Shards of crystal exploded toward them. Call tried to curl his body around to block Tamara. He heard her scream, and then suddenly everything was very dark and quiet.

For a moment, Call wondered if he was dead. But it didn't seem likely that the afterlife meant lying on a stone floor next to Tamara, while a black cloud hovered over them. Tamara was gasping, wide-eyed. Call rolled to the side awkwardly and stared.

Aaron was standing over them, his hand outstretched. Dark, nebulous chaos spilled from his palm, forming a wall around Tamara and Call, drawing into itself the flying bits of broken glass and crystal from the shattered chandelier. Call tried to call out to Aaron, but the chaos sucked away his voice.

He could feel a pull inside him — Call was Aaron's counterweight, and when Aaron used chaos magic, he felt it. The room beyond Aaron seemed to be wavering — and then Aaron dropped his hand and the darkness vanished.

Call staggered to his feet, reaching down to pull Tamara up after him. One of her cheeks had been cut by a piece of flying glass and was bleeding. Tamara was clutching his arm in a death grip, but now that she was standing, he thought she might be holding him up. Aaron was leaning against the wall, wide-eyed and breathing hard from exertion.

"What," he said in a raspy voice, "just happened?"

Before Call could answer, the doors flew open and the other partygoers flooded into the room.

CHAPTER FOUR

CALL'S VISION WAS swimming, making everything a little surreal. People streamed into the room, shocked and gaping. Voices, muttering and yelling, washed across his brain.

The chandelier looked like a huge dead animal collapsed in the middle of the room. Most of its arms were smashed off, and broken glass was everywhere in glittering, razor-sharp piles.

"What's going on in here?" a black-haired man shouted. Call had a vague memory from the ceremony that he was a teacher at the Collegium, and that his name was Master Sukarno. He was a big man, imposing, and his face was red with fury.

"That was chaos magic!" He whirled on Aaron and Call. "Were you *playing around* with void magic? How foolish can you be? Chaos magic is strictly controlled everywhere, but forbidden in these rooms. We're underwater and cannot risk the structural integrity of the school being compromised by arrogant children amusing themselves! We could all have drowned."

Tamara looked as if she might explode with rage. "How dare *you*!" she said. "No one was playing! We were just standing here in the room when the chandelier came down. It nearly crushed us. If Aaron hadn't done what he did, Call and I would be dead! Nothing's happened to your precious Collegium! It's fine!"

"What did you do to make the chandelier come down?" demanded Master Taisuke, one of the Masters at the Magisterium. "It's been hanging here for a hundred years. You three wander into the room and it comes crashing down?"

"That's enough!" It was Tamara's father. The Rajavis had levitated themselves over the wreckage to reach their daughter. On the other side of the room, Call could see Kimiya and Alex standing together, both watching the scene in wide-eyed horror. Tamara's mother dashed toward her daughter, pulling her away from Call, stroking Tamara's hair and looking at her worriedly. She dabbed at the cut on Tamara's cheek, blotting the blood with a handkerchief. And then Alastair was pushing through the crowd toward Call. He looked pale, much paler than Call would have expected. He didn't even bother levitating himself, just kicked a path through the smashed crystals and twisted metal and grabbed Call, pulling him into his arms.

"Callum," he said roughly. Over his shoulder, Call could see Aaron, still leaning against the wall. There was no one there to blot his cuts or put their arms around him. He was looking down at his hand, the one he'd used to unleash chaos, with a strange expression on his face.

"My daughter is not a troublemaker," snapped Mr. Rajavi. "In case you've forgotten, we're all here tonight to honor her heroism —"

"And the heroism of several other students," added Master North, who had shooed the onlookers back toward the walls so he and Master Rufus could examine the chandelier wreckage.

"I was against the awards ceremony from the start," said Taisuke. "Children shouldn't be rewarded for disobedience, even if the end result turns out positively."

Mentally, Call filed Master Taisuke into the category of Not a Fan of Mine. It was a growing file.

"Makars, especially, should be controlled," continued Taisuke. "As we saw from Constantine Madden, a young Makar who doesn't know his own power is the most dangerous thing in the world."

"So are you saying young Makars should be killed, as is the custom in other countries?" asked Master Rufus. He didn't speak loudly, but his voice was clear, powerful, and carrying. "Because someone's tried. The chandelier collapsed because the chain was tampered with. Someone was attempting to assassinate the Makars."

"Assassinate?" Master Sukarno said, deflating slightly.

Another teacher at the Collegium made a sharp gesture in the air and said an unfamiliar word.

A sudden, deafening roar went through the room. Alastair tightened his grip on Call, Tamara's parents grabbed her, and Master Rufus reached for Aaron. Some kind of alarm system seemed to have gone off — a path lit up suddenly in front of them, and Call could see doors that had been previously invisible illuminated in the walls. He, Aaron, and Tamara were hustled through one of the doors, down a corridor, and into a dimly lit, windowless room full of couches and chairs. Collegium staff raced around, securing the area.

Someone brought them blankets and mugs of sugary tea that seemed to be an apology on the part of Master Sukarno for accusing them of being careless delinquents. Anastasia Tarquin appeared with an energy bar and presented it to Aaron, telling him that using that much chaos magic, even with a counterweight, was likely to make him pretty tired.

For a moment, Call thought that meant that maybe the adults would leave them alone. Tamara was huddled on a couch with her parents, and Aaron was curled in an armchair looking miserable and exhausted. But of course, none of that mattered. The moment the staff bustled away, Master Rufus, Master North, Anastasia, and Graves all started asking endless awkward questions.

Why had Call come into the Trophy Room? Had anyone threatened him at the party? Did he know Aaron would follow him in?

There was no point embarrassing himself in front of the teaching staff of the Magisterium and the Collegium, never mind the Assembly, so Call lied. Nope, no one knew he was going to the Trophy Room. Nope, no one knew that Aaron would be with him. He just hated dancing and had been wandering around, checking out all the old stuff. He had totally not been stood up on a maybe date. He was definitely not a loser whose friends had almost been crushed under a chandelier of loserdom.

Then Celia and Jasper were allowed in with their parents trailing behind them. Celia's two mothers, Jasper's mom and dad. Mr. DeWinter gave Jasper a little shove and a stern look, as though warning him against doing anything potentially humiliating to their family name.

Call sighed, prepared for the worst. It had been bad enough when he'd imagined Celia explaining why she'd decided not to meet him, but explaining it in front of everyone was like an extra scoop of humiliation piled on top of his already overfull sundae of embarrassment. He wondered if it was bad to wish the chandelier had crushed him.

"You're friends with these three," Master North said to Celia and Jasper, indicating Call, Tamara, and Aaron. Celia looked pleased to hear this. Jasper looked as if he'd been accused of something. "Did you notice anything tonight, anyone behaving strangely toward them?"

"Jennifer Matsui was talking to Call," said Jasper. "Which is weird, because she's pretty and popular, and Call is hideous and unpopular." Jasper caught Alastair glaring at him, and flushed. "Just kidding. But I didn't think they knew each other."

"They do a little," said Tamara. "Jennifer's friends with my sister."

"She's *not* friends with Call, though," said Celia. She turned to Call. "Why would you be talking to Jennifer?"

Call had had it. "She was giving me the note," he said. "Your note."

"What note?" Celia looked totally baffled. "I didn't write you a note."

Call pulled the paper out of his pocket. "So what's this?"

Celia frowned at it. "But this isn't my handwriting. And it doesn't have my signature or anything — just my name written out. Did she say it was from me?" Then, she reread the words and flushed, her neck going red. "You thought you were meeting me? That's why you were in the Trophy Room?"

Tamara scowled. "You didn't tell us that."

"Callum," Master North said, his voice stern enough to make everyone else go quiet. "Let's go through what happened today again, very slowly. And this time *you're not going to leave anything out*. Do you understand me? This is too important."

"Okay," Call said, chastened. "It was just that I —"

"No excuses," Master North said. "Begin."

"I was looking for Alastair when Jennifer Matsui gave me a note and said it was from a . . . uh, pretty blond girl," Call said, wishing that he knew enough magic to make himself invisible or turn into a mist that could slither through the floorboards.

Celia beamed at him. *"Really?"*

Jasper started snickering. At Master Rufus's scowl, he tried to stop, but didn't seem likely to be successful.

"You're the only blond girl he knows," snapped Tamara, clearly far less amused. Nearly being crushed by ten tons of glass and crystal probably made her less interested in embarrassing Call.

Master North reached out his hand for the note and Celia gave it to him. He peered at it for a long moment, then looked at her. "And you didn't write this? You're sure?"

Celia shook her head. "I didn't. I mean —" She looked at Call unhappily. "I feel really bad someone used my name to try to hurt you."

"It was no problem," Call said, trying to seem as if he didn't mind one way or the other. Then he realized that saying that nearly being crushed by a chandelier was no problem was kind of bizarre. He looked helplessly at his dad. Alastair shrugged.

"Where is Jennifer Matsui now?" Master Rufus asked, clearly impatient with Call's dithering. "The person who gave her the note is likely to be the person responsible for tampering with the chandelier. Unless she did it herself."

"Jennifer?" Tamara said. "Why would she do that?"

Aaron frowned. "Why would *anyone* want to kill Call?"

"Well, he's a Makar," said Master Rufus. "Just like you."

Aaron, Tamara, and Call exchanged quick looks. It was true that Call was a Makar, but in Aaron's question, Call had heard the second question that everyone who knew his secret probably had. The question they couldn't ask or share. Because while everyone else was thinking that the person trying to kill Call had been targeting one of the Makaris, there was another possibility: that the person who had been targeting Call was trying to kill him because he knew what Call really was.

Maybe if the truth comes out, Call thought, *whoever tried to drop a chandelier on me will get an award, too.*

"Yeah, with his winning personality, it's hard to imagine who'd want to kill Call," said Jasper.

"Jasper!" said Tamara, but Call, for once, didn't mind it. Jasper being a jerk to him was normal, and right now, normal was all he wanted.

But that wasn't going to happen. A scream split the room — and then another, and another. Someone in the Collegium was shrieking in terror.

Tamara bolted to her feet. Aaron's energy bar went flying. Alastair looked horrified. "What's going on?" demanded Mrs. Rajavi, whirling to look toward the Masters.

Call was on his feet, too, running toward the door. His leg ached but he pushed past the pain — even so, he wasn't as fast as the others. He could hear voices, yells and cries, all echoing from one end of the Collegium. He followed the others as they ran back through the long corridor and down another hall, back into the War Room.

The room was full of people. The person who'd been screaming was still screaming. It was Kimiya. One of her hands was clutching the front of her dress, the other hand pointing up.

Outside the clear glass Call could see the water all around the Collegium, glowing a murky greenish blue. The schools of fish had vanished. There was only the water, and floating in the water was a body. A girl, barefoot in a dress that was partly wrapped around her, like seaweed. Her dark hair drifted in the current.

Tamara ran toward her sister, but Alex had already put his arms around Kimiya. There was an expression of horror on his face. "Jen," wept Kimiya, into his shirt. "Jen . . ."

Call felt as if his blood was fizzing with ice. The body in the water drifted and turned, and Call saw two things: First, that there was a long iron dagger plunged into the dead girl's chest. Second, that her face was familiar.

It was Jennifer Matsui, and someone had murdered her.

CHAPTER FIVE

THERE WAS A loud explosion. "Everybody *out*!" barked Master Graves, who had climbed onto the War Room table. One of his hands was raised, and fire glimmered in his palm. "Now!"

Master Rufus's face was lined and haggard in the blue light. Call wondered if he'd known Jen Matsui, what it was like for him to see a student die. He'd been Constantine Madden's teacher — he'd seen many students die. Call wondered if you got used to it. From Master Rufus's expression, he guessed not.

Rufus raised his palm. Light shone from his fingers, illuminating a pathway to the doors. "Move," he said in a voice that brooked no argument. The other Masters and several of the Assembly members surged forward, helping to herd the panicking, weeping, and shouting guests out of the War Room.

People poured into the hallway and then into the great hall. Anastasia Tarquin was there with several Masters, including Master Taisuke. They began directing people toward the stairs that led out of the Collegium. Call saw Celia disappearing up the steps with her moms and wondered if she was okay. Alastair, who had a hand on Call's shoulder, pushed him in that direction, gesturing for Aaron to follow.

Looking back, Call saw Tamara in some kind of intense conversation with her parents and the deWinters. Mrs. deWinter didn't seem happy and neither did the Rajavis. Mr. deWinter's expression was strange, though, like he was pleased and didn't want to show it. The crowd parted around them as it moved toward the exit. Assembly members apparently didn't have to follow orders.

"We didn't even get to say good-bye to Tamara," Call told his father.

"Not now," his father said, pushing with more force. "We need to get out of here before —"

"Alastair," said Master Rufus. "Wait."

Alastair paused. Call could sense him tensing with anger. He turned slowly, and so did Call and Aaron. The floating ropes had risen around them, cordoning off Aaron, Call, and Alastair.

"You can't just leave," said Master Milagros. "Call was attacked, and Jennifer murdered. Our apprentices need to be somewhere where we can keep them safe."

"Since you can't even keep the children safe at a party, I think it's a stretch to promise they'll be safe anywhere else just because you'll be there." Alastair's voice was cold.

"School begins in three days," Master Rufus said. "I expect

to see both the Makaris there and so does the Assembly. We will keep them safe — you're going to have to trust us."

Alastair turned to Rufus, some of the rage Call remembered from the Iron Trial lighting his face.

"It's been a long, long time since I trusted you, Rufus," Alastair said. "And look what happened then." His hand shot out, and the ropes surrounding them fell away to ash. Sparks curled between his fingers. Call looked at Aaron with wide eyes. "Let me know when you have found the person who did this, because until then I'll trust you as far as I can throw you. Come on, boys."

Call and Aaron scrambled to follow Alastair as he stalked toward the staircase. Amazingly, people shifted aside to let him pass, even the members of the Assembly. Probably because everyone thought he was the person who'd chopped off Constantine Madden's head and he looked about ready to chop off one of theirs.

Call and Aaron exchanged wide-eyed looks as Alastair dragged them toward the steps.

"Wait!" Tamara said, running up to them, pulling Jasper behind her like a tugboat. Her parents were still where she'd left them; they'd detached Alex from Kimiya and were comforting their daughter themselves. "I'm coming with you. We both are."

"What?" Jasper said. "No! I didn't think you were serious. Your hot sister needs a shoulder to cry on. I volunteer myself. I would be much better at that than staying in whatever hovel Call and his weird dad —"

Tamara kicked him savagely and he lapsed into a sullen silence.

Alastair regarded them both with surprise. "Well, you're welcome, but I don't think your parents would stand for it. I've know them for a long time and I'd be surprised if they agreed to let you out of their sight."

Tamara firmed her jaw, determination writ in every line of her face. "We have to take shifts watching over Call. I told them so and they agreed with me."

"Shifts?" Aaron said.

"Someone tried to kill Call," said Tamara. "That means we can't ever let him out of our sight. Someone has to be watching him constantly, twenty-four hours a day."

"Even when I'm sleeping?" Call asked.

Tamara fixed him with a gimlet eye. "Especially when you're sleeping," she said. "You're defenseless then."

Call wasn't thrilled about the plan. "What? No! I don't want Jasper watching me sleep — that's creepy. I don't want anyone watching me sleep!"

"We can discuss this later," Alastair said. "If you want to come with us, Tamara, Jasper, we're going now."

Call looked over at Aaron, but he wasn't paying attention to the discussion. He was staring past them, down the hall at the War Room and beyond, where Jen's body was floating. Call thought about their carefree summer of building robots and running through sprinklers and wondered if he'd been foolish to think that just because he'd tricked the mages into believing things had changed, they really had.

"Come on," Tamara said to Aaron, touching him on the shoulder and pulling his attention back to the here and now. Call allowed himself to be herded by his father toward the stairs. They passed the drinks table, now overturned, where Jen had handed Call the note.

When Alastair got to the stairs, he lifted Call in the air, moving him to glide swiftly and easily just above the steps of the staircase. He did it in a distracted, effortless manner, the same way he'd burned away the velvet ropes, as though he wasn't even really paying attention to what he was doing. Call was shocked. His dad had avoided using magic for so long that Call didn't think he really remembered how.

They reached the top of the steps and Alastair set Call gently down. He began striding ahead of the four kids, along the jetty, back toward where the car was parked.

They had just passed the giant weird statue of Poseidon when Jasper noticed Alastair's Rolls-Royce Phantom. He gave a long, appreciative whistle that ended abruptly — in a choking noise — when he realized that the car he was admiring belonged to Call's father.

"Not what you expected?" Call asked as Alastair opened the door and ushered them into the spacious backseat.

For once, Jasper didn't seem to have anything to say. They all piled silently into the car, Call crawling into the front seat beside his dad. As they pulled away from the boardwalk, Call looked back to see a group of mages standing at the edge of the ocean, near the Collegium entrance. As he watched, one of them walked into the water and disappeared.

"Water mages. They're retrieving the girl's body," said Alastair in a grim tone.

Call looked away. It was hard to believe that cheerful Jen, who'd teased him when she handed him the message, who Jasper had wanted to meet, was dead. The evening was supposed to honor the end of the war and somehow that made everything that had happened that much more grotesque. But could there ever really be peace, Call thought, when the Enemy of Death wasn't dead?

↑ ≈ △ ○ @

Somehow, back at the house, Alastair found enough pillows and blankets for all of them. Aaron abdicated his military cot so Tamara could move it into the den, because he was like that. Jasper claimed the couch, though he complained bitterly that it didn't fold out, and accused Havoc of giving the couch fleas. Call, who knew perfectly well that Havoc was flea-free, was back to hating Jasper. Aaron took a pile of blankets, made a makeshift bed on the floor at the foot of Call's, and went to sleep.

Call was almost asleep himself when there was a knock on his door. It was Tamara, looking faintly embarrassed. "Do you have anything I could sleep in?" she asked. "All I have is this" — she indicated her floaty dress — "and, yeah, I probably shouldn't . . ."

Call realized he was blushing. He wished it could be totally uncomplicated, having a girl best friend. It should be just like it was with Aaron. It shouldn't matter that Tamara was a girl. Still, he felt clumsy and stupid as he fished around in his T-shirt drawer until he found an oversize shirt that read WELCOME TO THE LURAY CAVERNS on it in Day-Glo yellow. He handed it over silently.

"Thanks," Tamara said. "I'll wash it and give it back to you —"

"That's fine, you can keep it —"

"— And, Call?"

"I mean, I've never worn it anyway, it's too big, and —"

"Call," Tamara said, again, looking at him with big, serious eyes. "We're going to keep you safe, okay?"

Call wished he could believe it. "Okay," he said.

↑ ≈ △ ○ @

They sat out in the yard the next day, Tamara back in her yellow dress, Jasper in a strange combination of Call's clothes and his own. It was brightly sunny, and Alastair had made them lemonade out of powder, which Tamara was giving the fisheye. Call suspected she didn't drink a lot of reconstituted things. Jasper was looking around haughtily at Call's small backyard and slightly overgrown grass.

Not that Alastair seemed to notice. He was seated on a rock, tinkering with a broken alarm clock. Even though there were digital alarm clocks and cell phones nowadays, people would pay decent money for old-fashioned phones and other gadgets that had been fixed up to run well.

"So what does it mean?" said Tamara. "If someone's trying to hurt Call because he's the . . ." She swallowed.

"Enemy of Death?" Jasper volunteered.

"I don't think it's a good idea to go around saying 'Enemy of Death' a lot," said Aaron. "We should come up with a code name. Like Captain Fishface."

Havoc barked. Call agreed with him that the name sucked. "Why Captain Fishface?"

"Well, you have a fishy look," said Jasper. "Plus, no one would ever guess what we meant because there's nothing scary about it."

"Fine, whatever," said Tamara, sounding as if she thought

the whole thing was a waste of time. "So who might know Call is Captain Fishface?"

"I refuse to be called that!" Call said. "Especially in light of recent events."

Tamara groaned as though this conversation was tormenting her even more than it was tormenting Call. "Okay, what do you want to be called?"

"How about Commander Pinhead?" Aaron asked. Jasper laughed, spitting out his lemonade.

Call put his head in his hands and took a deep breath, drinking in the smells of summer — the perfume of warm earth, cut grass, and machine oil. There was no winning. He was going to wind up with a dumb name no matter what. "Captain Fishface is fine."

"Good," Tamara said, rolling her eyes. "Now can we talk about who might know about Call?"

"His father," Jasper said, and they all glanced at Alastair, who seemed oblivious. He was whistling a jaunty tune in a slightly off-key manner.

"My dad is not trying to kill me," Call said. A year ago, he hadn't been so sure of that, but he was sure now. "And I don't think any of you are, either. Even you, Jasper. Who else?"

"Did any of us tell anyone?" Tamara asked, looking around at them.

"Who would I tell?" Jasper asked, and then blanched at their prolonged stares. "No! Okay? I didn't tell anyone! It's too big a secret, and I would get in trouble, too."

"Me neither," Aaron said.

Tamara sighed. "I didn't. But I thought I'd better ask. Okay, so then there's Master Joseph. He's got to be pretty mad at Call."

"I thought he needed Call," said Jasper. "Isn't Captain Fishface, like, his whole reason for being?"

Aaron grinned. "I think he hoped that either Call would be a lot more obedient than he is or that he could use Call to bring back Captain Fishface with all his memories intact."

Call, who thought pretty much the same thing, shuddered. "He might blame me for Drew's death."

"He probably blames me, too," said Aaron. "If it makes you feel any better."

Drew was Master Joseph's son. He'd gone to the Magisterium, pretending to be a regular student, but his real reason for being there had been to get close to Call. Drew had even helped his father kidnap Aaron and then swung him over a cage with a chaos elemental inside. The same chaos elemental that, ironically, wound up killing Drew. But Call had to admit that he'd had something to do with it as well. "Okay," Tamara said. "Top of our suspect list — Master Joseph."

Call shook his head. "I don't know. If he is out to get me, why not use the Alkahest? And, well, I just don't think he's ready to give up yet. He tried to save my life back in the tomb. I think he's still got hope that I am going to turn out . . . more like Captain Fishface."

"What about Warren?" Aaron asked. They all just stared at him for a long moment.

Call looked at him the way that Tamara had looked at her lemonade. "You think a lizard is trying to kill me? And he faked a note from Celia?"

"He's an elemental! And he was in the service of the Devoured who gave us that creepy prophecy." Aaron sighed. "Okay, it was a pretty out-there theory."

"It's okay," Tamara said. "We have to think outside the box. No matter how unlikely, we've got to put all our ideas on the table. Or at least on this stretch of grass."

"We don't have any suspects," Call said. "We don't have any ideas. We don't even know why I was being targeted. Maybe it was because I'm a Makar. Maybe it had nothing to do with being Captain Fishface. Maybe the person who tried to smoosh me with a chandelier was the same person who let out Automotones to kill all of us."

"That's what the mages are going to assume." Tamara sighed. "I guess it could be true."

"We're just going to have to stick together," said Aaron, smiling up at the blue sky. "And we're going to figure this out. We're heroes, right? We've got medals. We can do this."

Eventually, Call got out a pack of cards and they played a couple of rounds of a game that involved slapping one another's hands. They talked about going back to the Magisterium and what they hoped to accomplish that year. Havoc chased several bees, snapping at them until they buzzed lazily out of his reach. As the afternoon wore on, Stebbins arrived with suitcases for Tamara and a message from her parents that could only be delivered in private. Jasper called home on one of Alastair's restored chrome candlestick landline phones and then glumly reported that his family would send his things directly to the Magisterium. Call wondered if he'd tried to convince them to rescind permission for him to be there. Call wondered if his parents had forced him to come along in the first place and then quickly pushed away the thought.

"What are you looking at?" Jasper asked him gruffly when he noticed Call staring in his direction.

"Nothing," Call said. The last person he needed to be worrying about was Jasper.

That night, Alastair grilled steak and they ate it outside, on paper plates, along with buttered corn, snap peas, and cold slices of watermelon. Tamara threw watermelon at Aaron, who got seeds down his shirt. Havoc stood on top of Jasper when Jasper refused to give him a piece of steak. They took turns seeing who could make the sparks above the banked coals on the grill dance. It was almost like a party, except for the specter of Jen's death, which kept them from laughing too loudly or forgetting for too long that they could be next.

↑ ≈ △ ○ ◉

Two days later, Alastair drove them all to the Magisterium. Call sat in the front seat, gazing out the window, while Aaron dozed in the backseat. Tamara was listening to music on her phone and Jasper was reading the most recent comic book he'd found in Call's room and gotten obsessed with. Havoc was stretched out across their laps, dead asleep.

"You let me know if you want to come home," Alastair said to Call for what must have been the millionth time. "You've done enough. You know plenty of magic — enough to control your abilities. You don't need the Magisterium."

Call remembered the way Graves had insisted that Master Rufus give the Assembly updates on how Call and Aaron were doing. He remembered all the references to countries where mages with the ability to control chaos were killed or had their magic bound — even though the party was supposed to be in their honor. While Constantine Madden had been alive,

Makaris were awesome. They were desperately needed weapons. They meant the end of the war. But with Constantine Madden dead, Aaron and Call were just a reminder of that war and how it could happen again. Call doubted he would be allowed to quit attending the Magisterium, no matter what Alastair thought.

"It's okay, Dad," Call said. "I'll be fine."

As they neared the Magisterium, the roads grew narrower and more winding. They were completely unmarked: Only those who knew where the Magisterium was could find it. Call had often wondered what magic kept hikers and ordinary townspeople from nearby from happening across it. Something advanced, he guessed. Something to do with the earth. The trees grew thick along the sides of the road. Call couldn't help thinking about the Order of Disorder — it was clear that the Assembly knew about them and tolerated them, but he couldn't quite figure out why.

There was a beeping sound up ahead, bringing Call's attention back to the road. They pulled up into a clearing, where a school bus had already arrived. Students were pouring out of it, carrying suitcases and duffel bags. The main gate of the school was open: Call could see mages in their somber black, and various students already wearing their uniforms — red, white, blue, green, and gray — mixing with kids who had just arrived and were still wearing jeans and T-shirts.

Aaron woke up and he and Jasper and Tamara started poking one another, leaning out the windows as they recognized friends from previous years — Celia threw them a guarded smile as she headed through the gates with Gwenda, who was in her apprentice group with Jasper. Alex Strike was talking to

Anastasia Tarquin, who had pulled up next to the school bus in a white Mercedes. Call had seen the car before: She'd picked up Alex from the Rajavis' last year. Call had nearly forgotten: Anastasia Tarquin was Alex's stepmother.

Anastasia emerged from the car, looking elegant, as usual, in a white pantsuit. Alex was gesturing at her, looking annoyed, as a black van pulled up beside them. The back opened and two muscular young men leaped out, much to the delight of quite a few of the students of the Magisterium. They began carrying large pieces of furniture through the gates — a desk, a lamp, an immaculately white sofa.

"What's going on there?" Alastair wondered aloud as they all piled out of the Rolls. Call stretched to get the kinks out of his muscles. So did Havoc.

"The Assembly posted Anastasia at the school to keep an eye on things," said Alex, who had abandoned his stepmother to come say hello. He high-fived Call and Aaron, and smiled at Tamara. "She's moving into Master Lemuel's old office. She takes this stuff really seriously and, well, she also overpacks."

"Is she going to be looking for the spy?" Alastair asked.

"I don't think we're supposed to be talking about that," said Alex, looking over at Jasper worriedly. "I mean, no one is supposed to know."

Alastair raised his eyebrows. "Good thing she's being so discreet."

Alex looked back at his stepmother, who was supervising the carrying of several large steamer trunks into the caves. They were covered with old-fashioned stamps from faraway places — Mexico, Italy, Australia, the French Riviera, Provence, Cornwall. "She's got a cover story about making sure everything goes smoothly ridding Chaos-ridden animals from the forest."

Call put one hand on Havoc's back in what he hoped would be a reassuring manner. Havoc looked up at him, tail beginning to wag. A wave of anger passed through Call at the idea that anyone would want to hurt Havoc.

They better not, he thought.

Alastair turned to Call. "If you change your mind, you know how to get ahold of me," he said, then hugged Call tightly — a little too tightly, actually, making Call worry for his ribs.

"Bye, Dad," Call squeaked. Even if he had been squeezed a little too hard, this was the first time his father was okay with his attending the Magisterium. It was a great feeling.

Tamara had gone over and found Kimiya and was laughing with her. Jasper had headed toward Celia and Gwenda. Only Aaron had waited for Call. He gave him a slanted smile and Call wondered how hard it was for Aaron to be around other people's families all the time.

"Give me that," Aaron said, slinging Call's duffel bag over his shoulders and lifting his own luggage in his other hand. He started toward the school, seemingly not even weighed down a little bit by what he was carrying. Call walked behind him, stiff-legged from the trip, and thought about all the ways that life wasn't fair.

The caverns were humid but cool. Water dripped down from the jagged icicle stalactites to the melted-candle stalagmites below them. Sheets of gypsum hung from the ceiling, resembling banners and streamers from some long-forgotten party. Call walked past it all, past the damp flowstone and the pools shining with mica, where pale fish darted. He was so used to it that he no longer found it to be particularly creepy. It was just the place he went to school, as familiar to him now as the bang of metal lockers and the squeak of his sneakers on the gymnasium floor had been three years ago.

He wondered if they'd spot Warren, potential assassin, and if he'd have something creepy to say to them, but the little lizard was nowhere to be seen.

Call used his wristband, with all its new stones, to wave his way into their rooms. Aaron set down Call's luggage on their couch with a groan that made Call feel a little better about his own abilities and a little more guilty about Aaron's generosity. The room looked smaller than it had the year before and it took him a moment to realize it was because he'd grown, not because the room had shrunk.

The door opened and Tamara marched in, dragging her suitcases behind her. "I didn't know where you two had gone! You just wandered off!" she announced. Which was completely unfair, because she was the one who had wandered off, Call thought. She turned to Aaron. "And you know we're not supposed to leave Call alone!"

"I didn't," Aaron pointed out.

"Hmph," Tamara said before she stomped into her room. Call went off to his bedroom, which felt cold and dusty and unused, the way it always did at the beginning of a school year. He flung his suitcase open and put on his uniform — blue for third year. He snapped his cuff shut and looked at himself in the mirror on the wardrobe. There was a time when he'd been short enough that he could see himself completely in the glass; now his head passed the top of the frame and he had to crouch.

He went out into the common room and found Aaron and Tamara waiting in their uniforms. After promising Havoc some leftovers, they trooped off to the Refectory for dinner. Everyone but the Iron Year students — who were coming from their Trials and usually got to eat in their rooms — were settling in to their old tables and choosing from among the culinary options. Tonight's menu was a purplish mash, large mushrooms cut up so they seemed almost like slices of bread and slathered with some yellow paste, and three kinds of lichen — bright green, brown, and dark red. Call piled everything on his plate, along with a cup of liquid with a thin film of algae on it.

It was creepy how delicious the lichen was to Call. He forked it into his mouth like a starving man and wondered if it was possible for the lichen to have some sinister purpose. Like brainwash him into eating so much of it that he would become an entirely lichen-based life-form. Was that a thing that could happen? He gave his next forkful a long, suspicious look before shoving it into his face.

Jasper sat down next to Call, as though they were friends or something. "So, what's the plan?"

"What are you talking about?" Call asked.

"Oh, never mind," Jasper said with a roll of his eyes, then turned to Tamara. "I don't know why I even bothered asking him. What's the plan?"

"We can't talk here," she said, leaning in and dropping her voice. Call couldn't help noticing that the cut under her eye was still visible, a thin scabbed line. Every time he saw it, he thought of her fingers on his jacket, pulling him to safety. He thought of what he owed her.

He owed all his friends so much. He didn't know how he'd ever pay them back.

Aaron, who'd been talking to Rafe, another Bronze Year student, about the robots he and Call had built over the summer, seemed to notice something important was going on and broke off his conversation to join theirs.

"Tomorrow," Tamara said. "After dinner, let's meet in the library. We can discuss then."

"What are we talking about?" Celia asked, sitting down across from Call, her plate full of purple mush. "Is something going on?"

"No!" Aaron and Jasper said at the same time.

"Sure, that's not suspicious or anything." She stood back up. "If you didn't want me to sit here, you just had to say so. I'll go somewhere else —"

Call sprang to his feet. "Don't," he said before he could think of *how* to persuade her to stay. "We were just talking about the Gallery. But we hadn't decided to go. But I mean, we could. Go, that is."

"Are you asking me to go to the Gallery with you?" Celia inquired, her expression unreadable. The Gallery was where two people went when they were on . . .

A date. She is talking about a date. She thinks I am asking her on a date.

"I . . . don't know?" Call stammered.

"Well, maybe you should figure it out," Celia said, tossing her blond hair and stalking off to sit with Rafe, Kai, and Gwenda.

"The gauntlet is in your court, buddy," Jasper announced the moment she was out of earshot.

"You're mixing your metaphors," said Call. "It gives me a headache."

"Can we talk about saving Call's actual life instead of saving his love life?" said Tamara, looking fed up. "Until tomorrow night, one of us stays with Call at all times. It'll probably have to be either me or Aaron because if it's you, Jasper, everyone will think it's weird, since you don't like Call."

"Sure he does," said Aaron, looking surprised. "We're all friends."

"Whatever," said Tamara. "Tomorrow, after dinner, library. Bring some good ideas." She glanced over. "Alex Strike is gesturing at me. I'll be right back." She stood up and caught hold of Aaron's sleeve. "Come on. He probably wants to say hi to you, too."

"What —?" Aaron began as he was yanked off his feet and tugged toward the table where Alex, Kimiya, and their other Gold Year friends were sitting. They seemed like a somber group. Call couldn't blame them. Losing a friend like that —

"So do you like Celia or not?" Jasper asked, gnawing a piece of lichen. He had gotten a new slick-looking haircut before the awards ceremony, and a piece of dark hair fell into his eyes.

"How is that your business?" Call asked.

"Maybe *I'll* ask her out," said Jasper. "Did you ever think of that?"

Call hadn't. He goggled. "Do what you want," he said finally.

"I guess you *don't* care." Jasper's eyes gleamed with amusement. "Maybe because you like Tamara?"

"Jasper —"

"Do you? Like Tamara?"

"She's my best friend," Call said between his teeth.

"That doesn't mean anything." Jasper twirled his fork between his fingers. "People like each other all the time in apprentice groups. Look at Kimiya and Alex Strike. Or, you know, me and Celia. You could totally like Tamara —"

"What does it matter?" Call exploded, to his own surprise. He glared at Jasper, and in a low voice said, "Don't you get it? It doesn't matter. She'll always like Aaron better."

Jasper's eyes widened. "Whoa," he said. "Looks like I hit on an awkward truth there."

Call's head was swimming. Dimly, through the crowd, he could see Aaron and Tamara coming toward them. They were laughing together, like they always did.

"What I just said" — Call looked at Jasper — "don't repeat it."

Jasper leaned back in his chair. "Don't worry, Callum," he said with a sneer. "I keep all your secrets."

CHAPTER SIX

CLASSES THAT FIRST day were outside in the blazing sun, sitting on a half circle of boulders. Master Rufus felt that since the Assembly planned to start creeping around the woods, they needed to use the outside of the Magisterium as much as possible until that happened. Call missed the cool of the caves. His shirt was quickly soaked with sweat. Even the part on his head felt like it was getting a sunburn. Aaron's nose and cheeks had turned red, and Tamara was wearing one of her notebooks like a hat.

"Welcome to your Bronze Year at the Magisterium," Master Rufus said, pacing back in forth in front of them, his bald head shining. "You may not be the *most* trouble of all the apprentice groups I've ever taught, but you are certainly up there. Let's try to approach this year a little differently."

Considering that Master Rufus was referring to a previous apprentice group that had included Captain Fishface himself, that really was saying something.

"We all just got medals!" Tamara said, and received a stern look for interrupting him. She went on anyway. "We're the opposite of trouble."

Master Rufus's eyebrows did something complicated, rising and wiggling all at once. "Nonetheless, let's try to make sure that none of you get kidnapped or go on rescue missions or adopt more Chaos-ridden animals or leave the school for any reason."

None of them had anything to say to that.

"This year we will be learning about *personal responsibility*. You might not think that sounds like a particularly magical lesson, but this is the year that Constantine began his experiments with Master Joseph, trying to discover a path to immortality. It's the year when you leave behind the basics and begin to focus on what you might specialize in, so we want to make sure that every student — but especially Call and Aaron — consider what the wider implications of those specialties will be. It is a worthy goal to wonder about the limits of chaos magic. It is irresponsible and corrupt to use methods that put lives in danger to discover those limits. Like all schools, we are always interested in learning, in research, in pushing the limits of knowledge. But we must balance that with our duty to protect the world, even from ourselves.

"And," Master Rufus went on, "I want you to remember that you have walked through the gates of magic early in each of the preceding years. That should teach you not that you're better than other students but that the gates of magic open when the student is ready — not before. If you do not learn the Bronze Year lessons, you will remain in Bronze Year until you do."

Call looked over at Aaron and Tamara. They appeared as floored as he felt. He wasn't sure how any of what Master Rufus was talking about could be learned in school. It was remotely possible, however, that his brain was being slowed by heatstroke.

"One more thing," Master Rufus said. "About the spy in the Magisterium. Tamara, I don't know if I've spoken to you directly about this, but I am sure that Call or Aaron already told you, so I won't embarrass us both by pretending otherwise. You have every right to know. However, I insist — *insist!* — that you do not attempt to catch the spy yourselves. Leave this to us."

None of them said anything.

Master Rufus's eyebrows drew together more sharply. "Do you understand?"

Call nodded.

"Sure," Aaron said.

"Okay," said Tamara.

It was the most unconvincing display Call had ever seen. He wasn't sure if Master Rufus had been taken in or had just given up when the mage nodded and said, "Good! Now, I believe our first lesson should be about the element of water and how to balance it with air so that we can breathe underwater when we're swimming. I know just the lake we can practice in."

Call jumped up, pleased by the idea of cooling off. It was only as they started moving that he remembered Jen's body floating in the ocean and wondered if there was a reason that Master Rufus had put this particular lesson at the very top of his list.

Despite Call's dark thoughts, they spent a pleasant day bobbing around in the shallows of a small lake near the school. Master Rufus gave them amulets filled with air for them to hold and draw from while they were underwater. On the first few tries, Call couldn't focus and came up sputtering and choking. Aaron didn't fare better, though Tamara seemed serenely untroubled.

Finally, in frustration, Call grabbed the amulet and dived down toward the bottom of the pond. He'd always liked swimming — in the water, his leg didn't ache. He kept his eyes open. The lake was silty but fresh; he could see small fish darting around the plants that waved in the faint current. He could see Tamara and Aaron, blurred shapes in the water.

He thought, for some reason, of his father. He had seen in Master Joseph's memories how Alastair had climbed the side of a massive glacier to reach the scene of the Cold Massacre, where the Enemy of Death had killed dozens of helpless mages. Alastair had been climbing toward his wife and baby son, using water magic to form handholds and footholds in the glacier wall. It must have been exhausting. It must have seemed impossible.

Compared to that, this was nothing.

Call tightened his grasp on the amulet, squeezing it so hard he thought he felt it crack. *Air*, he thought. Air all around him, there was air in the water, all elements were one, *fire and earth, air and water. All are but one thing, not four, not two, and not three, but one.*

He opened his mouth and breathed.

It was like breathing damp, swampy air. He choked a little, letting his body drift upward as air filled his lungs. The second breath was easier, and by the third and fourth he was breathing normally. Standing on the bottom of the lake, breathing normally. Jubilantly, he tossed the amulet aside and swam upward, breaking the surface with a yell. "I did it!" he shouted. "I breathed underwater!"

"I know!" said Tamara, treading water. "I saw you!"

"Woo!" said Aaron. He punched the surface of the lake, making it spray up. "You rule!"

"Hello, we *all* rule," Tamara objected, as Call started swimming in circles, diving down to breathe and coming up again. He splashed water and grinned.

Sometimes magic really was just as awesome as he'd secretly hoped it would be.

↑ ≈ △ ○ @

That night, they were the only people in the library — Tamara, Call, Aaron, and Jasper, huddled around a table where a light glowed inside a lamp made from the shell of a huge underwater snail. They kept their voices down; sound tended to echo in the big, spiral stone room.

"So the question is whether whoever tried to kill Call at the awards ceremony is someone who'd be at the Magisterium," said Tamara, shuffling some papers. "I made a list of all the people who attend school here or teach here, as well as Assembly members who can come in and out."

Jasper leaned forward to look at the list. "You're not on it," he said.

"Of course I'm not!" Tamara flushed. "I didn't try to kill Call."

"Kimiya's not on it, either," said Jasper. "Or Aaron."

"Because they're not trying to kill me," said Call.

"You don't know that," said Jasper. "The list should be objective. I should be on it, too."

"Believe me," said Tamara. "You are."

Jasper made a face. "Good."

"Look, I know poking around when we're not supposed to is kind of our thing," Call said, interrupting them. "But maybe this time we don't try to catch the spy ourselves. Master Rufus says that there's some kind of plan in place and Alex's step-mom is here and is supposed to be setting a trap. Maybe we could leave it to them."

They all stared at Call as though he'd grown a second head. Finally, Aaron spoke. "Did you drink too much pond water today or something? There's no way you'd be saying that if it was one of us who was in danger."

"Think about it this way," Jasper said. "If the same person who released Automotones tried to drop the chandelier on you, then anyone standing next to you is just as likely to get killed as you are. So for my own sake, I want to look into this."

Call couldn't argue with logic like that.

"I've been thinking," Tamara said. "We need to get down in the tunnels where the huge elementals are kept. Then maybe we could figure out who had access to Automotones and how they got it. We can use this list and see if any of these people were down there — there's got to be some record of visitors or of who has clearance."

"Won't the mages have already looked into that?" Aaron asked.

Tamara shrugged. "Even if they have, they won't give us those names, so it's a place for us to start narrowing our suspect pool."

"Someone spent their summer rereading all their Nancy Drew mysteries," Jasper said.

Tamara gave him a toothy grin. "Someone is going to get a punch in their face."

"Do you have a better idea?" Aaron asked. "Because if not, don't criticize."

"How about Call makes himself into bait?" Jasper offered. "I mean, why wait around and do all this legwork when we can make the killer come to us? We just let everyone know Call is going to be somewhere remote and alone and then when the killer shows up to finish him off, we can jump —"

"Hey, wait a minute," Call said. "That idea is stupid."

"I thought we weren't supposed to criticize," Jasper said, grinning with self-satisfaction. "I think there's no way it could go wrong."

Tamara shook her head. "Call could get killed!"

"We'd still catch the spy," Jasper said, then winced after being kicked savagely under the table. "What? Not a lot of plans have that kind of built-in guarantee!"

"Let's try it Tamara's way first," Aaron said. Then, yawning, he stood. "After classes tomorrow, let's meet here again. We can look through the Magisterium maps and see if we can figure out where the elementals are kept. I'll take first shift tonight. Tamara, Call, you both get some sleep."

"See you then, suckers," Jasper said. He departed the library by taking the steps on the spiral staircase two at a time.

Call wanted to protest that one of them being awake, taking watch, was unnecessary, but no one was going to listen to him anyway. He got up with a sigh and followed Tamara and Aaron back to their rooms.

Halfway there, though, he straightened up with a jolt. "I know who'd be able to get to those elementals," Call said. "Warren!"

The little lizard was a fire elemental, after all, and while he couldn't entirely be trusted, he knew the layout of the Magisterium better than probably anyone or anything else. He'd led them through its labyrinthine corridors before — admittedly, bringing them to the attention of a more powerful and sinister elemental — but still, nothing *that* bad had happened.

And besides, last year they'd saved Warren's life. Master Rufus had set up a test of Aaron's chaos magic in which Aaron had been supposed to send the lizard into the void. Call wasn't sure what happened to things that got sucked into the void, but he was pretty sure they wouldn't survive. He'd helped Aaron to do some tricky magic so the lizard could escape. As far as Call was concerned, Warren *owed* them.

"Come on," he said, then about-faced in the middle of the hall. "This way."

The longer the spy was around, the longer his friends were going to hover over him like there was something wrong. He hated it. He didn't want them to be awake when he was asleep. He didn't want them in danger. If there was something to be done, he wanted to do it now.

"Where are we going?" Tamara protested as they headed back the way they'd come. "Back to the library?"

The corridor split in half. Call veered to the left. He remembered when he'd first come to the Magisterium how he'd thought he'd never learn the tunnels, the maze-like corridors that ran under and through the mountain. But he had, and now the paths through the upper levels of the Magisterium were as familiar to him as the streets of his hometown.

"Are we going to the river?" Aaron asked in a half whisper. The air of the tunnels was getting damper. They'd passed several of the rooms of other apprentice groups, only darkness showing under the doors. The Magisterium was asleep.

The rivers that ran through the school were its transportation artery. They carried students from classrooms to gates that led outside, to the Refectory and back to their rooms. Small boats moved on the rivers, powered by magic and assisted by water elementals. As Call, Aaron, and Tamara approached the water, the cave air grew colder, and Call could hear the rushing sound of the river.

Aaron and Tamara were muttering about whether Call was dragging them off to take a boat. The corridor opened out onto a pebbled underground beach. Phosphorescent moss clung to the walls and roof, lighting the space. Eyeless fish swam around under the water's surface.

"Warren!" Call called. *"Warren!"*

Aaron and Tamara exchanged a look. It was clear they thought Call had lost his mind.

"Maybe he needs sleep," said Tamara.

"Maybe he needs food," said Aaron.

"Warren!" Call shouted again. *"The end is closer than you think!"*

"Lizards don't come when you call them," Tamara said. "Let's get out of here, Call —"

Something scrambled down from the rocky overhang above them. There was a flash of fire, light on scales. Red eyes gleamed in the dimness. What looked like a tiny Komodo dragon with a beard and back ridge made out of fire crawled toward them across the rocks.

"Warren?" said Call.

"He really did come." Aaron sounded impressed. "Awesome, Call."

"Sneaking." Warren looked annoyed. "Sneaking and bothering Warren. What do you want, mage students?"

"We want you to take us to the sleeping elementals. The ones bound by the Magisterium," Call said.

"Right now?" Tamara demanded, whirling on Call. "I thought we were going to sleep!"

"Yes, sleep. Sneaking too dangerous," Warren said. "Tunnels too deep."

"You owe us, Warren," Call said. "We saved your life. Don't you remember?"

"I pay you back already," Warren muttered. "I warn you. *Ultima Forsan.*"

"That's not help," Call said. He knew what *Ultima Forsan* was: a Latin phrase that had been carved over the Enemy of Death's resting-place. It meant *the end is closer than you think.* He just didn't see how it was a warning in any useful way. "Taking us to the elementals, that would be helpful."

"Maybe you don't know how to get there," Aaron taunted the little lizard. Although he was the one who'd yawned back at the library, now his eyes glittered and he didn't look tired in the least. Aaron was someone who didn't like talking about doing things half as much as he liked actually doing them. "Is that the problem? Maybe you don't know that much about the Magisterium after all."

Warren's red eyes whirled. "I know," he said. "I know everything. But this is dangerous, little mage students. Dangerous business. I could take you, but you will have to trick the guardian."

"The guardian?" Tamara asked in tones of dread.

Call also would have liked some more clarification, but Warren, apparently deciding that his half of their conversation was over, sprang toward a shining mica wall and ran halfway up, before dashing toward the entrance to the other cavern.

"Follow that lizard!" Call announced, going after him.

Tamara groaned, but she followed.

He forgot that letting Warren lead you through the caves of the Magisterium — including some passageways that might never have been used by a single mage before them — was a frustrating and sometimes terrifying endeavor. The lizard led them along naturally forming cliffs and past lakes of what appeared to be boiling mud. He guided them into and out of rooms where they nearly choked on the sulfur smell and where they had to duck to avoid being scraped by the pointed ends of stalactites.

Call wasn't sure how far they'd walked when his leg started really hurting — the kind of burning muscle pain that was only going to get worse. He felt stupid for suggesting they do this, stupid for thinking he could walk this far. But he couldn't ask Warren to stop — the lizard was too far ahead of them, leaping from rock formation to rock formation, the crystals on his back ablaze.

And if Tamara and Aaron paused to wait for him, Warren might sprint ahead, leaving them lost in the caves. It had happened before.

Experimentally, Call drew on air magic, pushing slightly. He remembered the way Alastair had sent Call up the long winding steps of the Collegium. He remembered how he'd made his own way down them. All he had to do was concentrate and *push*.

Call went up into the air — fast enough that he had to bite the side of his cheek to keep from crying out — but after a moment, he was able to steady himself. He was floating just a little bit above the ground and none of the weight was on his leg. He felt amazing.

He pushed himself along with his mind, no longer stumbling like Aaron or Tamara did. He glided over the earth as though this was the way he was meant to walk. As they went along, the passages curling deeper into the mountain, the walls became smoother, the ground under their feet polished. It was as if they were making their way down the hallway of a museum. The doors set into the stone on either side were elegant, decorated with alchemical symbols and alphabets that Call didn't know.

At last, Warren stopped in front of a massive door made from the five metals of the Magisterium — iron, copper, bronze, silver, and gold.

"Here, mage students. Here is the locked door in the way of the way. The guardian is here. You must face her to go farther."

"What do we do?"

"Answer her riddles," Warren said, and, flicking out his tongue to nab a cave bug that Call hadn't seen until the lizard scooped it up, raced off along the ceiling. "Riddle her answers!" he called back before he disappeared.

"Crap," Aaron said. "This always happens. I hate riddles."

Tamara looked as though she was forcibly swallowing the words *I knew it* and not much liking their taste.

"Do we just knock?" Call lifted his fist and then hesitated.

"I'll do it." Tamara pounded on the door. "Hello? We're students and we've come to do a project —"

The door opened. Standing inside, in a white suit entirely untouched by her surroundings, was Anastasia Tarquin. Her cloud of silver hair had been pulled back tightly and silver earrings sparkled in her ears as though they'd been enchanted to do so. Her manicured eyebrows shot up at the sight of them and her mouth compressed into a thin line.

"*You're* the guardian?" Aaron asked incredulously.

"I don't know what you mean," she said, opening the door more widely. Behind it, they could see a long corridor that sloped downward. Two Collegium-aged boys in uniforms stood against the walls. *Guards*, Call thought. "What I do know is that you're not supposed to be down here."

"Master Rufus wanted us to start a project," Call began. "Like Tamara said. It's our Bronze Year and we're supposed to be figuring out our futures and our personal responsibilities, so we wanted to specialize in elementals. And, uh, we wanted to meet some."

"All three of you?" Tarquin asked. "Including two chaos magicians? You *all* want to specialize in elementals?"

"We're thinking about it," Aaron said quickly. "We don't want to rush into anything, but it's interesting. And we figure if we got to see some of the most amazing elementals around, we'll be sure one way or another."

Anastasia Tarquin didn't look like she believed them for a minute. "I'm afraid that while students might have — infrequently — been given access to the elementals bound here before, that privilege has been suspended for the moment for reasons that I believe you already know."

Automotones. Call remembered the massive metal monster rearing above them, tearing at the air with fire and claws.

"Now," said Anastasia, "unless you want me to discuss this with Master Rufus, I suggest you go back the way you came and we will all pretend we didn't see one another."

Call looked from Tamara to Aaron.

"So much for riddles," Aaron said under his breath. Then, unfailingly polite, he turned to Anastasia Tarquin. "We're sorry to have disturbed you."

She, however, didn't seem particularly charmed by him. Her eyes didn't lose their flinty look.

"Just one moment," she said, but she wasn't looking at Aaron. "Callum Hunt. Come inside. I would like to speak with you. Alone."

"Me?" Call asked, his voice going a little squeaky. He hadn't expected that, and with all the spy business, he wasn't sure he wanted to be alone with any member of the Assembly. But she was Alex's stepmother, and the Assembly had sent her to protect him. "Okay."

Tamara and Aaron looked at him mutely. Call was pretty sure they didn't want to change places right then.

He walked through the door and she closed it behind him with a heavy clang.

Anastasia put one hand on his shoulder. "You must be very worried, to come down here, looking for answers," she said, her voice softening in a way that made him nervous. He thought of the way snakes he'd seen on television did a little dance before they struck. "And I know how close you are to Aaron. You two look out for each other, don't you?"

"Yeah?" Call said. "I mean, yes. Aaron and Tamara and I. We all do."

"It's so good to have close friends," she agreed, nodding. "Especially when you have a parent who doesn't approve of magic."

"Alastair's coming around," Call said, trying to guess what this was about.

"When I married Alex's father, I swore I would never try to replace his mother. I had my own children from my first marriage and I knew how important it was not to try and impose myself where I wasn't wanted. I tried to be a friend, a guide, and a mentor. Someone who could answer his questions straightforwardly, as so many adults don't. I would be happy to do that for you as well, if you ever need someone to talk to."

"Uh, okay," said Call, puzzled by the whole conversation. He tried to glance past Anastasia a little, see what was hidden behind her. The two Collegium guards were completely silent, ranged along the wall of the room like suits of armor. There was a sofa with a newspaper on it, probably where she'd been sitting, and a corridor that stretched away behind. A deep red glow illuminated its walls. "So, you're definitely not going to let us in?"

Anastasia looked amused rather than angry. "You want me to say I would if I could, I imagine. But you have no idea how dangerous the great elementals are. It would be like tossing you into the mouth of a volcano. A friend would never put you in danger, Callum, do you understand?"

"Because I'm a Makar," Call said. "I get it, but —"

"No buts." Anastasia shook her head. "You and Aaron should go back to sleep. You are far too important to risk yourselves. Try to remember that."

With that, she opened the door. When Call stepped out to where Aaron and Tamara were waiting, he heard the door slam behind him.

CHAPTER SEVEN

YOU WENT WITHOUT me?" Jasper demanded, fork stabbing into the gray pudding on his plate.

It was afternoon. Call, Tamara, and Aaron had all slept through breakfast after their adventure in the tunnels the night before. Call had felt achy and fuzzy-headed through their lesson, nearly dropping a ball of fire on Tamara's head and singeing his own fingers. He'd forgotten to walk Havoc until halfway through class and had to clean up the resultant mess. Being back at school wasn't as easy as he'd hoped it would be.

"It was a spur-of-the-moment thing," Call said in a conciliatory manner. Then remembered to whom he was talking. "I mean, not that I would ever choose to bring you anywhere, but in this case, leaving you out of it was just a side benefit."

"Hey," Jasper said. "I am trying to save your life!"

"Don't mind him," Aaron interrupted. "He gets snappish when he's tired."

"So what did Anastasia do to you?" Jasper said. "My father always told me that she was some kind of stone-cold ice queen."

"She was really nice to Call," Tamara said. "It was weird. She had no time for me and barely looked at Aaron. It was all Call, Call, Call."

"I guess I'm the new-news Makar, you're the old-news Makar," Call said to Aaron. "I make this blue uniform look *good*."

Tamara laughed. Aaron sighed with deep resignation.

"Wow," Jasper said, looking at Call with wide eyes. "You didn't tell me he got delusional when he was tired."

Call took a deep drink of the brown tea-like substance in his wooden cup. He hoped desperately that it had caffeine in it. All summer he'd been able to indulge in as many espressos as he wanted — Alastair had repaired an old deco-style Gaggia machine that chugged like a train — but now that he really needed it, there was no coffee in sight.

He was tired. Tired of being watched by his friends, even if it was because they were trying to keep him safe. Tired of having a horrible thing about himself — a thing he had no control over — hanging over his head. He wanted to go to school like a normal person, and right then he was willing to do anything to make that happen.

"Okay," he said. "I will do your stupid plan."

"What?" asked Jasper, frowning at him. "Which stupid plan?"

With a slight wince, Call climbed up onto his chair, then from his chair onto the top of their table. He stood with his foot narrowly avoiding landing in Jasper's gray pudding, and surveyed the room.

"Oh no," Aaron said. "I think you were right about him getting delusional with tiredness."

Students were laughing and chattering with one another. Mages were munching on lichen. Then Rafe caught sight of Call standing on the table. He yelped and poked Gwenda, who was next to him. A murmur ran around the room and soon everyone was staring at Call, pointing and whispering.

"Call!" Tamara hissed in a stage whisper. "Get down!"

Call was having none of it. "GUESS WHAT," he yelled, making his voice loud enough to carry over the whole Refectory. "I AM GOING TO BE AT THE LIBRARY TONIGHT AT MIDNIGHT. ALONE."

He sat down again. His friends stared at him. Across the whole room, he could see other apprentices looking over at his table. Gwenda whispered something in Celia's ear and they both started giggling. Alex Strike wore an odd, concerned expression on his face. Master Milagros was staring at Call as if he'd been dropped on his head as a child.

"That — that — What was that?" Tamara sputtered. "Are you out of your mind?"

"He was making himself bait," Aaron said. He looked at Call with a serious expression. "I hope that was a good idea," he said. "The downside of letting everyone know you're going to be all alone so they can attack you is that everyone knows you'll be all alone so they can attack you."

"Pfft," said Tamara. "Nobody's going to be dumb enough to come after him because of that public announcement. They'd get caught right away."

Call shrugged and took a big bite of lichen. He felt oddly better. Things were back in their proper place — his friends all thought he was nuts and he was about to do something foolish. A grin started at the corner of his mouth.

"Someone sedate him quickly," Jasper said. "Who knows what he might do next."

But either the brown liquid Call had been drinking had caffeine in it after all or having something to do helped, because energy was zipping through his veins. He didn't feel tired anymore. He felt ready.

↑ ≈ △ ○ @

Call half expected there to be a group of avid onlookers when he arrived at the library that night, but it was empty. Tamara, Aaron, and Jasper did a sweep, looking behind bookcases, while Havoc nosed around under tables. The room was definitely deserted.

Call sat down at one of the tables, lit by a huge stalactite that had been driven through the center of the wood, pinning the table to the floor. Light swirled and glowed inside the stalactite.

"Okay," said Tamara, returning from the top floor of the spiral library. "You're on your own."

Aaron put his hand on Call's shoulder. "Remember," he said. "If you need to do any chaos magic, don't try to do it all on your own. I'm your counterweight. I'll be just outside with the others. Draw on me, on my chaos energy, like you'd draw on air if you were underwater."

Call nodded as Aaron let go of him and grabbed Havoc's ruff. His dark green eyes were worried.

"Try not to do anything stupid," Jasper said. As parting

supportive remarks went, it wasn't one of Jasper's worst. "Here, try to pretend like you're reading something instead of sitting here by yourself like a creeper." He dumped a bunch of books on the table in front of Call and turned to go.

Call watched as his friends trailed out of the room. A moment later, he was alone in the library. *Draw on me*, Aaron had said. But the truth was, Call was still afraid of using Aaron as a counterweight. It was what had turned Constantine Madden into the Enemy of Death. All chaos mages had to have a counterweight who was a human being, a living soul that would anchor them to the real world and keep them from sliding into chaos. Constantine's had been his twin brother, Jericho. Then one day his magic had gotten out of control. It had overwhelmed him and he'd reached for his brother's magic to anchor himself. But he'd succeeded only in destroying his brother.

Call couldn't imagine what that would be like, to kill someone you loved by accident. *I* should *know what it feels like*, he thought. After all, it was something that had happened to his soul — and surely that sort of thing ought to leave a mark. But Call didn't feel anything when he thought about it except worry that he might make the same mistake.

Maybe that was proof of what was wrong with him. He ought to be feeling pity for Jericho, who had died. But all his pity was for Constantine.

"Call?"

He nearly jumped out of his skin. Whirling around, he saw that someone had come into the library — a blond someone in jeans and a T-shirt, her hair in two ponytails. She had her hands awkwardly in the back pockets of her jeans.

"Call?" said Celia again. She stepped forward, closer to him. She was blushing, which immediately made Call also blush, as if blushing were something that was catching, like chicken pox. "You said you were going to be all alone in here, so I thought . . ."

"Um?" he said. What had Celia thought? Maybe that he'd lost his mind and needed to be taken to the Infirmary?

"I thought maybe you wanted to talk to me," she said, perching on a table across from his. "It's hard to talk alone anywhere. . . . The Refectory's always so crowded, and so is the Gallery, and I haven't seen you walking Havoc lately. . . ."

It was true. For a while the previous year, Call and Celia had walked Havoc every night together. But now he wasn't allowed out alone with Havoc. Tamara and Jasper were taking turns walking him.

"Yeah, I've been . . ." Call's voice trailed off. He wondered if it was possible to have a conversation entirely in sentences that trailed off. If so, he and Celia were definitely on their way to an epic example.

"Where did you get those?" Celia asked, suddenly laughing. Call glanced down and realized that she was pointing at the books on his table.

Fire Elements and Love Spells, a Primer.

The Alchemy of Love.

Water Magic and Commitment Spells: How to Get Her to Say Yes.

He was going to *murder* Jasper.

"I — well, I was just — it's for an assignment," Call said.

Celia put her elbows on her knees and looked at him meditatively. "If you want to ask me out, Call, just ask me out," she said. "We're third years now, and I've liked you since Iron Year."

"*Really?*" Call was amazed.

She gave him a tentative smile. "You couldn't tell? All those times walking Havoc together. And the kiss. I figured you knew, but then Gwenda said I should just tell you, so here I am."

"She said you should tell me?" Call felt very stupid, echoing her, but his mind had gone almost completely blank. Was he supposed to thank her, as though liking him was a compliment? That didn't seem right. Probably he should tell her he liked her, too — and he did like her — but what would telling her that *mean*? Would they be going out? Would they have to kiss? Would it mean they couldn't walk Havoc together and joke around anymore?

As Call opened his mouth to say something — although he still wasn't sure what — Tamara and Jasper raced up the stairs to the landing. Aaron and Havoc dropped from above. The Chaos-ridden wolf began to bark. Aaron looked ready for a fight.

"Stop right there!" Jasper shouted. Fire ignited in Tamara's palm.

Celia spun around, eyes wide.

The flame guttered out abruptly. Tamara clasped both her hands behind her back. "Oh, hi," she said with an awkward and slightly hysterical laugh. "We were just —"

"What are *you* doing here?" Aaron demanded. Some of the light of battle was still in his eyes and he didn't sound as kind as he usually did. They must have been really surprised when they saw that Call wasn't alone — surprised and scared.

"Call was about to ask me out," Celia said, confused and clearly upset. "Or at least I think he was. What are you all doing here? Why was everyone yelling?"

For a long moment, they were all quiet. Call had no idea how to explain any of this to her. *Maybe I should just be honest*, he thought. *Sort of honest anyway.* He didn't have to tell her about the whole Captain Fishface angle. But, then, he realized, none of it made any sense without mentioning Captain Fishface. Still, he had to say something. She was his friend.

"The thing is that someone is trying —" Call started, his whole body flushing hot with embarrassment. He was sure that he was going to say something stupid and that Tamara was going to see him do it and make fun of him. He was sure Celia wasn't going to understand.

"I came to ask you out," Jasper said suddenly, loudly, breaking in on Call's explanation. "That's why I said 'Stop right there.' Because, uh, I wanted him to stop asking you out before I got a chance. Don't go out with him! Go out with me."

Aaron's eyebrows shot up. Tamara made a choking sound. Call couldn't believe his ears.

Celia looked at Jasper in surprise. "You like me?"

"Yes!" he said, a little wild-eyed. "I definitely do like you."

Call remembered that when Jasper had asked Call if he liked Celia, he'd also said that maybe he wanted to ask her out. Did he? Or was he just trying to throw her off figuring out what was going on? Or was he trying to annoy Call? The last one seemed the most likely.

Celia cut her gaze to Call expectantly, as though he was supposed to say something or do something. He gazed back at her in total bafflement.

Finally, she sighed and turned to Jasper. "I'd love to go out with you," she said.

↑ ≈ △ ○ @

"Well, I think we can all agree that that was a total bust," Aaron said as they trudged back toward their rooms.

"Not for Jasper," said Tamara, who, to Call's annoyance, seemed to think the whole thing was a little funny. Actually a lot funny. She'd nearly exploded trying to keep herself from laughing after Celia had agreed to go out with Jasper. Call wasn't sure who'd looked more nonplussed, him or Jasper, but Jasper recovered quickly and began telling Celia what a great time they were going to have at the Gallery.

At that point, Call had given up. He'd left the library. Aaron, Tamara, and Havoc scrambled after him.

Tamara was dancing along beside Havoc now, making him jump up to put his paws on her shoulders. "This is going to be the best date ever," she said. "Jasper doesn't know anything about girls. He'll probably bring her a bouquet of eyeless fish."

"It's not going to be the best date ever!" Call snapped. "Jasper's doing this to *annoy* me. He'll probably be really mean to Celia. He'll hurt her feelings, and it'll be my fault."

"Oh, for goodness sake, Call," Tamara huffed. "He's not going to be mean to Celia. Not everything is about you."

"*This* is about me," said Call.

"Maybe not." There was an edge to Tamara's voice. "Maybe he just likes Celia."

"I think both of you are losing sight of the big picture

here," said Aaron as they rounded a corner where the corridor narrowed. "What if Celia's the murderer?"

"*What?*" said Call.

"Well, she came when she knew you'd be alone in the library," Aaron pointed out.

"To see if I was going to ask her out," Call said.

"That's her cover story. I bet she showed up and sensed something wasn't right, so she bluffed."

"Why would Celia want to kill Call?" Tamara demanded. They had reached their rooms, and she used her wristband to pop the door open. They went inside the dim living area. Havoc quickly leaped up on the sofa and stretched out luxuriantly, ready to sleep.

"Yeah," Call said. "Why would she want to kill me?"

"She could be working for an organization," Aaron replied stubbornly. "Look, Drew had a totally fictitious background. He wasn't who he said he was. Master Rufus said there was a spy. She could be the spy."

Call shook his head, unbuckling Miri from his belt and laying the knife down on the kitchen table. "Celia comes from an old magic family. She is who she says she is."

"How do you know?" Aaron continued. "Just because she told you about some aunt doesn't make it true. Or maybe the whole family supports the Enemy. Remember how you thought the note came from her? What if it *did* come from her? That's a simpler explanation than anything else. Besides, if you could tell she was a spy, she wouldn't be a very *good* spy, would she?"

"You might as well accuse Havoc of being a spy," said Call. They all looked at Havoc. He was asleep, his tongue hanging down to the floor. As he slept, his feet paddled as if he were going after an imaginary duck.

"I'm not saying we should drag her in front of the Assembly right now," Aaron said. "Just that we should keep an eye on her. In fact, we should keep an eye on anyone behaving weirdly."

"Wanting Call to ask her out isn't *weird*," said Tamara, rubbing Havoc's stomach. "Well, maybe a little weird, but not illegal."

"Thanks," said Call. "Thanks for the support." He picked up Miri and headed toward his bedroom, then turned around in the doorway to look back at Aaron. "I'm going to sleep."

"So am I." Aaron crossed his arms over his chest. "I'm sleeping on the floor in front of your room. In case anything tries to attack in the night."

Call slumped. "Do you have to?"

In answer, Aaron lay down on the floor in front of Call's bedroom door, recrossed his arms over his chest, and shut his eyes. Havoc flopped down beside him.

Traitor, Call thought. With a sigh, he retreated into his bedroom, shutting his door firmly.

The room was lit with dim phosphorescent light. Call kicked his boots off and went to sit down on the bed. His leg was aching. He felt tired and dispirited and more annoyed about Celia and Jasper than he would have anticipated. He could see his own reflection in the wardrobe mirror. He looked tired. The room was full of shadows behind him.

Call froze.

One of the shadows was moving.

CHAPTER EIGHT

CALL WANTED TO scream. He knew he *should* scream, but surprise and terror robbed him of breath. The shadow moved again, uncoiling against the uneven rock of the ceiling. As it slithered closer to the phosphorescent moss, Call's panicked hope that it was just a trick of the light was dashed.

It was a huge air elemental, whip-fast and insubstantial in places. It looked like an enormous eel from the deepest part of the ocean — if eels had huge, tooth-filled mouths on either side of their long bodies. It moved sluggishly, like dank, humid air at the edge of a storm.

"Aaron," he tried to yell, but his voice came out as a whisper too soft to be heard by anyone but the elemental. One of its heads pulled away from the ceiling with a wet, sucking sound and dangled down toward him. Its mouth opened, and Call could see that despite being formed of ephemeral air, the thing had teeth that seemed very real and very sharp. The skin around its mouth was pulled back so that its maw was in a perpetual rictus grin. It looked like it was going to bite him in half and then laugh about it. It had no eyes, just indentations in its head.

Miri, he thought. The knife Alastair had given him, the one made by his mother. It was on the nightstand, several feet behind him. Could the elemental see him? Call wasn't sure. Slowly, slowly, he edged back on the bed. He stretched his body flat, lying down in a way that exposed his most vulnerable parts — his neck and stomach. The elemental moved toward him as if sniffing the air.

Call swallowed, reaching up over his head, reaching until his fingers brushed the edge of Miri's hilt.

In the other room, Havoc began to bark.

The elemental sprang. A scream tore from Call's lungs as he seized the blade and sat up, slashing blindly forward. The heavy weight of the creature knocked him back on his bed. Its open maw snapped at his face while the dagger embedded itself just under the creature's jaw. He tried to push it back with the knife, but although the blade cut deeper into the elemental's airy flesh, it squirmed closer.

He felt those horrible teeth against his skin and the sharp talons razoring at his clothes and slicing skin. He rolled off his bed, feeling the warmth of blood. It didn't hurt yet, but he had a feeling it was going to.

If he survived.

The elemental whipped around, fast as a tornado, and dived for Call just as he leaped for the door. He could hear Havoc frantically barking on the other side, could hear Aaron's sleepy, confused voice. "What's going on? What's wrong, boy?"

Call yanked at the door. It didn't open.

"Aaron!" Call shouted, finding his voice. "Aaron, there's an elemental in here! Get the door open!"

"Call?" Aaron sounded frantic. The doorknob jiggled and the door shook in its frame, but it didn't budge.

"It's covered in locking spells!" Aaron shouted. "Call, get out of the way! *Back up!*"

Call didn't need to be told twice. He flung himself away from the door and rolled against his wardrobe, yanking the front of it open as the elemental dived. It hit the wardrobe door, sending splinters of wood in all directions. Call just had time to leap away and scramble under the bed as it lunged for him again. He kept moving, coming out on the other side of the mattress. The elemental was a coiling mass above him. One of its heads jammed itself under the bed, but the other drew back, hissing, clearly about to strike.

Call held up Miri just as there was a soft explosion around the door. The elemental whipped toward it, its mouth opening in hideous surprise. Darkness was eating away at the edges of the door — but not just darkness.

Chaos.

Call felt the pull under his rib cage and realized what was happening. Aaron was using his chaos power, drawing on Call as a counterweight. Call held still as the door began to crumble in on itself.

It vanished, sucked away into the void. Aaron exploded into the room, wild-eyed. *"Makar!"* he yelled, his own hand still raised in summoning, black light burning around it. "You idiot, use your magic!"

The elemental was whipping back and forth, clearly confused by Aaron's sudden appearance. Call scrambled to his feet and reached out toward chaos. He felt the wild, roiling emptiness of the void open. Darkness spilled into the bedroom.

The air elemental gave a puffing screech and sailed toward the opening to the common room. It slashed Aaron's shoulder as it went past, gliding toward Tamara's room.

She opened the door just as it lunged for her throat.

Tamara dropped, rolling beneath it with more agility than Call would have in a thousand years. Havoc bounded toward her, snapping at the creature. The elemental pivoted in the air, horrible legs quivering, horrible jaws opening wide enough to swallow any of them whole.

Aaron added his power to Call's. The chaos grew, tendrils of oily nothing snaking into the room. From the opening in the void, something emerged, smoke-colored and wearing the rough shape of a monstrously sleek cat with countless eyes.

A chaos elemental, springing into the room.

Call made a sound in his throat. Opening chaos was one thing — summoning a chaos elemental was another.

The air elemental spun around, sensing a new threat. It made a sound deep in its throat. Then it rushed at the chaos elemental at the same moment the chaos elemental went for it. They met in the air. The chaos elemental bit at the air elemental's underside as the chaos elemental coiled around and around it, squeezing.

The door to their rooms opened and Master Rufus hurtled in, followed by Master Milagros.

"Call —" Rufus started to shout. Then he caught sight of the elementals coiling together in the air. For a moment, he looked almost fascinated. Then he swept his hand into the air and blew.

His breath became a shock wave that swept over the elementals. The whole room shook. Call fell to the floor as the air elemental shuddered and came apart into eddies that spiraled like miniature dust storms. The chaos elemental splashed against the wall, like spilled ink. It did not re-form.

"Wow," Aaron said.

Call's heart thudded dully. He pushed himself to his feet. Tamara, in a pair of blue pajamas — now torn at the knee — crossed the room to him, putting her hand on his arm. He had to forcibly stop himself from leaning against her the way he suddenly wanted to.

He looked down at his chest, at his torn shirt and the blood still welling there. The injuries weren't deep, but they stung like bee stings.

Aaron was petting Havoc's head, staring meditatively at the spot where the chaos elemental had been.

"We heard all the shouting," Master Milagros said. "We didn't think — how badly are you hurt?"

"I'm okay," Call said.

Master Rufus sighed, clearly rattled. They all were, but it was unnerving to see Master Rufus anything but perfectly composed. Call felt stupid. Master Rufus had told them not to investigate, but they'd done it anyway. And then Jasper had come up with a totally ridiculous plan. How had none of them realized that by making it clear where Call was going to be, it *also* made it clear that he wasn't going to be in his room? Anyone wanting to break in knew exactly when to do it.

"Apprentices, let's all sit down," Master Rufus said. "You can tell me what happened. And then we can decide what to do next."

Master Milagros moved toward the hall door. "I am going to make sure no one else gets in or out of here," she said. "Absolutely no one."

She sounded kind of paranoid. It was very reassuring to Call. He was feeling kind of paranoid, too.

He went to the couch with Tamara and Aaron. As soon as they sat down, Havoc jumped up on Call's lap and started to lick his face. Tamara took point on explaining how they were all in the library, studying with Jasper, and then had come back to their rooms. She didn't mention Call's stunt in the Refectory, or their plan, for which he was grateful. He was feeling dumb and freaked out enough already.

Call explained how the thing had been in his room and how the door had been locked with a spell. When he started talking about it, he could feel his hands begin to shake and jammed them between his knees to hide the trembling from Master Rufus and his friends.

After hearing about the locking spell, Master Rufus went over to inspect what was left of the door. Since Aaron had pretty much disappeared the whole thing, there wasn't a lot to see.

After a few minutes, Master Rufus sighed. "We're going to have to bring a team of mages in here. And, in case something else has been tampered with, we're going to move the three of you to another room. Permanently. I know it's late, but I am going to need you to take whatever you had on you and bring only that. We will give you the rest of your things as soon as they're confirmed as safe."

"Do we really need to do that?" Tamara asked.

Master Rufus gave her his most stern look. "We do."

Aaron stood. "I'm ready to go, then, I guess. I didn't change my clothes or anything. Neither did Call."

Tamara got her uniform out of her room and padded back into the common space, holding her boots in her hands. Call looked around, at the symbols on the walls, the glowing rocks, the giant fireplace. These rooms were theirs, comfortable, familiar. But he wasn't sure that he could have gotten into bed and looked up at his ceiling without seeing that creature there. He shuddered. Right at the moment, he wasn't sure he was ever going to be able to sleep again.

↑ ≈ △ ○ ◎

The room that Master Rufus took them to didn't look too unlike their own. Call already knew that most of the student quarters were the same — two to five bedrooms grouped around common spaces where students could eat and work.

There were four bedrooms in the new space. They each took one, including Havoc, who flopped down next to the bed in his and went to sleep with his feet in the air. Call checked to make sure his wolf was fine, then came out into the common room to find Tamara and Aaron on the couch. Aaron had his sleeve rolled up, his arm stuck out. Tamara was looking critically at his forearm, where a big red splotch was visible.

"It's like a burn, but not a burn," she said. "Maybe some kind of reaction from being hit with all that chaos magic?"

"But he's a Makar," Call objected. "Chaos magic shouldn't hurt him. Why didn't you show your arm to Master Rufus?" It didn't look like a bad injury, but Call bet it was painful.

Aaron sighed. "Didn't feel like dealing with it," he said. "They'll get more freaked out, restrict us further, but they don't know what's going on any more than I do. They'll decide someone else needs to be guarding you twenty-four-seven, but nobody else is going to do as good a job as we will. Besides, it's not like you made a big deal out of the fact you're bleeding." He pulled down his sleeve. "I'm going to take a shower," he said. "I still feel kind of slimy from that thing touching me."

Tamara saluted tiredly as Aaron headed off toward the door that led down to the showering and bathing pools. "You okay?" she asked Call as Aaron left.

"I guess," Call said. "I don't really understand why we're safer in this room."

"Because fewer people know we're here," Tamara said. The sentence was clipped, but she didn't look angry at Call, just sort of tired. "Master Rufus must feel like there are very few people he can trust. Which means anyone could be the spy. Literally anyone."

"Anastasia . . ." Call began, but then the door opened and Master Rufus came in. His smooth dark face was expressionless, but Call had started to be able to read the tension in his teacher's posture, the set of his shoulders. Master Rufus was very tense indeed.

"Call," he said. "Can I talk to you for a moment?"

Call glanced over at Tamara, who shrugged. "Anything you have to say, you can say in front of Tamara," Call said.

Master Rufus was not amused. "Call, this isn't a movie. Either you let me talk to you alone, or you'll all be sorting sand for the next week."

Tamara snorted. "That's my cue for bedtime." She got up, her dark braids swinging, and waved good-night to Call as she disappeared into her bedroom.

Master Rufus didn't sit down. He just leaned his bulky frame against the side of the table. "Callum," he said. "We know that someone with access to complex magic is after you. But what we don't know is — why aren't they going after Aaron?"

Call felt obscurely insulted. "I'm a Makar, too!"

A corner of Master Rufus's mouth turned up, which didn't make Call feel any better. "I suppose I might have put that differently. I don't mean that you aren't a valuable target, but it's odd for someone to come after you *exclusively*, especially since Aaron has been a Makar longer. Why not attempt to kill you both?"

"Maybe they are," Call said. "I mean, Aaron was around during both attempts. Maybe the elemental would have gone after him once it had finished with me."

"And maybe the chandelier required a trigger before it fell and the assassin waited until Aaron was in the room . . . ?"

"Exactly," Call said, relieved that Master Rufus had come up with that on his own. He didn't like the sound of *assassin*, though. The word slithered around in his head, hissing like a snake. *Assassin* was much worse than *spy*.

Master Rufus frowned. "Maybe. But I think that ever since you arrived at the Magisterium, you've been keeping secrets. First your father's, now maybe one of your own. If you know who is targeting you or why you're being targeted, tell me so I can better protect you."

Call tried not to goggle at Master Rufus. *He doesn't know*

about Captain Fishface, Call reminded himself. *He's just asking a question.* Sweat started up on Call's palms and under his arms anyway. He did his level best to keep his expression neutral; he wasn't sure he succeeded.

"There's nothing I'm not telling you," Call said, lying as well as he knew how. "If someone is really trying to kill me instead of Aaron, I don't know why."

"Whoever it was had a way to get into your room," Master Rufus said. "No one should be able to do that, except for you three and myself. And yet there was only one elemental waiting — the one on your ceiling."

Call shuddered, but he didn't say anything else. What could he say?

Master Rufus looked disappointed. "I wish that you believed you could trust me. I hope you understand how serious this all is."

Call thought of Aaron and his weird not-quite-a-burn. He thought of the elemental and its terrible eyes, staring down at him through the dark, its claws sinking into his skin. He thought of the year before and all the things they'd never told Master Rufus about their failed quest to bring back the Alkahest. If he'd been a better person, he would have confessed to Master Rufus then and there. But if he'd been a better person, maybe there would never have been a problem in the first place.

"I don't know anything. I don't have any secrets," Call told Master Rufus. "I'm an open book."

CHAPTER NINE

THE NEXT FEW days passed uneventfully. Call didn't like their new rooms, which felt more like a hotel than a place that belonged to them. Books, papers, and new clothes were brought to them by the mages — every time Call passed their old door, he saw that it was closed with an iron bar. He tried his bracelet on the lock, but it didn't accomplish anything. He didn't like the fact that Miri was locked in there, and so far he hadn't gotten up the nerve to ask the mages to bring him his knife. Luckily, he'd managed to get Constantine Madden's wristband out by virtue of wearing it above his own, shoved up under the sleeve of his uniform or his pajamas. He knew he should take it off, maybe even get rid of it, but he found that he was having a hard time with the idea of giving it up.

His dislike of the room got way worse when Tamara turned up a photograph, wedged under one corner of her bed. It was a picture of Drew, grinning at the person taking the picture, one arm slung around Master Joseph's shoulders. Drew was young in the picture — maybe ten years old — and he didn't look like the kind of person who could have tortured Aaron just for fun. And Master Joseph, in the photograph, looked like one of those older, professory dads who wanted their kids to read picture books in the original French. He didn't look like a psycho who'd trained an even bigger psycho. He didn't look like a guy who wanted to take over the world.

Call couldn't stop looking at the photograph. It was ripped along one side, but an arm and part of a blue T-shirt showed there'd been another person with them. The shirt had black stripes on it. For a terrible moment, Call thought he might be looking at the arm of the Enemy of Death, before he remembered that Constantine Madden had to have died around the time Drew was born.

But it wasn't just the newness of the room and the loss of Miri and the photograph that made Call uncomfortable. He didn't like the way Master Rufus was looking at him nowadays either. He didn't like the way that Tamara glanced nervously over her shoulder all the time. He didn't like the new, worried frown line between Aaron's eyebrows. And he especially didn't like the way that none of his friends would let him out of their sight.

"Eight eyes are better than one," Aaron said when Call told him that he wanted to go alone to walk Havoc.

"I have *two* eyes," Call reminded him.

"Well, sure," Aaron agreed. "It's just a saying."

"You're just hoping to run into Celia, aren't you?" Tamara asked, prompting Aaron to give Call another stern look.

Celia's date with Jasper was that Friday and Aaron thought it would be the perfect opportunity to discover whether she was the spy. Tamara had managed to wheedle most of the details of the date out of Celia. It was going to be in the Gallery, and they were going to meet there at eight o'clock, after dinner, and watch a movie.

"Seems innocent," Tamara said with a shrug as they sat at lunch, forking up lichen pasta.

"Well, of course it *seems* innocent," said Aaron. "You wouldn't expect her to make her evil intentions known this early." He cast a glance toward Celia, who was giggling cheerfully with Rafe and Gwenda. Jasper was sitting with Kai and looked as if he was in the middle of an animated story.

"If it's Celia, how did she manage to get hold of a giant elemental?" Call demanded. "Without it, you know, killing and eating her?"

"Elementals don't eat people," said Tamara. "They absorb their energy."

Call paused for a moment. He was remembering Drew, who had been killed by a chaos elemental while Call had looked on in horror during Call's first year. He remembered how Drew's skin had turned blue and then gray, his eyes going empty.

". . . seems weird," Call heard Aaron say as he snapped out of his reverie.

"What's weird?" Call asked.

"The way everyone's looking at us," Tamara answered in a low voice. "Have you noticed?"

Call hadn't. But now that Tamara mentioned it, he realized that people were staring at them — at Aaron, specifically.

And not the way they usually stared at Aaron, with admiration, or with a sort of *Look, there's the Makar* expression.

This was different. Eyes were narrowed, voices lowered. People were glancing at him suspiciously, whispering and pointing. It gave Call a queasy feeling in his stomach.

"What's going on?" Aaron asked, bewildered. "Do I have something on my face?"

"Do you really want to know?" said a voice above their heads.

Call looked up. It was Jasper. "Everyone's talking about the elemental that almost ate Call —"

"Elementals *don't eat people*," Tamara insisted, cutting him off.

Jasper shrugged. "Fine. Whatever. Anyway, people are saying Aaron was the one who summoned it. Somebody told somebody that they overheard you two fighting and everyone saw Aaron summon all those chaos creatures last summer . . ."

Call gaped. "That's ridiculous," he said.

Aaron looked around the room. When he met other apprentices' gazes, they looked away. Some of the Iron Years started giggling. One began to cry.

"Who's saying that?" Aaron demanded, turning back to Jasper. His ears were pink and his expression was that of someone who wanted to be anywhere but where he was.

"Everyone," Jasper said. "It's a rumor. I guess because Makars are supposed to be unstable and everything, they figure you tried to kill Callum. I mean, some people think it's understandable because Call is so annoying, but other people figure that there's some kind of love triangle situation going on here with you two and Tamara."

"*Jasper*," Tamara said in her firmest voice. "Tell people that's not true."

"Which part?" Jasper asked.

"None of it is true!" Tamara said, her voice rising dramatically.

Jasper held up both his hands in a gesture of surrender. "Fine. But you know how gossip is. No one is going to listen to me." With that, he wheeled away from the table, back toward the food.

"Don't listen to him," Tamara said to Aaron. "He's ridiculous and he gets mean when he's scared. He's probably nervous about his date and taking it out on you."

Maybe, Call thought, but something really was going on. People were definitely cheating looks in their direction. Call got up and chased after Jasper, catching his elbow as he'd reached a large pot of cinnamon-and-clove-smelling brown liquid.

"Jasper, wait," he said. "You can't just tell us all that and then walk away. Who started the rumor? Who's making this stuff up? You've got to have a guess, at least."

The boy frowned. "Not me, if that's what you're implying — although I have to say, it got me thinking. Aaron told you two different stories about his past. That's pretty suspicious. We have no idea where he came from, or who his family really is. He just shows up out of nowhere and then, boom! Makar."

"Aaron is a good person," Call said. "Like, way better than either of us."

Jasper sighed. He wasn't laughing or sneering or making any of his usual pompous expressions. "Don't you think that's suspicious?" he asked.

"No," Call said, stomping back to the table. Fury boiled

inside him. Jasper was an idiot. In fact, everyone in the room was an idiot except for him, Tamara, and Aaron. He flung himself down at their table. Tamara was leaning in to talk to Aaron, her hand on his shoulder.

"Fine," Aaron was saying, his voice strained. "But I really think we should leave."

"What's going on?" Call asked.

"I was just telling him not to let this get to him." Tamara was flushed, red spots on both her brown cheeks. Call knew that meant she was furious.

"It's ridiculous," Call said. "It'll blow over. Nobody can believe something this stupid for long."

But Aaron's expression told Call that he wasn't reassured. His green eyes were darting around the Refectory as if he half expected people to start throwing things at him.

"I'm going to go back to the room," he said.

"Hold on there." It was Alex Strike, his long, lanky form casting a shadow across their table. His Gold Year band gleamed as he held out his hand. In the center of his palm were three round, reddish stones. "These are for you."

"You want to play marbles?" Call guessed.

Alex's mouth crinkled up into a smile. "They're guide-stones," he said. "The Masters are having a meeting tonight. You're invited." He wiggled his fingers. "One stone for each of you."

"We're invited?" Aaron said as the three of them plucked the stones out of Alex's hand. He looked nervous. "Why?"

"Search me. I'm just the messenger."

"So what do we do with these?" Call asked, examining his stone. Perfectly round and shiny, it did look a lot like a red marble. The big ones that you shot with.

"The Masters have been moving their meetings around to preserve security," said Alex. "Unless you have one of these, you can't find the room. The meeting starts at six — just let the stone take you where you're supposed to go."

↑ ≈ △ ○ ◉

Six o'clock found the three of them sitting in their new common room with Havoc, staring at the stones in their hands. They were all dressed in their blue school uniforms; Aaron had polished his shoes and Tamara had her hair down, gold barrettes clipped above her ears. Call's concession to fanciness was washing his face.

"Whoa!" Tamara said as her guide-stone lit up like a tiny Christmas light. Aaron's followed, flickering, and then Call's. They all stood.

"Havoc, stay here," Call told his wolf. After the previous meeting with the Assembly, he didn't want to give them any excuse to remember Havoc's existence.

Out in the hall, Tamara was using her stone to navigate. When she turned in the wrong direction, the glow of the stone dimmed.

"Master Rufus should have given us one of these when we went into the tunnels," Call said as they set off. "Instead of that vanishing map."

"I think that would have defeated the purpose of the lesson," Aaron pointed out, folding his fingers over his stone so he didn't have to keep squinting into its light. "You know, about finding your own way."

"Don't be superior," Tamara said, making an abrupt turn. All of their stones went to half-light.

"I think you, uh, missed the turn," Call said, pointing backward, into the large room with an underground waterfall that the stone seemed to indicate they should be heading into.

"Come on," she said, scrambling ahead, leaving Aaron and Call nothing to do but follow.

She ducked into the small entryway that led to a space with high ceilings and a small group of bats huddled together, making little nickering noises to one another. The whole room stank of them. Call pinched his nose.

"What are you doing, Tamara?" Aaron asked, voice low.

She hunched down and crawled into a tight passageway. Call and Aaron traded worried looks. It was dangerous to explore the caves without a map or a guide of some kind. There were deep pits and boiling lakes of mud, not to mention elementals.

Heading into the passageway after Tamara, Call really hoped she knew where she was going.

The rock was rough under his hands as he crawled along what seemed to be a naturally forming tunnel. It narrowed, and Call wasn't sure they were going to fit through. His heart began to thud as their only light faded dimmer and dimmer. After a few tense minutes, the area opened up into an unfamiliar but not particularly dangerous-looking room. Their stones brightened.

"Are you going to explain what all of that was about?" Call demanded.

Tamara put her hands on her hips. "We have no idea who's after you. It might be one of the Masters or someone who knows where the meeting is being held. We can't go the direct route. There might be a trap. The whole point of stones like these is to make sure we can't get lost."

"Oh, that's smart," Call said, trying to ignore the cold dread pooling in his stomach. He wanted to believe that whoever his enemy or enemies were, they weren't the current Masters at the school. He wanted to believe it was just some sneaky minion of Master Joseph or some random miserable Makar-hating mage. Or maybe a student who Call had annoyed in a big way. Call knew he could be really annoying, especially when he was putting effort into it.

Call was still mulling it all over when they arrived at the room the Masters had chosen for the meeting. They were late and the session had already begun. A group of Masters in black sat around a semicircle of smoothly polished marble. A long, low marble bench ran across the outside of the semicircle, allowing the Masters to face the center of the room. The stalactites that hung from the ceiling ended in round pendant bulbs of clear stone, each one glowing with a yellowish light.

"Tamara, Aaron, and Call," Master Rufus intoned as they filed into the room. "Please take your seats."

He indicated three heaps of jumbled polished rocks directly in front of the Masters' table. Call stared. Were they supposed to *sit* on those? Wouldn't the rocks just scatter, depositing them each onto the floor in an embarrassing pile?

But Tamara brushed past him confidently and sat on one of the rock heaps. She sank down slightly and crossed her arms, but the rocks didn't scatter. Aaron followed and Call went after him, throwing himself down on a rock pile. The stones hissed and clattered as his weight displaced them, but it was like sitting in a chair made out of taffy, though less sticky — the rocks molded and reformed around him until he was sitting as comfortably as his leg would allow.

"Cool!" Call exclaimed. "We need one of these in our common room."

"Call," Rufus said darkly. Call had the feeling Master Rufus still thought he knew something he wasn't saying. "Please restrain your commentary on the furniture; this is a meeting."

Really? I thought it was a party! Call wanted to say but didn't. Definitely, there couldn't have been less of a party atmosphere. Master North and Master Milagros flanked Rufus; Anastasia Tarquin, her steely silver hair piled on her head, sat near the end of the table, her dark gaze fixed on Call.

"What's this about?" Aaron asked, looking around the room. "Are we in trouble?"

"No," said Master Milagros at the same time that Master North said, "Maybe," and snorted.

"We're just trying to reason out how this attack could have happened," said Master Milagros with a sideways look in Anastasia's direction. "We had so many safeguards in place. We know you've gone through what happened before, but can you tell us all one more time, for the record?"

Call tried to tell them, tried to focus on details that might be helpful instead of the terror and helplessness he'd felt. Tamara and Aaron jumped in to explain their parts. Call made a particular point of highlighting how helpful Havoc had been, since he was still worried about the view the Assembly had taken on Chaos-ridden animals.

"Someone must be very determined. If anyone has an idea why, this would be a good time to tell us." Master Rufus gave Call a stern look from across the table, as if urging him once more to confess. After Call had brought the Assembly the head of the Enemy of Death, he'd thought that his secret was safe, but now it felt closer to the surface than ever before. If only he could just tell them. If only they'd believe that Call was *different* from Constantine.

Call opened his mouth, but nothing came out. It was Tamara who answered. "We have no idea why anyone would want to hurt Call," she said. "Call doesn't have any enemies."

"I wouldn't go *that* far," Call muttered, and Tamara kicked him. Hard.

"There's a rumor going around among the students," Master Milagros said. "We hesitate to bring it up, but we need to hear it from you. Aaron, did you have anything to do with the elemental attack?"

"Of course he didn't!" Call yelled. This time Tamara wasn't kicking him for sticking his oar in.

"We need to hear it from Aaron," Master Milagros said gently.

Aaron looked down at his hands. "No, I didn't do it. I wouldn't hurt Call. I don't want to hurt anyone."

"We believe you, Aaron. Callum is a Makar," said Master Rockmaple, a short mage with a bristly red beard. Call hadn't liked him at the Iron Trial, but he was glad Master Rockmaple believed Aaron. "There are any number of reasons those who oppose the Magisterium and what it stands for would attack a Makar. I think our primary concern should be discovering how a malicious elemental gained access to a student's room and — more importantly — how we can make sure it never happens again."

Call looked over at Aaron. He was still studying his

fingers, picking at the skin around his nails. For the first time, Call noticed that they were bit to the quick.

"It wasn't just any elemental," said Master Rufus. "It was one of the great elementals. One of those from our own holding cells. Its name was Skelmis."

Call thought about Automotones crashing through the house of one of his father's friends a year before, eager to destroy Call. Automotones had been another of the great elementals. It was disturbing to think that someone had been trying to murder Call for more than a year and that they seemed to be able to harness the most powerful creatures in the Magisterium to do it. Call wondered if it could be one of the Masters after all. He looked around the table and shuddered.

"Now, we may need you three to answer questions about specifics," said Master North. "And this may take some time. It is a formal inquest into Anastasia Tarquin and whether she was derelict in her responsibilities as the guardian of the elementals. Master Rockmaple will be recording our findings and sending them to the Assembly."

"I've already explained," Anastasia said. She was dressed in her customary white suit, her icy hair held in place with ivory combs. White-gold rings shone on her fingers. Even her wristband was formed from a pale gray leather. The only color on her face came from her eyes, which were red-rimmed with sleeplessness and worry. "The elemental Skelmis must have been released before I put up the safeguards. There are only two spelled stones that open the vaults to the elementals. One remained around my throat. The other was in a magically sealed vault in my room — locked with three separate locks.

I've carefully monitored everyone who's come in and out. You've seen the notations. You've spoken with the guards. Blaming this on me because it gives you an excuse to push an Assembly representative out of the school doesn't do any of us any good."

"So because you didn't notice anyone coming in, no one must have come in? Is that what we're supposed to believe?" Master North asked.

Anastasia stood, hands slamming down on the table, making Call jump. "If you intend to accuse me of something, just do it. Do you think I am in league with the Enemy's forces? Do you think I intentionally brought harm to this boy and his friends?"

"No, of course not," Master North said, clearly taken aback. "I am not accusing you of anything deliberate. I'm saying that you can brag about your safeguards all you want, but they didn't work."

"So you merely think me incompetent," she said, her voice icy.

"Which would you prefer?" Master Rufus said, stepping in. "Because it's one or the other. If Master North won't say it, I will. It was your job to make sure no one released an elemental from the vaults beneath the Magisterium. And yet one got out and nearly killed a student, one of my apprentices. That's on you, Tarquin, however you might not like it to be."

"It's not possible," she insisted. "I am telling you — I would never do anything to hurt Callum or Aaron. I would never let a student be put in danger."

Tamara gave a small snort at being left out of the declaration.

"And yet they were in grave danger," Master Rufus said. "So help us discover what happened."

Anastasia slumped back down onto her stool. "Very well." She reached around her neck and drew a chain from under her shirt. Hanging from it was a large cage . . . and inside the cage was a bronze key, its bow an alchemical symbol for a crucible. "When I took over guarding the way into the caverns of the deep elementals, I made sure the key never left my side."

"What about the other one?" Master North asked. "There are two keys. You said you locked the other up. Could anyone have stolen it and then returned it?"

"That's very unlikely," Anastasia replied. "You would need to get past three separate locking spells to get into my safe. And the safe itself was brought here with my other possessions. Master Taisuke himself helped me sink it into the stone."

"What kind of locking spells?" Master Milagros asked.

Anastasia hesitated, then sighed. "I suppose I will have to change them now anyway, even though I judge it very unlikely that anyone could have done what you suggest. Fine. The first safeguard is a password, which must be spoken aloud. And no, I won't tell it to you. I have told it to no one."

For a moment, she stared at her hands and her perfectly manicured nails. She was older than she seemed most of the time, older than Alastair, and in that moment, she looked it.

Then her head rose and her expression resumed some of its earlier sharpness. "The second is a clever little spell, triggered by the password. A hole appears in the safe, but were you to just stick your hand in, a snake elemental would strike, poisoning the robber with a lethal toxin. To bypass that, fire must be cast into the opening." A small, wicked smile turned up a corner of her mouth.

"Cool," Aaron said under his breath. Call agreed with him.

"And then, last, there is a final spell, created by me. You are the first people I have told of it and I am regretful that it must be replaced. Once fire is cast, nothing will change visually. At this point, you can reach through the hole so long as you move slowly. Should you jerk your hand out suddenly, alarms will sound and the vault will shut itself up again. However, there's an illusion of a snake elemental coiling out of the opening and drawing back to strike, so the temptation to withdraw quickly is understandable."

For a moment, they all sat in silence. Call was pretty sure they were marveling over her security, but he thought they might also be marveling at her deviousness, because those were some pretty inventive locks.

"Now, are we finished? There's something evil at work here in the Magisterium," said Anastasia, head held high. "We all know it. It's why I came. I suggest we find the source of it, rather than throw baseless accusations. Before it's too late."

Master North turned to Call, Aaron, and Tamara. "We want you to understand that nothing like this has ever happened at the Magisterium before and we're going to make sure it never happens again. You three are excused. We will continue on from here without you, but do not doubt that we will discover what happened."

It was clear that the mages might go on arguing all night, even though they had no actual leads on finding the spy. Call thought, suddenly, of Jericho Madden and how his death had been an accident — an experiment gone wrong. Was there an inquest after that? A lot of people uselessly pointing fingers at one another?

"I still believe that the safest thing would be to *teach* them," Anastasia said, the edge in her voice unmistakable. "You may believe me derelict in my duties, but that doesn't mean that you haven't neglected yours as well."

"I do teach them," Master Rufus said, turning his sternest look on her. "I teach them what they need to know."

"Ah," she said, and it seemed clear that she was no longer upset because she was sure she had the upper hand. "So Aaron and Callum know that they have the power to remove a living soul from its body? They understand how to do it? What a relief, because I thought you were so terrified of their abilities that you were planning on keeping them in the dark, even if it got them killed."

"I have excused our students," Master North said with unusual heat. "Tarquin, let them go. Defy me again and I will bar you from the school, no matter the Assembly's orders."

Outside the meeting room, Call turned to Aaron and Tamara. Tamara raised her eyebrows in a gesture that seemed to capture how completely weird that meeting had been. Aaron shook his head. After walking a short way, they saw a familiar path, which was good, since it turned out the stones were only for a one-way journey and they would lead back to the meeting again and again.

Finally, Aaron spoke. "Good thing we got out of there before Jasper's date. I was getting worried."

"You don't really think that Celia's the one, do you?" Call asked. "I mean, not *really*, right?"

"I know you don't want it to be her," Aaron said, walking past moss that fluoresced blue when their breath touched it. "I know you think she's your friend, but we've got to be careful. Celia did something odd around the time of both attacks. It could be coincidence. Or maybe not."

"So how is the date going to help?" Tamara asked. "Even if it is Celia, Jasper's not a target."

"Jasper promised me that he'd say stuff about Call. If she takes the bait, then we'll know."

Tamara rolled her eyes. She probably thought that Call wouldn't notice in the dim light of the moss, but he did.

↑ ≈ △ ○ ◎

They arrived breathless at the Gallery, which was lit up for the night with spangled streamers of moss, glimmering blue and green. Students splashed in deep pools of water that glowed turquoise. Call remembered the first time he'd been there: Celia had invited him during their Iron Year, and it had been one of the first things about the Magisterium that he'd really liked. It had made him catch his breath and realize he was looking at stuff no ordinary person would ever see.

Now he looked around the place with more familiarity. He certainly recognized people — there was Alex, lounging in a corner with Tamara's sister and another Gold Year girl. Gwenda and Rafe were jumping out of one of the pools of water, splashing each other. Kai was over by the glass tubes that dispensed fizzing candy, digging through a mountain of sweets with one hand and holding up a book with another.

"Look at me!" someone yelled. For a second Call thought

he saw a skinny, brown-haired figure in a worn T-shirt, beckoning toward him. Someone whose eyes glowed black in a face that was too pale.

Drew.

Call blinked, and the vision resolved itself into Rafe, cannonballing into a pool. Water went everywhere. People clapped and cheered; Aaron leaned over and whispered to Call and Tamara, "There they are."

He pointed to where Jasper and Celia sat on a big overstuffed purple couch. Celia looked pretty in a pink dress, her hair tied up in a ponytail. Jasper looked like Jasper.

A stone bowl floated between them. Celia dipped her fingers in, and when she brought them out, they shone. She blew on them, and multicolored bubbles spiraled up toward the ceiling. She giggled.

"Ugh," said Call. "Celia's staring at Jasper with googly eyes. This is so weird. She doesn't even *like* Jasper. Or at least if she does, she's never mentioned it before."

"She's leading him into her clutches," said Aaron.

"You're both idiots," said Tamara, sounding resigned. "Come this way."

They crept around the big bar full of snacks and candy, keeping to the wall. It was dark; Call followed the light of Tamara's glinting gold barrettes. When they emerged on the other side, they were behind the purple couch, much closer to Celia and Jasper. It was Jasper's turn with the bowl, apparently. He gave Celia a meaningful look, then blew on his fingers. Bubbles in the shape of hearts rose into the air.

"Oh, gross," said Call. "I'm going to puke."

Tamara had to slap a hand over her mouth to smother her

laughter. "It's a date," she said when she'd stopped wheezing. "On dates, people are supposed to have fun."

"Or pretend to," Aaron said, narrowing his eyes at Celia. He really seemed to think she might be guilty.

"How is staring at each other fun?" Call demanded.

"Okay," Tamara said, giving both boys an unfathomable look. "If you two jokers were taking somebody out, what would you do?"

Call watched Celia's cheeks go pink as Jasper leaned in and said something to her. It was weird to watch. For one thing, it was bizarre to see Jasper be nice to someone. Usually, even when he was in his not-a-total-jerk guise, he had an edge to the stuff he said. But with Celia, he seemed like he was acting like a normal person.

And she seemed into him.

Which was *totally unfair*, since the only reason that Jasper even asked her out was to cover up what they'd really been doing in the library.

Come to think of it, Celia had always said that Call was overreacting when he talked about what a jerk Jasper was. Maybe she'd liked Jasper! Maybe she'd only been pretending to like Call to get closer to Jasper.

"I don't know," Aaron said. "Whatever she wanted to do."

Call had forgotten the question that Aaron was answering. For a moment, Call kind of hoped Celia was the spy after all. It would serve Jasper right if she were.

Tamara poked Call in the shoulder. "Wow. You must really like her."

"What? N-no!" he sputtered. "I was just lost in thought! About how Jasper is a total sucker."

Aaron nodded sagely. Jasper and Celia were dipping their fingers at the same time and blowing, causing illusions of butterflies and birds to fly up in the air. Both of them started to laugh, just before one of Jasper's birds swooped down to eat one of Celia's butterflies.

That was more like it! Call grinned. He wondered what would happen if he conjured the illusion of a cat to chase all the birds.

"You should just ask her out if you like her that much," Tamara said slowly, thinking through her words carefully. "I mean, I think she'd forgive you if you explained."

"Explained what?" Aaron asked.

Call overheard Jasper start to complain to Celia about Fuzzball, Gwenda's ferret. And even though Celia had told Call all about Jasper's allergic reaction to Fuzzball *last year*, so Jasper had to know she knew, Celia still totally pretended this was new information. Jasper ate it up. He went on and on about the dumb ferret and how much he didn't like it and she acted like she was *fascinated*.

Call wanted to scream.

"Ooh, look," Celia said when Jasper had finally exhausted the ferret topic. "Alex Strike is starting up a movie. Do you want to go watch?"

Alex was an air mage, and one of the ways he deployed his talent was to shift and shape colored air against the wall of the Gallery cave, creating the illusion of popular movies. Sometimes he changed the endings to amuse himself. Call had a clear memory of an Ewok and droid and ghost Darth Vader conga line in Alex's version of *Return of the Jedi*.

Jasper took Celia's hand and helped her off the couch. Together they went over to the west side of the room, where rows of low stools had been set up. They found two seats together just as the light in that part of the cave dimmed and the first scenes of a movie started to play against the wall.

"Here we go," Aaron whispered. "She's going to take advantage of the dark to knock him unconscious."

Call suddenly felt tired of the whole thing. "No, she's not," he said. "I've been alone with her dozens of times. If she'd wanted to hurt me, she could have. We should just give up on this. The only danger on this date is Jasper boring Celia to death."

"Or us being bored to death," muttered Tamara. "Call's right, Aaron. Jasper promised to grill her about Call, but I think we can safely say that he's forgotten all about that."

Shapes moved against the wall, casting strange patterns of light. Call could see Alex sitting in the back, moving his hands slightly to make the images dance. From what Call could tell, the movie was a combination of *Toy Story* and *Jurassic Park*, with toys being chased across the screen by velociraptors.

"This is a dead end," Call said. "But I have an idea of what we could do tonight."

That made Aaron look over in surprise. "What?"

"If someone went down into the elemental prison and freed Skelmis, then there are at least some witnesses. There have to be."

"The other elementals," Tamara said, realizing what he meant instantly. "They're imprisoned down there. They would have seen what happened."

"But wouldn't the Assembly already have asked them?" said Aaron.

"Not necessarily," said Call. "Most people are pretty afraid of elementals. They don't think of them as creatures you can talk to. And they're hard to fight off. But with two Makaris . . . and an elemental in a cage . . ."

"It's a crazy plan," said Tamara, but her brown eyes were alight.

"Are you saying you don't want to do it?" said Call.

"No," said Tamara. "I'm just saying it's a crazy plan. How would we get down there?"

"Anastasia practically gave us the whole rundown on how to do it during the meeting," said Call. "She said she keeps a key in her room, and one around her neck. All we have to do is get into her room when we know she isn't there and grab the key."

"And the guards?" said Aaron. "What about the guards at the door?"

"We'll worry about that when we get there," Call said. "The spy got in. There must be a way. And if we don't do it tonight, she's going to change all her locks. We won't have this chance again."

Aaron gave Celia one last suspicious look and nodded his head. Together, they crept out into the hallway. As they started toward the area where the Masters' rooms were, Call realized there were three complications to his plan. One, he wasn't sure which room belonged to Anastasia Tarquin. Two, he didn't have a way in. And three, once they were inside, they were going to have to guess her password.

How hard can it be? he asked himself. Her password was probably something completely obvious. Something they could figure out just from looking at her stuff.

And her room might be obvious, too. He glanced over at Tamara and Aaron. They seemed ready to be convinced that this was a plan that could work. Maybe they'd already thought of a way. And at least they were all doing something, not just waiting around for the spy to strike again.

Call sighed. If the Masters and the Assembly couldn't be relied upon to solve this, then it was down to them.

CHAPTER TEN

IT DIDN'T TAKE them long to reach the corridors where the Masters lived. It wasn't a part of the Magisterium that Call had ever been to before. Though it wasn't forbidden, the only students who generally braved the area were assistants like Alex running errands or students carrying messages for Masters. Going there otherwise was too much of an invitation to get in trouble.

Call, in fact, was having a hard time looking confident and walking as he normally did, which had been Tamara's advice. He kept wanting to slink along the walls, out of sight, though very few other students passed them. No Masters did. They were all still holed up in their meeting, trying to figure out what had gone wrong, which was good news for Call's plan. It did make things a little spooky as they turned onto the set of corridors where the Masters' sleeping quarters were, though.

They had some fun guessing whose door was whose. Master Rockmaple must be the massive door studded with brass, Master North must be the plain metal door, Master Rufus the door of brushed silver. The door with a picture of a kitten dangling from a wire that had the message HANG IN THERE underneath obviously belonged to Master Milagros.

Anastasia's was just as easy to spot. A thick white mat had been placed in front of it, and the door itself was made of pale marble veined with black that looked like smoke. Call remembered her having all her expensive, pale white furniture carried inside on the first day of school.

"This is her," Call said, pointing. "It has to be."

"Agreed." Aaron drew close, tapped his fingers against the marble. He examined the seams of the door, but like all doors in the Magisterium, it didn't have hinges, just the flat pad where you were supposed to wave your bracelet to get in. Eventually Aaron stepped back, raising his hand. Call felt a familiar pull underneath his rib cage.

Aaron was about to use chaos magic.

"Wait," Call said. "Don't — not unless we absolutely have to."

The pulling feeling went away, but Aaron gave him a look that was almost hurt. "What have you got against chaos magic all of a sudden?"

Call tried to form his jumbled thoughts into words. "I think it brings the Masters running," he said. "I think they have some way of sensing it, at least when it's used in the Magisterium."

"I figured it was the racket that Skelmis made in our room

that got them there so fast," said Tamara thoughtfully. "But they did race over pretty quickly for just some noise. Call could be right."

"Okay, then," said Aaron. "What do you suggest?"

For the next ten minutes they went at the door with everything they could think of. Tamara cast a fire spell, but the door was impervious. It didn't react to freezing, either, or to "Open sesame," or to the unlocking spell Tamara had used on the cages in the village of the Order of Disorder. It just sat there, looking at them, being a door.

It didn't react to being kicked, either, Call discovered.

"Seriously?" Aaron said, after they'd exhausted their ideas and were leaning sweatily against the opposite wall. He glared at Master Milagros's kitten poster. "All this worrying about the safe and we can't even get past the door."

"Somebody got past *our* door," Tamara pointed out.

"So it's possible," said Call. "Or at least it should be. I mean, we knew it wouldn't be easy. These doors are the Magisterium's security. We shouldn't be able to wave just any wristband at one of them and have the door open." He waved his arm at the door for emphasis.

There was a click.

Tamara stood up straight. "Did that just —"

Aaron took two strides across the hallway and pushed. The door slid open smoothly. It was unlocked.

"That's not right." Tamara didn't sound pleased; she sounded upset. "What was that? What happened?" She whirled on Call. "Are you just wearing your regular band?"

"Yeah, of course, I'm —" Call pushed up the sleeve of his thermal shirt. And stared. His wristband was on his wrist;

that was true. But he'd forgotten the wristband he'd shoved up above his elbow.

The wristband of the Enemy of Death.

Tamara sucked in a breath. "That doesn't make sense, *either*."

"We're going to have to figure it out later," said Aaron from the doorway. "We don't know how much time we have in her room." He looked agitated but also a lot happier than he'd been a moment before.

Call and Tamara followed him in, though Tamara's expression was still worried. Call felt as if the Enemy's wristband was burning on his arm. Why hadn't he left it back home, with Alastair? Why had he wanted to wear it to school? He *hated* the Enemy of Death. Even if they were in some way the same person, he hated everything Constantine Madden stood for and everything he had become.

"Wow," Tamara said, shutting the door behind them. "Check out this room."

Anastasia's room was stunning. The walls were glittering, veined with quartz. A thick white pile rug covered the floor. Her sofa was white velvet, her table and chairs were white. Even the paintings on the wall were done in shades of white and cream and silver.

"It's like being inside a pearl," said Tamara, turning in a circle.

"I was thinking it was like being inside a giant bar of soap," said Call.

Tamara gave him a withering look. Aaron was stalking around the room, looking behind the china cabinet (white, with white dishes) and behind a bookshelf (white, lined with books wrapped in white paper) and under a (white) trunk on the floor. Finally, he approached a long tapestry hanging on one wall. It had been woven in threads of cream and ivory and black, and it depicted a white mountain of snow.

La Rinconada? Call wondered. *The Cold Massacre?*

But he couldn't be sure.

Aaron twitched the tapestry aside. "Got it," he said, lifting the tapestry up and away. Behind it was a massive safe, made of enameled steel. Even it was white.

"Maybe her password is some variation on the word *white?*" Aaron suggested, looking around. "That's definitely her thing."

Tamara shook her head. "In this room, that would be too easy for someone to say by accident."

Aaron frowned. "Then maybe the opposite. Jet? Onyx? Or a really bright color. Neon pink!"

Nothing happened.

"What do we know about her?" Call asked. "She's on the Assembly, right? And she's married to Alex's dad, whose last name is Strike, so obviously she didn't take his name."

"Augustus Strike," Tamara said. "He died a few years back. He was pretty old, though. She'd been filling in for him a lot by then, my parents said."

"And she said something about a husband before that — and having kids," Call said. "Maybe they got a divorce, but if not, that's two people who married her and died. Maybe she's one of those ladies who kills her husbands for their money."

"A black widow?" Tamara snorted. "If she killed Augustus Strike, people would know about it. He used to be a very important mage. She has her seat on the Assembly because of him — before her marriage she was just some no-name mage from Europe."

"She could just be unlucky," Call said. He hadn't realized Alex's dad was dead. He wondered if Tamara's parents had dissuaded Kimiya from seriously dating him because of his lack of connections. This year, Alex and Kimiya seemed to be close again, but Call wasn't sure what that meant.

"Alexander," he said aloud. "Alexander Strike."

That wasn't the password, either.

"Do we know where they were from?" Aaron asked. "Europe is a pretty big place."

"France!" Call yelled. Nothing happened.

"Don't just yell *France*!" Tamara scolded him. "There are a lot of other countries."

"Let's look around and see what we find," Call said, throwing up his hands. "What do people use as their passwords? Their birthdays? The birthdays of their pets?"

Tamara found a notebook, bound in a light gray leather, under a stack of books. It held notes on the comings and goings of guards, names of elementals, and a half-composed note to the Assembly explaining how security measures at the Magisterium and Collegium could be tightened while the two Makaris were still apprentices.

Tamara dutifully read out anything that seemed like it could be a password, but the safe didn't change.

Aaron discovered a small stack of photos with several grim-faced people, two small babies and a very young woman with dark hair standing off to one side in a baggy dress. The photos were grainy and nothing in them was familiar. The landscape was rural, with fields of flowers behind them. Was one of the children Alex? Call couldn't tell. Babies all looked pretty much the same to him.

There was nothing written on the backs of the photographs. Nothing that could possibly help them discover a password.

Finally, Call looked under her bed. At this point, he was starting to feel a little desperate. They were so close to getting the key and being able to talk with the elementals, but increasingly he was feeling as though figuring out the password of someone they barely knew was impossible.

There were a few white shoes with low heels and a single cream-colored slipper. Behind them was a wooden box. It might have been the only thing in the whole room that wasn't some variation on the color white. As Call scooted closer to it, he wondered if the box was hers at all. Maybe it was a leftover of the last person who'd used the room.

He pushed it out the other side and went around the bed to inspect it. Worn wood and rusty hinges — not at all her style.

"What did you find?" Aaron asked, coming over to Call. Tamara sat down next to them.

Call lifted the lid . . .

. . . and the face of Constantine Madden stared back at him.

Call felt as if he'd been punched in the stomach.

It was Constantine in the photograph, no doubt about it. He knew Constantine's face as well as he knew his own, for all sorts of reasons.

Not all of him was visible. Half his face was young and still handsome. The other half was covered by a silver mask. It wasn't the same mask that Master Joseph had once worn, to fool everyone into believing he was the Enemy. This one was smaller — it concealed the terrible burns Constantine had gotten escaping the Magisterium, but that was all.

Constantine was standing among a group of other mages, all wearing the same dull green uniforms. Call recognized only one of them: Master Joseph. Master Joseph was younger in the photo, too, his hair brown instead of gray.

Constantine's clear gray eyes stared right at Call. It was as if he were smiling at him, down the years. Smiling at himself.

"That's the Enemy of Death," said Aaron in a hushed voice, leaning over Call's shoulder.

"And Master Joseph, and a bunch of Constantine's other followers," said Tamara, her voice tight. "I recognize some of them. I'm starting to think . . ."

"That Anastasia Tarquin was one of them?" said Call. "There's definitely something weird going on. The Enemy's wristband opened her door, she has pictures of him . . ."

"She might not be keeping it because it's him in the photo," said Tamara. "It could be because of any of the other people."

Call stood up on legs that felt wobbly. He faced the safe, his hands in fists at his sides.

"Constantine," he said.

Nothing happened. Tamara and Aaron stayed where they were, half crouching over Anastasia's opened box, looking up at him. They both had matching expressions on their faces — the expression Call thought of as their Dealing with the Fact That Call Is Evil expression. Most of the time they could ignore or forget that Call's soul was Constantine Madden's.

But not always.

Call thought of the followers of the Enemy of Death. What had drawn them to Constantine? The promise of eternal life, of a world with no death. The promise that loss would be reversed and grief erased. A promise that the Enemy had made to himself when his brother died, then extended to his followers. Call had never experienced real loss, and couldn't imagine what it would be like — he didn't even remember his mother — but he could imagine the kind of followers that Constantine had undoubtedly attracted. People who were grieving, or frightened of death. People to whom Constantine's determination to get his brother back would have been a symbol.

Anastasia had lost several husbands, after all. Maybe she wanted one of them back.

Call raised his hand, looked at the Enemy's wristband, and then, again, at the safe.

"Jericho," he said.

There was a click, and the safe opened.

Call, Tamara, and Aaron went still at the sound. The safe was unlocked. They were going to be able to sneak down to see the elementals. The plan had worked. But Call was still nervous enough to make his hands shake.

Anastasia had seemed like a nice, non-murderous person, but despite that, it seemed that she was either trying to kill him or she was on his side for terrible reasons. He didn't like either option.

"So . . . you better cast fire into the lock," Tamara said. "Before that poisonous snake elemental crawls out."

"Oh, yeah." Call fumbled to get his thoughts straight. Snapping his fingers, he kindled a small flame between them.

Then, approaching the opening, he let it grow into a long, thin bar of flame — like an arrow without a quiver or bow. He tossed it through the open hole of the safe. It whuffed, briefly seeming to grow and burst in the enclosed space. Call couldn't tell if there was an elemental in there, coiling around. Had he sent enough fire to destroy it? Did it disperse or just slither into some corner?

Call reached out his arm toward the hole in the safe.

Don't flinch, he told himself. *Don't move fast. If you see a snake, it's an illusion.*

His fingers edged forward as he heard an intake of breath behind him.

"Call," Aaron warned, "don't go too fast."

The snake's head slithered out of the hole just as Call's hand skimmed the edge. It was the bright green of poison, with black eyes like two droplets of spilled ink. A tiny orange tongue flicked out, testing the air.

The hair on his arms rose. His skin crawled at the feeling of a snake sliding over him, cool and dry. Was that an illusion? It didn't feel like an illusion. Every muscle in his body clenched as, against all his instincts, he reached deeper into the safe. He felt around for a moment, encountering more coils of something that felt like smooth rope.

He shuddered involuntarily. Outside the safe, the snake began to wind its way up his arm.

"Anastasia wouldn't have lied to the Masters, would she?" Call asked in a voice that quavered only a little. "This is an illusion, right?"

"Even if it isn't, I don't think you should startle it," Tamara said, her voice sharp and nervous.

"Tamara!" Aaron scolded. "Call, we're sure. It's an illusion. Just keep going. You're almost there."

Aaron should probably have been the one to do this, Call thought. Aaron definitely wouldn't have been seriously considering giving a high-pitched scream and bolting out of the room, not even worrying about the alarm.

But along with that thought came a tiny thread of doubt. If Aaron did want him dead, what better way than to tell Call to do something stupid. What better way than to encourage him to be brave and dumb.

No, Call told himself, *Aaron isn't like that. Aaron's my friend.*

The snake had reached Call's neck. It started to twine, making itself into a snaky necklace . . . or a noose.

At that moment, Call's finger touched what felt like a key. The jagged metal bit was cool against his skin. He closed his palm over it.

"I have it. I think," he said, starting to withdraw his hand.

"Go slow!" Aaron commanded, almost making him jump.

He glared in Aaron's direction. "I am!"

"We're almost there," Tamara said.

Call's arm emerged, then his hand, with the key in it. As soon as he was free, the snake disappeared in a puff of foul-smelling smoke, and the safe resealed itself.

They'd done it. They had the bronze key.

↑ ≈ △ ○ @

They closed up Anastasia's room as fast as they could and hurried toward the deep passage of the Magisterium where the elementals were kept. Call kept glancing nervously back over his shoulder as he went, half expecting Rufus or one of the other Masters to have discovered what they were doing and come after them.

No one was there, though. The corridors were quiet, and then even quieter as the stone around them smoothed out, the walls and floor turning into marble that was so polished it was slippery. Doors carved with alchemical symbols flashed by, but this time Call didn't pause to look at them. He was sunk into thoughts of Anastasia Tarquin, of the photo in her room. Of Master Joseph. Was Anastasia Tarquin one of his servants? Was she the spy in the Magisterium, looking out for Call because he was — despite everything that had happened — still Master Joseph's Chosen One, the soul of the Enemy of Death?

Tamara came to a stop in front of the massive door made from the five metals of the Magisterium — iron, copper, bronze, silver, and gold. It shone softly in the ambient light of the corridor. She turned to look at Call and Aaron, a determined expression on her face. "Let me handle this," she said, and knocked once, sharply, on the door.

After a long pause it swung open. One of the young guards Call remembered from the last time they'd been there squinted out at Tamara suspiciously.

"What's going on?" he asked. He looked like he was about nineteen, with shaggy black hair. The uniforms of the Collegium were a deep navy, with stripes of different colors down the sleeves. Call suspected the colors meant something — everything in the mage world did. "What's up, kid?"

Tamara restrained her annoyance at being called "kid" admirably.

"The Masters want to see you," she said. "They said it's important."

The boy swung the door wider. Behind him, Call could see the antechamber, with its sofa and dark red walls. The tunnel leading away into the distance. His heart pounded. It was all so close.

"And I'm supposed to believe that?" the boy said. "Why would the Masters want me to leave my post? And why would they send a runt like you to get me?"

Aaron exchanged a look with Call. If the Collegium guy didn't cool it, Call thought, he'd end up on the floor with Tamara's boot on his neck.

"I'm Master North's assistant," Tamara said. "He wanted me to give you this." She held out the guide-stone. The boy's eyes widened. "It'll take you to where the meeting is — you need to give evidence about the protections here. Otherwise you could be in trouble, or your boss could be."

The boy took the guide-stone. "It wasn't her fault," he said, sounding resentful. "Or any of the guards'. That elemental came from somewhere else."

"So go tell them that," said Tamara.

Clutching the guide-stone, the boy stepped out into the corridor. He slammed the door behind him, and Call heard the tumblers of a dozen locks as they slid into place.

"Better scram," the boy said, glancing briefly over the three of them, and then headed off down the hall.

When the guard was out of sight, Call fumbled the key out of his pocket.

There was a spot in the huge door into which it fit neatly, and when it was placed there, an entire tracery of symbols began to glow all over the door. Words Call had not seen before revealed themselves: *Neither flesh nor blood, but spirit.* As Call was puzzling over that, the door opened, swinging inward.

They headed inside, passing quickly through the antechamber and into the dark red corridor. It was short, leading to a second, massive set of doors that went up and up, reaching over Call's head, the size of the doors of an enormous cathedral.

But there was a spot in them, too, a tiny hole, almost too small to notice. Call swallowed and fit the bronze key into the spot. The second set of doors opened with a groan.

They stepped through.

Call didn't know what to expect, but the sudden heat of the room beyond surprised him. The air was heavy and smelled sour and metallic. It felt like a place where a huge fire was blazing, but no fire was visible. He could hear the rush of water in the distance and the roar of flames, much closer. Arched doorways in the stone led in five different directions. Chiseled in the rock were familiar words: *Fire wants to burn, water wants to flow, air wants to rise, earth wants to bind, chaos wants to devour.*

"Which way?" Call asked.

Aaron shrugged, then spun around with one arm out, letting himself point randomly, like a weather vane. "There," he said when he'd stopped. The arch he was pointing toward seemed to be much the same as the others.

"Warren?" Call called under his breath. It seemed like a long shot that the little lizard would hear them down there, but Warren had shown up in strange places and at odd times before. "Warren, we could really use your help."

"I don't know about that," Tamara said, heading in the direction Aaron had picked. "I don't trust him."

"He's not so bad," Call said, but he couldn't help thinking of how Warren had led them to Marcus, Master Rufus's former Master, now one of the Devoured, drawn into the element of fire by using its power too much. Still, Marcus hadn't hurt them. He'd just been scary.

It was dim beyond the archway, less a corridor than an empty space of tumbled stone with a path cutting through it, leading into further darkness. A torch was embedded in one wall, burning greenly; Aaron took it down and led the way, Call and Tamara just behind him.

The path sloped downward, becoming a ledge over a deep pit. Call's heart started to thud. He knew that large elementals were imprisoned here, knew that theoretically mages were able to approach them without getting eaten — that was the whole point of the imprisonment. But by the dim light of Aaron's torch, Call couldn't help feeling a little bit like they were approaching a dragon's den instead of a holding cell.

A little farther and an alcove dipped into the wall. When they passed it, they saw a winged serpent hovering inside. It was covered in feathers of orange and scarlet and blue, vivid even in the gloom.

"What's that?" Call asked Tamara.

She shook her head. "I've never seen one before. Looks like an air elemental."

"Should we wake it up?" Aaron whispered.

There must be restraints, Call reasoned, but he didn't see any. No prison bars, no anything. Just them and a deadly elemental, a few feet away.

"I don't know," he whispered back. He racked his brain, thinking over monsters in books he'd read, but he couldn't think of what this was called.

One of its eyes opened, its pupil large and black, the iris around it a bright purple and star-shaped.

"Children," it whispered. "I like children."

The "for breakfast" went unsaid, but seemed clear to Call.

"I am called Chalcon. Have you come to command me?" The eagerness with which it asked the question made Call very nervous. He wanted to command it. He wanted to force it to tell him everything it knew — or, even better, find and devour the spy. But he wasn't sure what the price might be. If he'd learned one thing during his time in the Magisterium, it was that magical creatures were even less trustworthy than mages.

"I'm Aaron," Aaron said. Trust Aaron to introduce himself politely to a floating serpent. "This is Tamara and Call."

"Aaron," Tamara said, between her teeth.

"We're here to question you," Aaron went on.

"Question Chalcon?" the serpent echoed. Call wondered if it was very bright. It was definitely big. In fact, he had a feeling it was bigger than it had been a few seconds ago.

"Someone broke in here a little while ago and freed one of you," said Aaron. "Do you have any idea who it was?"

"Freed," Chalcon echoed wistfully. "It would be nice to be freed." He swelled a bit more. Call exchanged an anxious glance with Tamara. Chalcon was definitely getting bigger. Aaron, standing in front of it with his torch raised, seemed very small. "If you free Chalcon, he will tell you everything he knows."

Aaron raised an eyebrow. Tamara shook her head. "No way," she said.

There was a loud thump. Chalcon had flown at them suddenly, his star-shaped eyes burning red with anger. Aaron jumped back, but the serpent was thrashing against an invisible barrier, as if a sheet of glass separated them.

"This guy's not going to tell us anything," Call said, edging sideways. "Let's try to find a different elemental. Someone more cooperative."

Chalcon growled as they moved away from his cell — it was a cell, wasn't it, Call thought, even if it didn't have a door or bars? He kind of felt bad for the winged creature, meant to fly but stuck down here instead.

Of course if Chalcon actually flew around, he would probably pick Call off and snack on him like a hawk nabbing a tasty field mouse.

They moved downward and into a bigger space — a massive hall lined with alcoves, each imprisoning a different elemental. Creatures squeaked and flapped. "Air elementals," said Tamara. "They're all air elementals — the other four archways must have led to the other elements."

"Over here," Aaron said, pointing at an empty cell. "This is where Skelmis was — its name is engraved in the plate. So the elementals in this room had to have seen something."

Call walked up to one of the cells, and a creature with three big brown eyes on long eyestalks and a body that seemed more miasma than solid looked back at him. He wasn't even sure it had a mouth. It didn't look like it had a mouth.

"Did you see who freed Skelmis?" Call asked it.

The creature just stared back at him, floating gently in its prison. Call sighed.

Tamara went up to a cell that opened into an enormous space where three eel-like elementals swam through the air. They were the same elementals that had carried Call, Tamara, Aaron, and Jasper back from the Enemy of Death's tomb in their bellies, only much smaller now. Maybe all elementals could change their size like Chalcon could.

Remembering flying inside the elementals also made Call remember where Jasper was now. On a date. With Celia. Who was almost definitely not trying to kill Call, but who might not be his friend anymore, either.

"Are air elementals all pretty dumb?" Call asked, annoyance at Jasper bleeding into his voice. They had only a short amount of time before the Masters figured out who'd sent the guard and came down here, ending the whole operation. If they didn't have anything by the time the Masters arrived, the trouble they were going to be in would be for nothing.

"Harsh," Aaron said.

"Harsh, but fair." Tamara was watching the placid movements of the eel-like creatures. "Let's try the earth elementals. They're friendlier."

They backtracked up the path, past Chalcon, who stared hungrily at them, trilling in a super-eerie way. Call's leg felt as if it were full of jabbing knives. They'd done a lot of walking, but taking the steep slope up made his muscles burn. By the time they were back in the main corridor, despite this being his plan, he kind of wanted to give up. Tamara was studying the stone, trying to figure out if there were markings so they could tell which archway led to the earth elementals. Aaron was frowning, like he was trying to puzzle this whole thing through.

"I hear you there, apprentices," someone said from the

farthest archway, a voice that seemed ominously familiar. "Come and find me."

Call froze. Was it the spy? Had they stumbled on the person who wanted him dead?

Aaron whirled with the torch. The archway was empty, the space beyond it glowing a deep red-black, like old blood. The corridor seemed full of ominous shadows.

"I know that voice," Tamara whispered. Her eyes were wide, her pupils enormous in the darkness.

"Come and find me, Rufus's children," the voice said again. "And I will tell you a secret."

Aaron raised his torch over his head, the fire spitting and crackling. In the greenish glow his expression was determined.

"This way," he said, and took off, running toward the sound, Tamara right behind him.

That's what heroes did, Call guessed. They ran straight toward danger and didn't ever give up. Call wanted desperately to go in the other direction, or just lie down and cradle his leg until it hurt less, but he wasn't about to let Aaron have to fight without his counterweight.

Aaron wasn't his enemy.

With a gasp, trying to ignore the pain, he followed them.

It was immediately evident what element they'd fled toward. Oppressive heat blasted from the archway and the corridor beyond. The walls were made of hardened volcanic rock, black and full of ragged holes. The roar of fire was all around them, like the blast and crash of a waterfall.

Aaron was standing partway down the hall, Tamara beside him. He had lowered the hand that was holding the torch, though it was still shedding a weird greenish light over them. "Call," he called, and there was a strange note in his voice. "Call, come here."

Call limped down the hall, passing different cells in which fire elementals were imprisoned. Their cages weren't closed off by clear walls but by gold-colored bars sunk deep into the earth. Behind the bars, he could see creatures made out of what looked like black shadow with burning eyes. One was a circle of flaming hands. Another was a cluster of fiery hoops linked together, drifting and pulsing in the air.

The heat was so oppressive that by the time Call reached Aaron and Tamara, his shirt was soaked in sweat and he was close to passing out. He could see immediately, though, why Aaron and Tamara were so still. They were staring through the bars of a cage at a sea of flames, and in the center of that sea of flames, a girl was floating.

"Ravan?" Tamara said in a cracking voice that Call had never heard before. "H-how are you here?"

Ravan. Call felt a shock of horror go through him. Ravan was Tamara's sister. He knew she'd been swallowed up by the elements, becoming one of the Devoured, but it had never occurred to him that she would be down here.

"Where else would I be?" the flame-girl asked. "They lie to us, you know? They tell us that the pitiful magic we learn in the Magisterium is the whole of what we can do, but I am so much more powerful now. I no longer call up fire, Tamara. *I am fire.*" The iris of her eyes flickered and danced with what Call at first thought was a reflection of the flames — but then he saw there was fire behind her eyes, too. "That's why they have to lock me up."

"A touching family reunion," a voice said from the other side of the room. Call whirled. Marcus the Devoured was looking out at them from an almost identical cage, grinning. "Callum Hunt," he said in his crackling, roaring voice. "Aaron Stewart. Tamara Rajavi. Here you are. It seems not all my prophecies have come to pass yet, have they?"

Call remembered Marcus's words from two years ago, a terrible echo of his own fears: *One of you will fail. One of you will die. And one of you is already dead.*

They knew, now, which of them was already dead: Call. He had died as Constantine Madden. *Already dead.* The words hung in the air, a terrible proof that what Marcus had said was the truth.

"Marcus." Aaron frowned at him. "You said you had a secret for us."

Tamara couldn't seem to wrench her gaze away from Ravan. Her fingers reached out for her sister's burning hand, as though she couldn't quite accept that her sister wasn't human anymore.

Marcus laughed and the fire around him leaped and danced, flaring up volcanically. Even Tamara turned at that, jerking her hand back as though just realizing what she'd been about to do.

"You seek the one who freed Automotones and Skelmis, yes?" Marcus asked. "The one who is trying to kill Callum? For they are one and the same."

"We knew that," Aaron said. "Tell us who it is."

"An answer you will not like." Marcus grinned a flaming grin. "It is the greatest Makar of your generation."

Tamara looked even more stricken. "*Aaron's* trying to kill Call?"

Call felt the words like all the air went out of the room. Aaron couldn't be the spy. But hearing Marcus's words, Call felt stupid. They were fated to be enemies. Aaron was fated to be the hero and Call was fated to be the villain. It was as simple as that. Call had never had friends like Aaron and Tamara before, and sometimes he wondered why they liked him. Maybe the answer was simple. Maybe Aaron wasn't actually his friend.

"No!" Aaron said, throwing his arms wide in a gesture that nearly put out the flame in his torch. "Obviously I'm not!"

"So I'm trying to kill *myself*?" Call asked Aaron, unable to stop from blurting out what he was thinking. "That makes no sense. Also, there's no way anyone thinks I'm the greatest Makar of my generation."

"You don't really think that I want to hurt you, do you?" Aaron demanded. "After everything — everything — I learned about you and had to accept —"

"Maybe you didn't accept it!" Call said.

"That chandelier almost hit me, too!" Aaron yelled.

"Free me," Ravan said to Tamara, her face pressed against the bars. "Free both of us and we'll help you. You know me. I might be a different creature now, but I am still your sister. I miss you. Let me show you what I can do."

"You want to help us?" Aaron said. "Get Marcus to tell them I'm not the spy!"

"Everyone calm down!" Tamara said, turning her gaze on the Devoured Master and then toward her sister. "We don't know how much of any of this is true. Maybe Marcus is making this up. Maybe he just wants what every elemental down here wants — a ticket out."

"Is that all you think I want?" Ravan put her hand on her hip. "You think you're so great, Tamara, but you're just like Dad. You think that because you break the rules and get away with it, you can sit in judgment of everyone who gets caught." And with that, she let the flame overtake her, becoming a flaming pillar and falling backward into fire.

"No, wait!" Tamara said, rushing over to her sister's prison, hands grabbing the hot bars and holding on for a desperate moment, even though when she released them Call could see the pink skin on her palms where she'd burned them. "I didn't mean it! Come back!"

The fire leaped around, but it didn't coalesce into any human form. If Ravan was still there, they couldn't pick her out of the rest of the dancing flames.

"I know you won't release me, little apprentices, not yet — although I could teach you much. I taught Rufus well, didn't I?" There was something hungry in Marcus's gaze that made it hard to look directly at his face. "Well and yet not well enough. He doesn't see what's right under his nose."

His gaze was fixed on Call. Call flinched. He couldn't look at Tamara and Aaron. He stared at Marcus. "You've been at the Magisterium a long time," he said.

"Long enough," said Marcus.

"So did you know Constantine? The Enemy?"

"Whose enemy?" Marcus said with contempt. "Not mine. Yes, I knew Constantine Madden. I warned him, just like I warned you. And he ignored me, just as you have ignored me." He smirked at Call. "It is unusual to see the same soul twice."

"But he wasn't like me, was he?" Call said. "I mean, we're completely different, aren't we?"

Marcus just smiled his hungry smile and sank down into the flames.

CHAPTER ELEVEN

THEY'D ALMOST MADE it back out into the hallway when the Masters burst into the guardroom, magic blazing in their hands. They were wild-eyed, ready to fight. At the sight of Tamara, Aaron, and Call, the crackling ball of white energy hovering in front of Master North slipped and crashed to the ground in a shower of sparks.

"Apprentices?" he demanded. "What are you doing here? Explain yourselves!"

Master Rufus strode forward, grabbing Aaron's collar in one hand and Call's in the other. "Of all the reckless, ridiculous things you have ever done — this one, *this one* is the worst! You have put not just yourselves, but the entire Magisterium, in danger."

Tamara, not yet being hauled along by Master Rufus, dared to speak. "We thought one of the elementals might know who let Skelmis out. I know you made us promise not to investigate, but that was before Call was attacked!"

Master Rufus turned a look on her that Call worried might actually scorch skin. "And so you broke into an Assembly member's room and stole property from her locked safe? Property that could then be stolen from you? Did you consider that?"

"Uh," Tamara said, having no good answer.

"Oh, don't be too hard on them," Anastasia said, her voice cool as ever. She had to know they'd found her photographs and guessed her password, but she appeared entirely unruffled, as though she had nothing at all to feel guilty about or to fear. "It's difficult to feel powerless when someone is hunting you. And they're heroes, after all. It must be twice as hard for heroes."

Master Rufus twitched at the word *hunting* but didn't loosen his grip on Call or Aaron.

Tamara was watching Anastasia. Call could tell she was tempted to say something about what they'd found in her room, but it was difficult to go against the one person on your side. Besides, she was still reeling from having seen her sister, locked up like just another elemental.

"We can't let this slide," Master North said. "Discipline is important for apprentices and for mages in general. We're going to have to punish them."

Anastasia's chilly hand patted Call's cheek. He felt vaguely frostbitten. "Tomorrow is soon enough, surely," she said. "I'm the wronged party, after all. I ought to have some say."

"I will personally escort these three back to their rooms," Master Rufus said. *"Now."*

With that, he dragged Call and Aaron toward the gates. Tamara followed, probably happy Master Rufus had only two hands. Call looked back at Anastasia. She was standing with the others but not speaking with them. Her gaze rested on Aaron, watching him with a fascination that made Call's stomach knot without quite knowing why.

↑ ≋ △○ @

Call kept expecting Master Rufus to burst through the doors of their new sleeping quarters and yell at them for breaking into the elemental prison. He slept fitfully all night. He woke again and again, gasping, hand to his chest, out of a dream where something he couldn't quite see was about to drop down on him.

Havoc, who had given up sleeping in the fourth bedroom, licked Call's feet sympathetically each time he cried out. It was a little gross, but also kind of reassuring.

By the time the bell rang, tired as he was, Call was almost relieved not to have to battle sleep any longer. He pulled on his uniform, yawning, and stepped out into the common area. Havoc was at his heels, eager for a walk.

Tamara sat on an arm of the sofa in a bathrobe, a towel covering her head. Aaron was next to her, in his uniform, hair sticking up from sleep. With them on the sofa was Master Rufus, his face grave. They'd clearly been waiting for Call to emerge.

Well, he'd been anticipating this. He sat down heavily next to Aaron.

"You know that what you did last night was inexcusable," Master Rufus said. "You broke into an Assembly member's chamber and you sent the guard away from the elemental gate — a boy who, by the way, fell into a crevasse and broke his leg. If he hadn't, I would have found you a lot sooner."

"He broke his leg?" said Aaron, looking horrified.

"That's right," said Master Rufus. "Thomas Lachman is now under the care of Master Amaranth in the Infirmary. Luckily, he was spotted by a student, nearly unconscious at the bottom of a dry ravine. As you can imagine, after his discovery, the Masters' meeting was thrown into disarray. If we hadn't been distracted, your little adventure in the elementals' domain would have been cut even shorter than it was." He looked coldly from one of them to the other. "I want you to know I hold you personally responsible for the boy's injuries. Had he remained there longer, he might have died."

Tamara looked stricken. She was the one who'd given Thomas her guide-stone. "But we — we wander around the caves all the time and nothing ever happens."

Master Rufus's expression grew even colder. "He wasn't an apprentice here. Anastasia selected him because he was an outsider, educated at a different Magisterium, so he wasn't familiar with the caves, while you are."

Unbidden, Call remembered his father's warnings about the Magisterium and the caves: *There's no light down there. No windows. The place is a maze. You could get lost in the caverns and die and no one would ever know.*

Well, they'd found Thomas. At least Alastair had been wrong about that part.

"We're sorry," Call said. He meant it, too. In a way that maybe Rufus wouldn't understand, he was sorry they'd ever gone to the elementals' caves. He wished he'd never heard Marcus say that the person trying to kill him was the best

Makar of their generation. He wished Tamara hadn't seen her sister, or at least what was left of her. She'd been horribly silent and tearless when Master Rufus had left them in their chambers after frog-marching them back from the guardroom. She'd slammed her way into her bedroom and locked the door. Call and Aaron had faced each other awkwardly for a moment before going to bed themselves.

"We really are sorry," said Aaron.

"It's not me you need to apologize to," said Rufus. "Assemblywoman Tarquin has considered your punishment and decided that you must all pay a visit to her room and apologize to her personally." He held up a hand, forestalling any comment. "I'd suggest you do it tonight. You are lucky to be getting off so very lightly."

Too lightly, Call thought, *and not because of luck.*

↑ ≈ △ ○ @

When Call, Aaron, and Tamara entered the Refectory, a hush fell over the room. Apprentices who had been lined up to fill their bowls with lichen and mushrooms and spicy yellow cave tea froze in place, staring.

"What's going on?" Tamara whispered as they hurried to their usual table. "Is it me or is everyone acting bizarre?"

Call glanced around. Alex was looking at them from a table full of Gold Years. He gave a short wave and then looked down at his plate. Kai, Rafe, and Gwenda were staring — Gwenda was pointing at Celia and then at Aaron, which didn't make any sense. As for Celia herself, she was settled at a table with Jasper, holding hands with him over a plate of what looked like wet leaves. They seemed to only have eyes for each other.

"I don't think I even know what normal is anymore," Aaron said under his breath. "Do you think they know about last night? That we broke into the elementals' prison?"

"I don't know," said Call. Under regular circumstances he might have gone and asked Jasper, but lovestruck Jasper seemed incapable of doing anything but staring at Celia, saying stupid things to Celia, and drooling a little.

Call wondered how long Jasper was going to be a lovestruck idiot. He wondered if whatever was happening to Jasper would have happened to him if he'd gone on the date instead.

"Let's just sit down," Tamara said, but her voice wasn't steady. She was obviously shaken, in a way Call hadn't seen since the day she'd discovered who he really was. He wished they were somewhere they could talk about her sister. He wished that everyone would stop staring at them.

"Tamara." It was Kimiya, standing over their table with her arms crossed. "Why don't you come and sit with me?"

Tamara looked up sharply, her big dark eyes widening. She seemed stricken speechless at the sight of her sister. "I — but why?"

"Come on, Tamara," Kimiya said. "Don't make me do this in front of everyone."

"Do what?" said Call, suddenly angry. Kimiya was acting like he and Aaron didn't exist.

"I don't want to move," Tamara said. "I want to sit with my friends."

Kimiya jerked her chin toward Aaron. "He's not your friend. He's dangerous."

Aaron looked shocked. "What are you talking about?"

"Your dad's in jail," Kimiya said bluntly. Aaron recoiled as if she'd smacked him. "Which is bad enough, but then you lied about it. To everyone."

"So what?" said Call. "You're not entitled to know private things about Aaron."

"I am if he's staying at my house!" Kimiya snapped. "My parents deserved to know, at least." She glared at Aaron. "After everything they did for you —"

Rage went through Call, white-hot; some of it was for Aaron, and some of it was *at* Aaron. Because he couldn't quite shut up the nagging voice inside him that said *What if, what if, what if,* and he hated everything about not trusting Aaron. Including Aaron himself. He pushed himself to his feet, glaring at Kimiya.

"Your parents sucked up to Aaron because he was the Makar," he snarled. "And now you're acting like that means he owes you something? He doesn't owe you anything!"

"Stop it! Both of you, stop it!" Tamara whirled on her sister. "Did you tell Mom and Dad?"

Kimiya looked offended. "Of course I did. They have a right to know what kind of person the Makar is."

Aaron dropped his face into his hands.

"Tattletale," Tamara snapped at Kimiya, her face reddening. "Who told you about Aaron's dad? *Who?*"

"I told only three people," said Aaron, his voice muffled. "Call and Jasper and you."

"Well, I didn't hear it from any of them," said Kimiya irritably. "Look —"

"Jasper told Celia." It was Alex, appearing behind Kimiya

and putting a hand on her arm. "And Celia told everyone. Sorry, Aaron."

Aaron lifted his head. His green eyes were darkly shadowed. "What am I supposed to do now?"

"Everyone's wound up," Alex said. "After what happened to Jen, and the elemental attack on you guys. They want someone to blame, and, well, you're a Makar. It makes you potentially scary."

"I didn't hurt Jen! And I'd never hurt Call," Aaron protested. "Or anyone."

Alex looked sympathetic. "Just stick it out," he said. "People will find something else to talk about. They always do. Come on, Kimiya."

With a reluctant sigh, Kimiya let him lead her back to the Gold Years' table.

Tamara lifted her chin. "We go get food," she said, "and if anyone says anything to our faces, we set them straight. If they whisper behind our backs, they don't deserve our attention. Okay?"

After a moment, Aaron rose. "Okay." As they made their way toward the food tables, he spoke to Call under his breath. "Thanks for sticking up for me."

Call nodded. He felt bad for even considering Aaron might be the spy.

And yet, the thought of it wouldn't go away.

By the time they got through the line for food, Call's plate was piled high with lichen, mushrooms, and tubers although both Aaron's and Tamara's plates remained uncharacteristically bare. The three apprentices slid into their usual spots at the same table where Jasper and Celia were, but they took care to pick seats as far from them as possible. Celia looked away from Jasper long enough to glance in their direction with pity, but Call's evil glare made her turn away fast. He'd always known she liked to gossip, but he'd never thought that she'd tell everyone something like this. Of course, Jasper had probably made Aaron's family seem worse than it was, to impress her. Probably Jasper and Celia deserved each other. Call hoped they'd suck face for so long they ran out of oxygen and choked.

"We need to find the spy," Aaron said, bringing Call's thoughts back to the here and now. "None of this is going to go away until the real spy is caught. And we — especially Call — won't be safe until then, either."

"Okay," Call said slowly. "I mean, I'm in favor of that plan, except for the part where it's more of a declaration of the end goal and not a plan at all. *How* are we going to find the spy?"

"Anastasia must know something," Aaron said. "I mean, given what we found, she has to be involved in some way."

"Her password is the name of the Enemy of —" Tamara began whispering and then stopped herself. "I mean, Captain Fishface. Her password is Captain Fishface's brother. She has a picture of Fishface himself in her room. So she's got to be on the side of his people. The only problem with this theory is that they're not the people who want Call dead."

Call opened his mouth to object, but Tamara interrupted him. "Or at least they didn't want him dead when Automotones was sent to kill Call. Even if Master Joseph's changed his mind since then."

"Maybe she *hates* Master Joseph, *hates* the Enemy, and keeps that stuff around to remind her of her quest for revenge,"

Aaron suggested. "Maybe she sent Skelmis after Call because she knows he's really Captain Fishface."

"She doesn't seem like that," Call objected.

"Yeah," Aaron said, his voice brittle. "That's the same thing you said about Celia. Stop acting like the spy is going to be someone who's mean to you or who you hate. You can't just believe that because someone is acting like your friend, they really are your friend!"

"Oh, really?" Call asked, letting Aaron's words hang in the air.

Aaron sighed and put his head down on the table, cradled in his hands. "That's not what I meant. That came out wrong."

"Maybe we should let my sister out. Maybe she could help us," Tamara said in a small voice.

Call turned toward her, shocked. "Are you serious?"

"I don't know," she said, pushing at some greens on her plate with a fork. "I need to think more about it. After Ravan became one of the Devoured, everyone — my parents, her friends — acted like she was dead, so that's how I thought of her. I mean, sometimes I tried to picture her happy, swimming around in the lava of a volcano or something, but I never thought she was trapped here in the Magisterium. And now, seeing her, I feel like everyone lied to me. I feel like we didn't try hard enough. And I feel like I don't know how to feel." Tamara let out a ragged breath.

"If you want to get her out, we'll get her out," Call said, with feeling.

"But we need to be careful," Aaron cautioned. "We need to know more about the Devoured. In our Iron Year, we promised you, Tamara, that we wouldn't let you be drawn into becoming one of them. I think that promise extends to not letting you be drawn in *by* them. Once someone is Devoured, are they still themselves? How much of them is left? If it was a relative of mine standing there, I would want to believe it was really them."

"You're right," Tamara said, but she didn't look totally convinced. "I know you're right."

"We've got a morning class today, right? The first thing we need to do afterward is go to Anastasia's room and apologize to her," Call said.

"And if she is the spy, we have to make it out alive," added Tamara.

"Master Rufus knows where we're going to be, though," Aaron said. "It would be crazy to attack us. She'd get caught."

"Depends on whether she's going to stick around after," Call said. His arm ached — he was still wearing both wristbands, even though he was extra conscious of the Enemy's now. "Look, either she's out to get us and she's been nice to me to lull us into a false sense of security, or she's in league with Master Joseph and she's being nice to me *because* I'm Captain Fishface. Either way, she's dangerous."

"You're not Captain Fishface," Tamara hissed under her breath.

"You know what I mean." Call sighed.

"We'll get in and out of her room fast," Aaron said. "Eat nothing, drink nothing, stick together. We deliver an apology, then we go. And we stay on high alert the whole time."

Call and Tamara nodded. As plans went, it wasn't the greatest, but with Tamara worried about her sister and the whole room whispering about how chaos mages were bad news, it was the best they were likely to come up with. Call couldn't help remembering what he'd realized after the Collegium ceremony: that there was a problem with the Enemy of Death being considered officially dead and the war over — in this new world, where Makars weren't desperately needed, they made everyone afraid.

↑ ≈ △ ○ @

Call wondered how class would go that morning with Master Rufus when all three of them were in such a somber mood, but to his surprise, a special guest lecturer had been scheduled for their group.

To his even more extreme surprise, it was someone he knew: Alma from the Order of Disorder. The last time he'd seen her, she'd been trying to kidnap Havoc so she could add him to her massive stable of Chaos-ridden animals in the middle of the forest.

She still didn't look like a dognapper. She looked like a kindergarten teacher. Her white hair was braided into a coil against her dark skin. She wore a gray shirt over a dark green skirt. Several long strands of jade beads hung around her neck. When she saw the three of them, her gaze went immediately to Aaron. She smiled, but the smile didn't quite reach her eyes, which remained deep and watchful.

"This is my old friend Alma Amdurer," Master Rufus said. "She taught at the Magisterium when I was an apprentice and knew my Master, Marcus."

Call wondered if Alma knew what had become of Marcus. Her expression didn't change at the mention of him.

"She knows a great deal about chaos magic. Far more, I am sorry to say, than I do. Call and Aaron, you are going to spend the morning working with Alma while I teach Tamara alone. I have been thinking a great deal about what Assemblywoman Tarquin said at the meeting of the mages and I've decided that, as much as I don't like to admit it, she was correct. You need to know things, and I don't believe I am the right person to teach them. Alma agreed to come here on very short notice, so I want you to be polite and listen very attentively."

The whole speech made Call more than a little nervous. Alma had been thrilled when Aaron had turned up at the Order of Disorder. She'd been dying to get her hands on a Makar. He recalled her trying to talk Aaron into returning to the Order of Disorder so she could experiment on him. Now, Master Rufus was practically handing him over.

"Okay," Aaron said slowly, not sounding entirely enthusiastic.

"We're going to stay here and work, though, right?" Tamara sounded as if she shared Call's concerns and didn't want to leave Aaron alone.

"We'll be next door." Master Rufus waved, and the stone wall parted, rock groaning and opening a crack, wider and wider, to clear a way for himself and Tamara. He turned back to Alma. "Let me know if you need anything."

"We'll be fine," she said, with a glance at Call and Aaron.

Call watched Master Rufus and Tamara step into the next room. They looked distant and faraway through the hole Rufus had made. Tamara was trying to communicate something to Call with her face — her eyes wide and her hands making a gesture that looked like a dying bird — when the rock slammed back into place and they both were removed from view.

Without any choice, Call turned to Alma.

"You both look very skeptical," she said with a laugh. "I don't blame you. Can I tell you something that might surprise you? Master Rufus didn't tell anyone else that he was inviting me to teach you. Not Master North. Not the Assembly. Not anyone. The Order of Disorder isn't exactly respectable these days and neither am I."

"You threatened my wolf," Call said. "And my friend."

Alma was still smiling. "I hope your friend here doesn't take it personally that you mentioned the wolf first."

"I don't," Aaron said. "Call knows I can take care of myself. But neither of us trusts you. I hope you don't take *that* personally."

"I wouldn't expect you to." Alma backed up until she was leaning against Rufus's stone desk. She crossed her arms. "Two Makars," she said. "The last time there were two Makars alive at the same time, it was Constantine Madden and Verity Torres. They wound up in a battle to the death."

"Well, that won't happen to us," said Call. Alma was starting to seriously get on his nerves.

"Two Makars in the same Magisterium, the same apprentice group — do you know how much trouble Rufus gets from the other Masters for that? They feel like he cheated them somehow at the Iron Trials." She chortled. "Especially picking you, Call. Aaron was an obvious choice, but you're something very different."

"Are we going to learn anything here?" Aaron asked. "Besides teacher gossip, I mean."

"You might just learn the most important lesson of your life, Makar," said Alma sharply. "I'm going to teach you how to see souls."

Aaron's eyes widened.

"You are each other's counterweights," she went on. "And you are both chaos mages. Each of you can work the magic of the void, and that is why you bear black stones in your wristbands — it is what, I would guess, everyone has told you since the moment you were revealed as Makars. But there is another magic you can work as well. The magic of the soul. The human soul is the opposite of chaos, of nothingness. The soul is everything."

Her eyes were burning with a fanatic light. Call glanced sideways at Aaron; he seemed fascinated.

"Most human beings will never truly see the soul," she went on. "We work like the blind, in darkness. But you can see. Call and Aaron, face each other."

Call turned to face Aaron. He realized with some surprise that they were about the same height; he'd always been a bit shorter than his friend. He must have shot up an inch or two.

"Look at the other person," said Alma. "Concentrate on what makes them *them*. Imagine you can see through skin and bone, blood and muscle. You're not looking for their heart — you're looking for something more than that." Her voice had a lulling cadence. Call stared at Aaron's shirtfront. He wondered what he was supposed to be seeing. There was a dark spot on the shirt where Aaron had spilled tea at the Refectory.

He flicked a glance up at Aaron's eyes and found Aaron looking at him. They both grinned, without being able to help it. Call stared harder. What made Aaron *Aaron*? That he was friendly; that he always had a smile for everyone; that he was popular; that he made bad jokes; that his hair never stuck up like Call's? Or was it the darker things he knew about Aaron — the Aaron who flew into rages, who knew how to hotwire a car, who had hated it when he turned out to be the Makar because he didn't want to die like Verity Torres?

Call felt his vision shift. He was still looking at Aaron, but he was also looking *into* him. There was a light inside Aaron, a light that was a color Call had never seen before. He couldn't describe it, the new color. It was shifting and moving, like a glow cast against a wall, the reflected light of a lamp that was being carried.

Call made a noise and jumped back in surprise. The light and color vanished, and he found that he was just looking at Aaron, who was staring back at him with wide green eyes.

"That *color*," Aaron said.

"That's what I saw, too!" Call exclaimed. They grinned at each other recklessly, like two climbers who had just made it to the top of a mountain.

"Very good," said Alma, sounding pleased. "You two have just seen each other's souls."

"This seems awkward," said Call. "I don't think we should mention it to anyone."

Aaron made a face at him.

Call felt giddy. Not only had he mastered the magic on the first attempt, but seeing Aaron's soul had made his brief suspicions of Aaron seem ridiculous. Aaron was his friend, his best friend, his *counterweight*. Aaron would never want to hurt him. Aaron needed him, just like he needed Aaron back.

The relief was overwhelming.

"I think that's enough for today," Alma said. "You both did very well. Next, I want you to interact with souls. You're going to learn the soul tap."

"I am not doing that," Call said. "I don't know what it is, but I won't like it."

Alma sighed as though she thought that Master Rufus must be pretty long-suffering to put up with Call, which was pretty unfair since, before, she'd said other Masters wished they'd picked him.

"It's a method of knocking an opponent unconscious without doing them any real harm," she said. "Are you still against it?"

"How do we know it doesn't hurt them?" Aaron asked.

"It doesn't appear to," Alma replied. "But, as with all soul magic, there hasn't been enough study for anything to be entirely certain. When Joseph and several others and I began our research, we thought that chaos magic held the potential for doing much good in the world. Because there are so few Makaris born into each generation and because chaos magic has always been considered dangerous, we just don't know enough about it."

The greatest Makar of your generation. The words came back to Call, rankling him. He didn't mind Aaron being better than him, but he didn't like the idea of someone being better than Aaron.

Alma went on, warming to her subject. "You have to understand how exciting it all was. We were discovering entirely new things. Oh, chaos mages had seen souls before — a few had even learned how to rip souls from bodies. But no one had attempted to touch a soul. No one had tried to put chaos into an animal. No one had tried to switch a soul from one body to another."

"So did Joseph go crazy or what?" Aaron asked. "I mean, how come he didn't stop Constantine before he killed his brother? Was he just excited by all the magic?"

Jericho Madden. Call felt his head swim. Although all this was the distant past, it felt closer than ever. Lately, Call felt as though it was about to push him out of his own life, the way Master Joseph had wanted to push his soul out of his body.

Alma's eyes clouded. "To tell you the truth, I look back on that day and I don't know what happened. I've turned it over and over in my mind, and I can't help coming to the conclusion that Jericho died because Joseph wanted him to die."

That got Call's attention. "What?"

"Constantine was a young man. He had other interests than the study of chaos magic — or rather, he felt as if he had his whole life to study it. And, of course, Rufus was his Master, not Joseph. I think that Joseph wanted Constantine to be committed to the cause."

Call was horrified. "Master Joseph arranged for Jericho to die so Constantine would be more committed to the idea of using chaos magic to bring back the dead?"

Alma nodded. "And so Constantine would hate the Magisterium, which he blamed for Jericho's death. Of course, I don't think Joseph knew he was creating a monster. I think he just wanted to ensure loyalty. I think he wanted to be the one who made the discoveries, wanted his name to go down in history."

Call thought of Master Joseph in Constantine's tomb, the curl of his lip and the mad light in his eye. Call wasn't so sure that Master Joseph hadn't known, hadn't wanted a monster.

"People remember the Enemy of Death," said Alma. "But they forget the man who made him who he was. Constantine may have been evil, but he was also tragic. He wanted his brother back. Master Joseph, on the other hand, what he wanted was power. Just power. And those are the most dangerous people in the world."

CHAPTER TWELVE

HOW DO I look?" Call asked. "Repentant?"

He was standing in front of Anastasia Tarquin's door in the hallway that housed the Masters' chambers. Call, Aaron, and Tamara had decided they ought to clean up a little before descending on the Assemblywoman. She was something of a terrifying presence, with her jewels and her cultured, contemptuous attitude. Call felt she would take their apologies more seriously if they dressed up, so he and Aaron were wearing the jackets from the outfits they'd worn to the awards ceremony and Tamara was in a black sundress.

Havoc hadn't come with them. Havoc, Call pointed out, had nothing to apologize for.

Tamara exhaled hard enough to blow a lock of hair off her forehead. "You look fine," she said. "For the umpteenth time." She shivered. "It's cold in here," she complained. "Knock on the door already."

Aaron raised an eyebrow. "Is everything okay?"

"I don't know," said Tamara. "Ever since I saw my sister, she's all I can think about." She swallowed. "And then today's lessons. I don't like being separated from you two as if there's something wrong with me because I'm not a Makar. Plus, Master Rufus was twice as hard on me as he usually is."

"Well, we're doing it again Monday," said Call. "Alma's coming to teach us something creepy called the soul tap."

"I don't like her," Tamara said. "She gives me the creeps."

Aaron stepped up to the door. "We'd better get this over with."

He knocked. The sound seemed to boom and resound in the corridor. Anastasia's door opened. She stood before them wearing a white silk robe of great magnificence over a gown that was even fancier. Her feet were in white leather slippers. "I was beginning to expect you'd never arrive," she said, raising one silvery eyebrow.

"Um," Call said. "Can we — come in? We want to apologize."

Anastasia opened the door wider. "Oh, of course. Come right it." She smiled as they filed past her. "This should be an interesting conversation."

Tamara gave Call a significant look. Call shrugged. Maybe Anastasia was bent on murder — they were going to find out, either way, and that was kind of a relief. The Assemblywoman slammed the heavy door behind her with a satisfying bang and joined them in the living room. She was tall — tall enough that her shadow, cast against the far wall where the safe had stood, was enormous and spidery. The safe itself had been removed; Call wondered where the Masters had put it.

"Do please sit," she said. Diamonds sparkled in her ears, glimmering against her hair.

Call, Tamara, and Aaron settled themselves on her white couch. Anastasia sat opposite them, on an ivory chair. On the coffee table in front of them were five cups and a teapot on a tray inlaid with something that might have been bone.

"Can I offer you some?" she asked. "I have a lovely lavender and lemongrass tisane that you might enjoy after all the fungus and lichen you're served up in the Refectory." She made a face. "I never acquired a taste for underground cuisine myself."

They all leaned away. "Under the circumstances," Tamara said, "I think we'll pass."

"I see," Anastasia said, with a pinched smile. "Now, does that make sense? You're the ones who broke into my room and stole my belongings. You broke into the elementals' prison. Isn't it more likely that you're a threat to me than that I'm a threat to you?"

"We're students," Tamara said, looking outraged. "You're an adult."

"You're Makars," said Anastasia. "Well, two of you are." She gestured toward Call and Aaron. "And I was speaking rhetorically. I know you mean me no harm. But equally, I mean you no harm. I've only ever looked out for you. I don't deserve suspicion."

Call felt his eyebrows fly up into his hairline. "Really? So why do you have a photograph of Constantine Madden in a weird box under your bed, and why is the password to your safe the name of his brother?"

"I might as well ask you how you managed to obtain Constantine Madden's wristband and, having obtained it, what in the world would make you actually wear it?" She gave Call a significant look.

Call blanched, his hand going to the wristband, shoved up under the sleeve of his jacket. Now that he was paying attention, he saw there was a subtle outline where the fabric pulled over it. "How did you know?"

Anastasia lifted the teapot and poured herself a cup. The pleasant scent of lemongrass filled the room. "Without it, you wouldn't have been able to get into my room in the first place. The reason is simple — long ago, I used magic to synchronize our wristbands. I knew him, you see, when he was a boy. I know, to children of your generation, the idea of the high-and-mighty Enemy of Death as a mere boy is shocking, but he was just a child when he came to the Magisterium.

"I hold myself partially responsible for what happened to him and to Jericho. Reminders of Constantine and Jericho are reminders of my own failure." She looked down. "I should have seen what was happening, should have stopped Joseph before he pushed the boys too far. In a way, I am responsible for Jericho's death and for what Constantine became. I won't allow myself to forget that."

She took a sip of her tea. "I owe those boys a debt. And the way I will repay it is by making sure that the next generation of Makaris remain unharmed. I am an old woman and I have lost a great deal, but before I die, I want to know that you're both safe. Callum and Aaron, you are my hope for a better future."

"So that's why you volunteered to come here and help find the spy?" Tamara asked her.

She nodded slowly. "And if I knew who it was, believe me, I wouldn't hesitate to act."

"We're sorry," Aaron said. "I mean, that's what we came to say, but we really are. We shouldn't have gone through your things or broken into your room or any of it. I mean, we can't apologize for trying to keep Call safe, but we're sorry for the way we did it."

Tamara nodded. Call felt uncomfortable that everyone was sticking out their necks for him.

Anastasia smiled, the way all adults smiled when Aaron turned on his charm. But before she could respond, there was a knock on the door. Call, Aaron, and Tamara looked at one another in alarm.

"There's no need to worry." Anastasia rose to her feet. "That's our fourth guest. Someone I invited to join us."

Master Rufus? Call wondered. *Someone else from the Assembly?* But when Anastasia opened the door, it was Alma Amdurer who stood on the threshold. She was wrapped in a dark red poncho, and she slipped into the room, letting Anastasia shut the door behind her.

"Hello, children," Alma said with a smile. "Has Anastasia explained everything to you?"

"I haven't," said Anastasia, moving to stand beside Alma. With her all in white, and Alma in dark crimson, they reminded Call of the Red Queen and White Queen from *Alice in Wonderland*. "I thought you'd better do that."

Alma fixed her dark eyes on them. "You know, of course, of the Assembly's plans to round up Chaos-ridden animals and dispose of them?" she said, without preamble.

Call blinked, wondering what this had to do with Anastasia — or any of them.

"It's horrible," he said.

Alma smiled. "Good. Most people don't think so. But the Order of Disorder agrees, and we're willing to do whatever we need to do to keep those animals safe."

"Well, we'd like to help," Aaron volunteered. "But what can we do?"

"We know when the animals rounded up in the woods here are being transported," said Alma. "We need the help of a Makar to assist us in moving them from the transportation vehicles to a safe place."

Tamara held up a hand, stopping Aaron and Call before they could volunteer. Her eyes were flinty. "No way. It's too dangerous."

Alma looked hard at the three friends. "If you care about Havoc, then you should help me. These are his brothers and sisters in chaos. Perhaps even literally."

"If we're going to help you — and yes, I come, too, even if I'm not a Makar — then you need to do something for us," Tamara said.

"Well, that would only be fair," said Anastasia, with a small smile.

"Anastasia has told us of your difficulties," said Alma. "And of course, we hear things. The Order is not entirely disconnected from the world of the mages. We would be willing to help you find the spy."

Aaron sat up straight. "What makes you think you can find the spy?"

"Because," said Alma, "we have a witness we can interrogate."

"But there haven't been any witnesses!" Call protested. "The Assembly hasn't found any —"

"There's Jennifer Matsui," said Alma calmly.

There was a silence. "She's dead," Tamara said finally, looking at Alma as if she'd lost her mind. "Jen is dead."

"The Order has been studying chaos magic for years," Alma said. "The kind of magic practiced by the Enemy of Death. The magic of life and death. Master Lemuel has learned a way to speak to the dead. We can talk to Jennifer Matsui and find out who attacked her, if you help us with the Chaos-ridden animals."

Call looked from Tamara's stunned face to Aaron's hopeful one. Aaron probably wanted to find the spy more than any of them, Call thought. More even than Call did himself.

"Okay," Call said. "What exactly do you need us to do?"

↑ ≈ △ ○ @

That night, Call and Tamara went outside the caves to walk Havoc. Aaron had been willing to come, but it was obvious he didn't really want to — he was sitting on the couch, bundled up in a blanket, reading comics that Alastair sent Call from home. When some people were upset, they ran around and yelled a lot, but Aaron curled into himself in a way that Call found more worrying.

"This isn't your fault, you know," Tamara said to Call as Havoc nosed a patch of weeds. The wolf knew that as soon as he chose a tree or whatever and did his business, they were going to take him back inside, so he was lingering as much as possible.

"I know that." Call sighed. "I didn't ask to be born — or reborn, or whatever."

She snorted. The night was clear, the stars bright, and the air less chilly than it should have been that time of year. Tamara wasn't even wearing a jacket over her uniform. "That's not what I meant."

With a deep breath, he went on. "I just feel like something happened way back when, with Constantine and Master Joseph and even Master Rufus and Alastair. They discovered stuff, back at the Magisterium. Important stuff. I mean, the Order of Disorder knows how to talk to the dead? That's huge. And yet no one else seems to know that."

"No one *wants* to know it," Tamara said. "No, scratch that. I bet it's the Assembly that doesn't want people to know."

Call blinked at her. "What about your parents? They're on the Assembly."

"They didn't even want me to know about Ravan." Tamara kicked a clod of dirt with the toe of her boot. "You're right. Anastasia and the Order of Disorder all knew Constantine when he was at school, which means they know more about what happened than we do. Lots more."

"And they know more about how chaos magic really works." Call called to Havoc, urging him back inside. "And maybe they know something about the spy, too."

"The greatest Makar of our generation," Tamara said thoughtfully. "So someone else, here at school, is using chaos magic. They just haven't gotten caught doing it yet."

"Not by us," Call said. "But they will."

The wind picked up, blowing the trees hard enough to send a cascade of leaves down on them. It tossed Tamara's unbound hair and carried away their voices when they called to each other. After a moment of frustration, Call pointed toward the Magisterium and they bent their heads and started back toward the mission gate, Havoc racing behind them.

As they went inside, into the darkened halls and the narrow cavern passageways, Call couldn't help but be conscious of the heavy weight descending on his shoulders the deeper into the caves he went: the weight of, once more, not knowing whom he could trust.

↑ ≈ △ ○ @

On Monday, Master Rufus announced that there would be a test that Friday, one in which the entire Bronze Year would be competing with one another. Master Rufus even had purple armbands for Tamara, Aaron, and Call, proclaiming them a three-person team.

Callum groaned. He'd never liked the tests, not since they'd had to fight wyverns in his Iron Year. After running away during Copper Year and coming back with the head of the Enemy of Death, he'd been able to opt out of a few more, but now it seemed like his test-avoiding luck had run out.

Aaron was too sunk in the gloom of being disliked, or at least suspected, by everyone in school to do more than solemnly accept his armband. Call wanted to tell Aaron that he'd never been popular and he was perfectly fine, but he worried that maybe Aaron wouldn't find his words all that reassuring. Still, gloomy Aaron was even less likely to argue than regular Aaron.

"Can you tell us anything about the test?" Tamara asked. "Anything at all?"

Master Rufus shook his head. "Most certainly not. You three are considered — for many reasons — to be an extraordinary group. If you don't acquit yourselves well, you will be letting many people down, myself included. I expect you to do your best. And I expect that you will be able to do so without any *hints*."

Tamara shrugged and grinned. "You can't blame me for trying."

Master Rufus gave her a look that said he most certainly could, but he didn't belabor the point. Instead, he launched into a lecture about what to do when one seems to have an abundance of magic and a spell starts getting bigger than was intended. The short answer: It was that person's responsibility to control it.

Everything they learned was about responsibility and control these days. And none of it helped at all.

↑ ≈ △ ○ ◉

On the way back to their new rooms, they saw Gwenda lurking in the hallway. It was chilly in the corridors, and she was wearing a heavy sweater and jeans, as well as an irritated expression on her face. She brightened up when they approached, rubbing her hands up and down her arms to warm herself.

"I hoped I'd catch you," she said.

"What's up?" Tamara asked. Aaron hung back, looking worried that she'd snap at him or glare. But she only looked hopeful.

"I need to talk to you guys," she said. "Can we go to your new room?"

The three of them glanced at one another. Call could see his own spark of excitement mirrored in the eyes of his friends.

Maybe Gwenda knew something about the spy, had seen something or suspected someone?

They ushered her into their common room, and Call directed Havoc to guard the door just in case anyone tried to break in. Havoc took up his post with a vigilant air.

"Look," Gwenda said, once the three of them had settled onto the couch and were looking at her expectantly, "the thing is . . ."

"Go ahead, Gwenda," said Tamara. "You can tell us anything."

"I want to move in with you!" Gwenda burst out, a flush rising on her dark brown skin. "I know apprentices in the same group are supposed to share rooms, but I looked it up and you can change if you want to. I heard you had an extra room free, and the thing is, I can't *stand* it anymore!"

"Stand what?" asked Aaron.

"Jasper and Celia!" Gwenda said in exasperation. "They're always cuddling on the couch, kissing, slobbering into each other's ears. It's horrible."

"So tell them to stop," said Call, disappointed. Tamara, on the other hand, looked entertained.

"They won't stop," said Gwenda. "I've tried; Rafe has tried, and it's totally hopeless. They don't listen. This is why interapprentice group relationships suck for everyone."

"We'd have to ask Master Rufus," said Aaron, who was a sucker for a sob story and was probably also glad that Gwenda preferred his criminal background to Jasper's facesucking ways.

Call glared. He liked Gwenda fine, but given the amount of plotting and sneaking around he, Aaron, and Tamara did, he didn't see how having her in their rooms would be anything but an inconvenience.

"My parents were an interapprentice group relationship," he said.

"Well, I bet whoever else was in their group hated them," said Gwenda ungraciously.

Call was about to open his mouth to tell her that they'd shared a group with the Enemy of Death and his brother, but decided not to. It wasn't exactly a secret, but neither was it something everyone knew. Call felt like the less people talked about him in connection with Constantine Madden, the better.

Also, if she started implying that the Enemy of Death was driven to becoming an evil overlord because of Call's parents' being gross in a romantic way, he might have to kill her.

"Gwenda . . ." Tamara started, evidently having some of the same doubts as Call.

There was a banging on the door. Gwenda jumped, then looked hopeful. "Is that Master Rufus?" she said. "You could ask him right now."

Aaron shook his head. "Master Rufus just walks right in," he said, getting to his feet. He went across the room and flung the door open.

It was Jasper.

"Oh, my God," said Gwenda. "Why can't I get away from you?"

Jasper looked puzzled. "Why would anyone want to get away from me?"

She whirled on Call and Tamara. "Does he come over here all the time? Like dropping in unannounced like this?"

"Constantly," said Tamara.

"It's a problem," Call seconded.

Gwenda threw her arms up. "Forget it, then," she said. "Forget the whole idea."

She stalked out of the room, past Jasper, who looked puzzled.

"What was all that about?" he asked.

"Mostly that you suck," Call replied. "Although we knew that."

Jasper came into the room, the door swinging shut behind him. He was drawing in a breath to say something when Havoc sprang, knocking him to the ground. Jasper yelled.

"Whoops," Call said. "We told Havoc to guard the door, so . . ."

Jasper yelled some more, which Call thought was uncalled for. There was no indication that Havoc was going to hurt him. Havoc knew Jasper. He was just sitting on Jasper, his tongue hanging out, looking thoughtful.

"Get . . . him . . . off . . . me," Jasper said through his teeth.

Call sighed and whistled. "Come on, Havoc," he said. As Havoc sprang off Jasper and went over to Call to get praise and ear rubs, Jasper got to his feet, ostentatiously dusting off his sweater.

"Okay, Jasper," said Tamara. "Spill. Why are you here?"

"Or just leave," Aaron said coldly, getting to his feet. "That would be okay, too."

Tamara's eyebrows went up. Call's mouth had dropped opened a little. Aaron just didn't talk to people like that. Aaron didn't usually look at people the way Aaron was looking at Jasper, either: like he was going to punch him square in the face.

Call found himself with an overwhelming desire for popcorn.

Jasper seemed uncomfortable. "I wanted to apologize."

Aaron didn't say anything.

"I know you think that I started the rumor," Jasper went on. "I mean, not that it was a rumor exactly, about your dad. It's true."

Aaron looked, if possible, more menacing. "It was a secret," he said. "And you knew that."

"Yes." Jasper had the grace to look ashamed.

"And the rest of it is lies," said Aaron flatly. "I'd never hurt Call. He's my best friend. He's my counterweight."

"I know," Jasper said, to Call's surprise. "And I didn't tell anyone you would. I really didn't! I told Celia the part about your dad, yes, and I shouldn't have done that. I'm really, *really* sorry. It's just that everyone was talking about you and I got caught up in it. But I didn't say any of the rest of it."

"So do you think I'm the spy?" Aaron asked.

Call remembered Jasper's words in the Refectory: *Aaron told you two different stories about his past. That's pretty suspicious. We have no idea where he came from, or who his family really is. He just shows up out of nowhere and then, boom! Makar.*

Jasper looked over at Call. He was probably remembering them, too.

"I don't think so," Jasper answered. "I wondered, after the rumors got started. But the only person I ever told that I thought you might be is Call."

Aaron turned a stricken look on Call, before turning back to Jasper. "You don't *think* so?"

"No," Jasper said. "You're not the spy, okay? I don't believe you're the spy, and I am sorry for telling Celia about your dad. And for what it's worth, she's sorry, too. She never thought things would get so out of hand. She only told two people, and she swore them to secrecy, but then it spread."

Aaron sighed and the fight went out of him. "I guess it's okay. You really didn't start the rumor about me being out to get Call?"

Jasper pulled himself up in a weirdly formal manner and placed one hand over his heart. "I swear it on the deWinter family name."

Call snorted and received a very enjoyable glare from Jasper. Things felt almost normal.

"Oh, no," Tamara said. "If you want things to be okay, you have to do something for Aaron. And Celia has to help."

"What's that?" Jasper looked at Tamara worriedly, which was pretty much always a good idea but was an especially good idea now, when she was staring at him with a glimmer in her eye.

"Celia's on the rumor circuit," Tamara said. "Find out if there could be another Makar at the school, or anywhere. Someone operating in secret. And see if there's anyone Drew talked to a lot, okay?"

"And find out who did start the rumor," Call put in.

Jasper nodded, holding his hands up to ward away their being mad at him. "Done."

"Good. Apology accepted." Aaron flopped down on the couch. "You've got bigger problems than us anyway. Gwenda was here because she wants to move out of your rooms."

"Because of me?" Jasper said. "That's ridiculous."

"Maybe she's not a big fan of romance," Tamara said with a sly smile.

Jasper took a seat next to Aaron without being invited. "She's just jealous because she doesn't have a boyfriend like me. I am a great boyfriend. I know exactly how to keep a girl happy."

Tamara rolled her eyes. Call was glad she didn't find this convincing. After Celia's defection, he wasn't sure what impressed girls.

"As a proof of how sincerely I am sorry, I could give you some of my best romantic tips," Jasper offered.

Call, who'd been about to perch on one of the arms of the sofa, started laughing so hard that he fell. He hit his bad leg against the floor — which hurt — but not enough to keep him from howling with mirth.

Tamara was smiling, but clearly trying not to. Her lips kept twitching up and down at the corners.

"Are you okay?" Aaron asked, leaning over to help Call up.

"Yes!" Call managed to say before he started laughing again. He dropped onto the couch on Aaron's other side, still wheezing. "Fine! I'm fine!"

"Number one," Jasper said, with a frown at Call, who clearly didn't appreciate the wisdom that was about to be dispensed, "when you talk to a girl, you have to look her right in the eye. And you *can't blink*. That's very important."

"Doesn't that mean your eyes start watering?" Aaron asked.

"Not if you do it right," Jasper replied significantly. Call wondered what that meant. Were you supposed to develop a second eyelid, like a lizard?

"Okay, so tip one is that you stare right at a girl," said Call. "If you like her."

"Tip two," Jasper went on, "is to nod at everything she says, and laugh a lot."

"Laugh at her?" said Tamara dubiously.

"Like she's hilarious," said Jasper. "Girls like to think they're charming you. Tip three: Smolder at her."

"*Smolder?*" Aaron echoed in disbelief. "What's that, exactly?"

Jasper straightened up, tossing his hair back. He lowered his eyelashes and stared directly at the three of them, his mouth turned down in a grim scowl.

"You look mad," Call said.

Jasper squinted even harder, closing one of his eyes and staring meaningfully out of the other.

"Now you look like a pirate," said Tamara.

"It works on Celia," said Jasper. "She melts when I do that."

"She must like pirates," said Aaron.

Jasper rolled his eyes. "Tip four is to have the right haircut, but that's obviously hopeless for both of you."

"There's nothing wrong with my hair!" said Aaron.

"It's all right," said Jasper. "Call's looks like he cut it with a sharp rock."

"Is there a tip five?" asked Tamara.

"Buy her a cat calendar," said Jasper. "Girls love cat calendars."

Havoc barked. Tamara burst out laughing. She rolled to the side of the sofa and kicked her heels up. Call didn't think he'd ever seen her have such a good time.

"Oh, and if your mind wanders while she's talking, you should tell her you were distracted by how beautiful she is," Jasper added. "And whatever she's wearing, tell her it's your favorite color."

"Won't she notice you have different favorite colors?" asked Aaron.

Jasper shrugged. "Probably not."

Tamara's giggles were trailing off into hiccups. "Jasper," she said. "Do me a favor."

"Yes?" Jasper said.

"Never like me like that."

Jasper looked indignant. "None of you get it," he said, rising to his feet. "Well, my mission here is done. I've apologized and I've given you tips."

"*And* you've promised to have Celia look out for useful information," Call reminded him.

Jasper nodded. "I'll talk to her."

"Don't forget to smolder!" Tamara yelled from the couch as Jasper walked toward the door. He made a face at her as he pulled it open, then frowned.

"There's a note stuck to your door," he said, detaching a piece of paper. "It's addressed to Call and Aaron."

It was a folded note, with spidery handwriting across the front. *Callum Hunt and Aaron Stewart.*

"I'll take it," Aaron said, bounding to his feet. But Jasper, with a sideways smile, was already trying to flick it open.

"Ow!" he said. A small spark, like a jolt of static electricity, had leaped from the paper and shocked his hand.

"It's got a spell on it," said Tamara, sounding pleased. "Only Call or Aaron can open it."

Jasper looked grudgingly impressed. "Pretty cool," he said, grabbing up the note and tossing it to Aaron. "See you later."

He vanished into the corridor. Aaron opened up the note as the door shut. His eyebrows drew down as he looked at it. "It's from Anastasia Tarquin," he said. "She's asking us to meet her at the Mission Gate at ten to midnight on Friday. She says to bring Havoc."

"That's the same day as our test," Tamara said, sitting upright. "What does she want to talk about?"

"I don't think she wants to talk," Aaron said, still looking at the paper. "I think that's when we're going to do it. That's when we're going to steal the Chaos-ridden animals."

CHAPTER THIRTEEN

THERE WERE FOUR days before Friday, and Call, Aaron, and Tamara spent them alternately worried about Alma's plan and the test. Master Rufus kept saying cryptic things during classes and assigning them bizarre coursework. That week, Call had learned how to (a) catch fire Tamara had thrown at him, (b) breathe after Aaron used air magic to choke off his oxygen, and (c) dry his clothes after Master Rufus got him really wet. The last part, unfortunately, had not been done with magic.

It didn't help that everyone was moody. Tamara kept looking into flickering candle flames and fireplaces, as though she might see the face of her sister there. Aaron kept looking around the Refectory like he was waiting for everyone to throw their food at him. And Call kept jumping at shadows. It was getting so bad that he was freaking out Havoc.

It didn't help that Jasper continued to be useless in the

rumor department. According to Celia, Drew hadn't had many friends. He'd kept to himself, occasionally trailing after some older students for advice on how to deal with Master Lemuel. Alex Strike had, apparently, told Drew that he should go to Master North, but he hadn't. Probably his orders had been to lay low, not to go complaining to the head of the school.

As for the person who'd started the rumors about Aaron, Jasper didn't know anything yet. He promised to have more information by the end of the week.

By the time Thursday night rolled around, Call was just ready for Friday — no matter how bad it was — to happen. Anything to be closer to some answers. But at the Refectory, Master Rufus told them they were going to have a late-night lesson, as Alma had returned.

"Tamara, it's a lesson in chaos magic, so —" he began, but she cut him off.

"I want to watch," she said. "It'll be interesting. Not that many people get to see chaos magic in person and I've seen a lot of it. I want to know more about how it works."

He nodded, although he didn't look entirely happy. Of course, Master Rufus's resting expression was usually a gloomy one, so maybe that didn't mean anything.

After finishing up their lichen and mushrooms and cloudy gray underground smoothies, they gathered in the usual classroom. Master Rufus paced back and forth. Alma leaned on a short staff and spoke. "As you know, the opposite of chaos, or void, magic is the soul. In the last lesson, you learned to see a soul. Now I want you to learn to touch another person's soul with your magic — a brief tap is all."

"I believe I previously stated my objection to doing this,"

Call said. "It's creepy and weird and we don't even know what it does to the other person."

Alma gave a long-suffering sigh. "As I said before, you're rendering them unconscious. Nothing else. But if you are too squeamish, then I suggest that Aaron start. He can practice on you."

"I, uh —" Call began.

Tamara got up from where she'd been sitting, against a rock wall. "I'll do it."

"You can't!" Call said. "Also, what is the deal with everyone wanting to knock me out?"

"It must be something about your face," Tamara said, shaking her head as though he was being even more ridiculous than usual. "But what I actually meant was that I'll let Aaron practice on me. I volunteer to be soul-tapped."

Aaron gave her a dubious look. "Why? I don't want to hurt you!"

She shrugged. "I want to know how it works and maybe I won't be able to tell much, but maybe I will. And since you're worried about it hurting, I can tell you."

Call hesitated. He felt stupid for objecting to the whole thing. Learning how to tap people into sleep was pretty awesome, so long as it didn't scramble their souls. If someone was annoying him, a little soul tap would take care of that. He could make Jasper pass out constantly.

"Fine, fine," Call said. "Teach me how to do it, too."

Tamara gave him a dirty look, but Alma was all smiles. "It's easy," she told him.

It wasn't. Alma understood the theory but had never done it herself, and the last time she'd had a Makar to experiment with was almost two decades before. According to her, the act took a massive amount of focus, first to see a soul and then to reach out the thinnest sliver of chaos magic to touch it.

Call got paired with Alma, much to his annoyance, while Aaron got Tamara. The idea of touching the soul of someone he barely knew made him feel cold and shuddery and strange.

He had to try, though. He closed his eyes and tried to do what she said, tried to see her soul like he'd seen Aaron's. But it wasn't the same. Aaron was one of his best friends. This was like playing hide-and-seek when everything was dark, grabbing around randomly. But he caught hold of her soul without quite meaning to. He wasn't just tapping it; he could feel the silver length of it wriggling like a fish out of water. He had the impression of iron will and enormous sadness and sudden terror, before he pulled his thoughts away from her. Gasping, he opened his eyes just in time to see hers roll up in her head.

She collapsed onto the pile of pillows that Master Rufus had conjured from some other area of the Magisterium.

He glanced over to see Aaron catch Tamara in his arms as she swooned gracefully. Aaron held her for a moment before her eyes fluttered open and she laughed and straightened up, grinning at Aaron.

Rufus had hurried to Alma's side. "She's still unconscious," he said. "But she's all right." He looked grim. "Good work, everyone."

Call had done it. He had tapped someone's soul. He just didn't feel good about it. Not at all.

↑ ≈ △ ○ @

Friday dawned. Callum was awoken by Havoc licking his bare feet, which was gross and also tickled. Call twisted around, still half-asleep, trying to protect his toes by scooting them under the covers. But that just made Havoc leap onto the bed and lick his face.

"Off — murpf — come on!" Call sputtered, covering his head with one hand and pushing the wolf back with another. Sometimes knowing where Havoc's tongue had been was worse than not knowing.

Pulling on his uniform, still drowsy, he wondered if he could soul-tap Havoc back to sleep for another fifteen minutes, but then he decided what with him being Chaos-ridden and all, probably enough had been done to Havoc's soul.

Call padded into the common room and banged on Tamara's door. It was her turn to accompany him on morning walks. A groan came from inside and a few minutes later she opened the door, looking as bleary-eyed as he felt, wearing her purple armband. That reminded Call to go back for his. They staggered out into the hall, holding a leash no one had bothered to attach to Havoc.

"Today's the day," Tamara said, pointing to her armband, when they were halfway to the Mission Gate. "Everyone's going to be expecting big things from us at this test, but I've been talking to the other students, and Master Rufus has been spending so much time teaching us about *personal responsibility* and teaching you two about chaos magic that I don't think we're ready."

Call had been concentrating on not tripping. His leg was always stiff in the mornings and it was tricky to put too much weight on it before it limbered up. He nodded. Call always suspected he wasn't ready for things, but he didn't like Tamara agreeing with him.

"Maybe we can use chaos magic," he suggested. "It can be our not-so-secret weapon."

She snorted. "Sure, if you want everyone to think you cheated."

"It's not cheating!" Call insisted. "It's Aaron's and my magic."

Tamara raised her eyebrows. "Is that what you'd think if you weren't a Makar?"

"Probably not," Call said reasonably. "But I *am* a Makar."

She made the face at him that meant she was either annoyed or amused. Call was never sure in which direction the expression was weighted — all he knew was that she wore it a lot, especially around him.

Havoc did his business as Call drank in the fresh air and kicked at some leaves. Then they went back inside, where they discovered that their stuff had finally been deemed harmless by the mages and returned to them. Although Call was tempted to look through everything, he grabbed Miri, sheathed the knife, and headed for the Refectory with Tamara. They found Aaron already at their table, with Jasper and Rafe. Aaron's whole body was hunched over his plate, as though he were trying to disappear.

Tamara flopped down in a chair and regarded Jasper. "Well? Did you find out anything useful?"

Japer raised an eyebrow at her. "Go away, Rafe," he said.

"Why?" screamed Rafe. "For the love of God, why?" He seized his plate and moved to another table as Jasper looked after him with raised eyebrows.

"Never mind him. He's always grouchy in the morning," he said. "Anyway, I did talk to Celia. I had to really pull out my full range of charms to get anything out of her."

Aaron looked alarmed. Call rolled his eyes. "Please, no more masculine tips," Aaron begged. "Just tell us what she said, if she said anything."

Jasper looked mildly deflated. "There aren't any rumors about any Makars other than you two. Although apparently there's a lot of chatter about you guys, if you're interested. How you took down the Enemy. Whether you're going to start experimenting with your powers. If you have girlfriends."

"Why would they have girlfriends?" Tamara sounded shocked.

"Vote of confidence there, Tamara," said Call.

"I just meant — well, it's not like you have *time*."

"When it's love, you make the time," said Jasper, gazing at them in a superior manner.

Tamara groaned. "And the rumors? Who started them?"

Jasper shook his head. "Still don't know. Celia said she thought maybe one of the older kids."

Tamara sucked in her breath. "Do you think it could have been Kimiya?" she said. "She was horrible to Aaron."

"But why would she make up stuff like that?" Aaron said. "She knows me — a little a least."

"I don't think it was her," said Call. "She acted like someone who was shocked that Aaron might not be who she thought. Not like someone who had already started a rumor about him."

Jasper tossed a mushroom into the air and munched it. "It's only been a week. I'll find out more."

"Great," said Aaron. "We might actually get some answers if we survive the test today."

Call had almost forgotten about the test. He groaned.

Master Rufus headed them off as they were leaving the Refectory. He had a sinister smile on his face and a big bag slung over his shoulder. "Come, apprentices. I think you're going to like what we've got in store for you today."

↑ ≈ △ ○ @

Call did not like it.

They were back in the enormous room where many of the tests took place, including fighting wyverns in their Iron Year. But this time it was *on fire* — okay, maybe not all of it, but a lot of it. Call felt heat encase him immediately, roasting his edges gently, like a marshmallow about to singe.

In the center of the room were leaping flames. They weren't random, though. They were set out in a pattern. Lines of flame ran parallel to each other, leaving what looked like pathways between them. It reminded Call of pictures he'd seen of hedge mazes, people wandering around inside labyrinths made of trees and bushes. But this one was made of live flame.

"A fire maze," Aaron said, staring. Tamara was staring, too, her eyes dancing with reflected flames. The fire rose and fell, scattering sparks. Call wondered if Tamara was thinking of her sister.

One of the Gold Year students, probably Master North's apprentice, passed by and carefully handed Master Rufus three canteens from a pile she was carrying. Rufus nodded and turned back to his apprentices. "These are for you," he said, indicating the canteens, each of which was carefully engraved with initials: *AS. CH. TR.* "Water is fire's opposing element. These are filled with a small amount of water for you to draw on as you navigate the maze. Remember that you can use it all and charge through the walls or save your magic. I am not going to tell you which one is the wiser course. You are to use your own judgment."

Call was pretty sure that Master Rufus *was* telling them which was preferable, even if he didn't want to admit it.

"The only thing absolutely not allowed is flying up above the maze. That will result in immediate disqualification. Understood?" Master Rufus gave them each a stern look.

Call nodded. "Because it's cheating?"

"And dangerous," said Tamara. "Heat rises. The air above the maze will be scorching."

"Quite right," Master Rufus said. "One more thing: You will be going in individually." He looked long and hard into each of their shocked faces. "Not as a group, but alone."

"Wait, what?" Tamara said. "But we're supposed to be protecting Call! We haven't been letting him out of our sight."

"We thought this was a team challenge," Aaron put in. "What about the armbands?"

Master Rufus glanced toward some of the other Masters standing with their apprentices, readying them for the maze. Some of the older students were weaving between them, handing out canteens, answering questions. Assistants. Call saw the flash of gold and silver wristbands, caught sight of Alex and Kimiya. Kimiya looked over toward them and gave Tamara a small wave, but Tamara didn't wave back. Her dark eyes were flinty.

"It is a team challenge — your scores will be averaged," Master Rufus said. "This test is to demonstrate that it's important for each and every one of you to take responsibility for the educations of the other apprentices in your group. And while it's important for you to know how to function in a group, it's also important to know how to function on your own.

"Don't worry about Call," Master Rufus added. "Worry about yourselves and your scores. Each one of you will enter from a different part of the maze. Your job is to make it to the center. The first person who gets there will win an entire day free of classes, to be spent in the Gallery with the rest of their team."

Call felt a sudden spur of fierce desire to win. A whole day off, lying around in the hot pools, watching movies and eating candy with Tamara and Aaron. That would be amazing!

He also was grateful not to be looked after for the test. He appreciated what his friends were doing, but he wasn't used to never being alone and it wore on him. This was a test, created and run by the Masters. That meant *no one* was safe. But, probably, he wasn't in any more danger than the rest of them.

Master North's voice came booming across the field of fire, amplified by air magic. He told them the rules again, emphasizing the no-flying part, and then began to read off their individual starting places. Call looked for his chalk mark: *BY9*.

"Good luck," he told Aaron and Tamara, both of whom were clutching their canteens and looking at him worriedly. Call felt a surge of warmth, and not from the fire. Both his friends were about to enter a blazing labyrinth, and both of them were worried about him, not themselves.

"Be careful," Aaron told him, clapping Call on the shoulder. His green eyes were reassuring.

"We can do this," Tamara said, some of her old enthusiasm back. "We'll be splashing around in the Gallery before you know it."

She and Aaron took their places. Call heard Master North's voice rising above the crackle and clamor of the flames. "Ready, set, and go, students!"

Apprentices darted forward. There were multiple pathways into the maze. Call followed his own track, leading him deep into the fire. It blazed up all around him. He could see the other students only as shadows through the licking orange and red fire.

The maze branched off into two different paths. Call picked the left one at random and headed down it. His heart was beating hard and his throat felt like it was burning from the superheated air he was inhaling. At least there was no smoke.

Fire wants to burn. He remembered his own ironic retort to that the first time he'd heard the Cinquain. *Call wants to live.* At that moment, the flames burned down lower and Call was able to look out across the maze.

He saw no one. His heart sped up as he realized not one single other student was visible. He seemed to be alone in the labyrinth, though he could still see the Masters standing against the walls.

"Aaron?" he called. "Tamara?"

He strained his ears to hear above the snapping of the fire. He thought he caught his name, faint as a whisper. He lunged toward the sound, just as the flames shot up around him again, now burning as high as telephone poles. Nearly caught by a blast of rising fire, Call staggered free, the edge of one of his sleeves burning. He put it out with a slap, but his eyes were stinging, almost blinded, and he was coughing hard.

He reached for his canteen and thumbed it open, expecting to see the familiar glint of water. Water that he could draw on, whose power he could use to douse the flame.

But it was empty.

Call shook it right next to his ear, hoping he was wrong, hoping for the familiar slosh of liquid. He tipped it over against his hand, hoping for even a single drop. There wasn't. There was nothing, except a tiny hole in the base. It looked as though it had been drilled through.

"Master Rufus!" he shouted. "My canteen doesn't have any water! You have to stop the test!"

But the flames only leaped up around him. A blast of it shot out in his direction and he had to jump to one side to avoid it. Call stumbled and went down hard on one knee, only narrowly avoiding face-planting into a wall of fire. Pain raced up his side. For a moment when he stood up, he wasn't sure if his bad leg was going to hold him.

"Master Rufus!" he yelled again. "Master North! Someone!"

Why did he think it would be okay to be on his own? Why had he trusted the Masters to keep him safe? If Tamara or Aaron were with him, he could have borrowed some of their water! But then his thoughts veered abruptly: What if neither Tamara's nor Aaron's canteen had water? What if the same person who'd targeted him wanted to make *sure* they couldn't have helped, no matter what.

He had to find them.

Call started walking again, trying to ignore the growing heat all around him. Balls of fire worked their way loose at intervals and flew in random directions, like flares. He dodged one as he made his way around a corner. He turned another and found himself standing in front of a wall of fire.

He'd come to a dead end.

Skidding to a halt, he turned around, ready to retrace his steps, only to find a wall there, too. The maze had changed and the fire all around him seemed to be reaching out with tongues of flame, singeing him, making the air stink with burned hair and burned cloth.

Call's anguished howl was swallowed up by the fire. *Of course* the maze changed. Otherwise, there was barely any need for the water — there had to be places where magic was required.

Just then one of the walls shifted closer. Call could see the metal rivets on his boots glowing orange red. Unless he wanted to be barbecued, Call had to find a way out of the maze. He couldn't fly up; Tamara was right, it would be even hotter in the air right above the flames.

Air. *Wait*, Call thought. *Fire needs air, right? Fire feeds on air.*

He had an idea.

He thrust out his left hand, the way he'd seen the mages do when they were summoning power into their spells. The way he'd seen Aaron do it. He reached out, farther than the fire around him, farther than the stone under his feet. Farther than the water running in the brooks and creeks miles above them. Farther than the air. He reached through space that existed and didn't, reaching past it into nothingness. Into the heart of the void.

The heat of the fire faded away. He could no longer feel his skin burning and prickling. In fact, he was cold. Cold as outer space, where there was no warmth, only nothingness. In the center of his palm, a black spiral began to dance. It rose up and up from his skin like a coil of smoke set free.

Fire wants to burn.

Air wants to rise.

Water wants to flow.

Earth wants to bind.

Chaos wants to devour.

The chaos rose up from Call's hand, faster and faster now. It had become a black tornado, spinning around his wrist and hand. He could feel it, thick and oily, like quicksand that would pull you under. He thrust his hand up higher, as high as it could go, until he was reaching toward the top of the flames.

Devour, he thought. *Devour the air.*

The smoke exploded outward. Call gasped as a noise like a sonic boom punctured the air. The flames began to sway wildly back and forth as the black smoke ran across their tops, spreading like a cloud layer, devouring oxygen. Fire needed oxygen to live. Call had learned that in science class. His dark chaos was eating away at the oxygen surrounding the flames.

He could hear other noises now: other apprentices, shouting in surprise and fear. The flames made a noise as if they were being turned inside out — then vanished, collapsing down to heaps of charred ash. Suddenly, the whole room was visible — Call could see the other students spread out across the floor, some of them clutching their canteens, all of them looking around wildly in shock.

Call's smoke was still hovering in the air. Dark and sinuous, it appeared to have fattened up on the air it had swallowed. Call started to gasp, remembering something else he knew from science class: Fire might need oxygen to survive, but so did people.

The smoke began to drift down, questing, coiling. Master Rufus was striding toward the destroyed maze, shouting, "Call! Get rid of it, Call!"

In a panic, Call flung his hand out again, reaching for the chaos, trying to pull it back toward him. He felt it resist. It wanted to push back and be free. It wanted him to leave it alone. He was stretching out his hand so hard his fingers were turning into aching claws. *Come back.*

Suddenly, the dark chaos smoke swirled into a tight coil and sprang toward the ground. Call gave a yell — then saw that it was arrowing down toward Aaron, whose hand was also raised. It vanished into his palm and disappeared.

Master Rufus skidded to a stop a few feet from Call. Aaron slowly lowered his hand. Call could see Tamara, her cheeks streaked with ash, her mouth open. Across the heaps of ash and the huddles of frightened students, Call and Aaron looked at each other.

↑ ≈ △ ○ @

Tamara was the only one of the three of them who went to the Refectory for dinner that night. She brought back food for Call and Aaron — a tray piled with lichen, mushrooms, tubers, and the purple pudding Call liked.

"How was it?" Aaron asked.

She shrugged. "Fine, I guess." Tamara could lie pretty well, so Call had his eye on her, ready to believe that no matter what she actually said, the truth was much worse. "Everyone had questions, but that was it."

"What kind of questions?" Call asked. "Like, am I crazy? Am I going evil?"

"Don't be paranoid," Tamara said.

"Yeah, they probably think *I'm* the crazy one," Aaron put in with a sigh. The weirdest part was that Call had to acknowledge that this was probably true. Even though Aaron had saved everyone — *from Call*, which made him recollect his Evil Overlord list of last year, because almost murdering all the Copper Year apprentice groups would have gotten him mad points — his use of chaos magic had probably still scared them.

"This is almost over," Tamara told them. "We're going to help Alma and she's going to get Jennifer to . . . okay, I don't know what she's going to do exactly. But we're going to know who killed Jennifer and that means we're going to know who's after you. So eat up. You're going to need your strength."

"So who won?" Call asked.

"What?" Tamara looked flummoxed. "What do you mean?"

"Who won the test?" Call repeated. "Who gets to go to the Gallery? Like, did they pick the person who was closest to the center or did they decide to give up on the whole thing?"

"We get to go," she said slowly, as though she was trying to be very sympathetic to someone to whom she was giving bad news. "You won, Call."

"Oh," he said. He wasn't sure how to take the news. No one had congratulated him at the time. Master North had come roaring over the empty fire to shake Call's shoulders and demand to know what he'd been thinking. When Call showed him the empty canteen with the hole in the bottom, though, his expression had gone shuttered and strange.

Master Rufus had looked around coldly, as though thinking about what he might do to the culprit. Call knew how that felt, although it worried him that for a moment Master Rufus's gaze seemed to have settled on Anastasia.

Sometimes when Call looked around the Refectory, he thought it was impossible that a person who wanted to kill him could blend in with everyone else.

"Tamara's right," Aaron said, lifting a large forkful of lichen. "We need to rest and get ready for tonight. We already used enough magic that I need a nap or I am going to fall asleep with my arms around a Chaos-ridden bear and get eaten."

Call, who fell asleep with his arms around a Chaos-ridden wolf a lot of the time, snickered. Then he dug into the food. He and Aaron polished it off in very little time. By then, he was feeling drowsy, too, and light-headed, and as though his skin wasn't quite his own. He remembered Aaron being sick and passing out after large expenditures of chaos magic, but he'd never felt this way before. He lurched up and went to lie down.

When he woke, tangled in his sheets, his uniform and boots still on, he couldn't even remember hitting the bed. Outside the door were voices. The summons must have come.

Call pushed himself to his feet and went out into the common room.

Alex was sitting on their couch, talking to Tamara. Both of them were dressed in black, like ninjas. Alex's brown hair was half-concealed under a dark cap, and Tamara was wearing an oversize black sweater and leggings. Her hair was in glossy braids tied with black bows. Alex was smiling at her in a new way, a way that Call had only previously seen him smile at Kimiya.

Call didn't like it.

"My stepmother sent me to help," Alex said, turning to Call. "Are you sure you want to do this? This whole — midnight caper? This is serious stuff."

"I didn't actually know you were going to be involved," Call said, and Alex blinked a little, as if surprised by Call's tone. Tamara gave Call a reproachful look.

"He's Anastasia's stepson," she pointed out. "And he's an air mage. We could use him."

Aaron came into the room, also dressed in black, though he hadn't covered his bright hair. He nodded at Call. "We let you sleep as long as we could."

"That was some pretty serious chaos magic you laid down at the test today," Alex said. "I can see I'm going to have a hard time keeping up with you two."

Call and Aaron exchanged a look. It was a look that said that neither of them were exactly looking forward to being called on to use their Makar powers again. Call felt completely tapped out.

"You'd better go change into something dark," Alex added. "We don't want to be seen by the highway."

Call went back to his room and changed into black jeans and the darkest sweater he could find, which was navy. Almost as an afterthought, he took Miri from her place on his nightstand and slid her through the belt of his jeans. Then he woke up Havoc, who was asleep on the bed with his tongue lolling on the comforter.

"Come on, boy," Call said. "Time for an adventure."

When he went back into the living room, Havoc bounding at his heels, the others were waiting for him. Alex opened the door to leave. With a look back at Call, Tamara followed.

Call stepped out into the corridor and glanced around in surprise. Everything was ordinary — the rock walls of the hall, the path stretching away on either side — but there was a strange shimmer in the air, as if it were vibrating around them.

"Camouflage," Alex said in a low voice. He had his right hand up, his fingers making a series of complicated movements, as if he were playing the piano. "Changing the molecular makeup of the surrounding air makes it harder for people to see us as we go by."

Call looked at Tamara with a raised eyebrow, as if for confirmation. She shrugged, but was clearly impressed. Which was also annoying — if anyone had done any impressive magic that day, it was definitely Call.

Though he probably shouldn't think about it that way.

He couldn't help wondering if Aaron was thinking the same thing, though, since a second later a coal of fire bloomed from Aaron's palm, illuminating their way. "Let's go," he said. "Out through the Mission Gate?"

Alex nodded. They set off, Aaron's light throwing their shadows against the wall — tall Alex, then Aaron, then Call and Tamara, and, behind them, the trotting shadow of Havoc.

They encountered only a few people on their way to the gate, and just as Alex had said, no one seemed able to see them or their shadows. Celia was standing with Rafe, talking about something in low tones. When they passed her, she frowned but didn't otherwise react. Master North even walked by, his face buried in a stack of papers, and didn't glance up once.

Call wondered when Master Rufus was going to teach them a trick as awesome as this and realized, gloomily, that the answer was probably never. Master Rufus was not a person who liked to stack the deck against his ability to find his own apprentices.

They exited through the Mission Gate. Havoc, used to being taken this way to be walked, started toward his regular trees and patch of weeds. Alex was gesturing in the other direction.

"This way," Call called to his wolf, as loudly as he dared. "Come on, boy."

"Where are we going?" Aaron asked.

"Alma's waiting for us," Alex said, leading them toward the dirt road the bus took up the hill to the Magisterium at the beginning of every year. It was a steep decline, but a fast one — much faster than sneaking through the woods, the way they had in their Copper year, or stumbling through them in a panic, the way Call and Tamara had after Aaron had been kidnapped in their Iron Year.

Roads are great, Call thought meditatively, vowing to take them more. *Less being kidnapped by elementals. More roads.*

They turned a corner and saw a van idling near a large group of rocks. Alma leaned out the window. "I didn't think you kids would have the guts to turn up," she said gruffly. "Get in."

Alex heaved open the van door and they piled inside in a tumble of bodies. As soon as the door shut, Alma took off, driving much faster than Call thought was strictly necessary. Havoc began to whine.

"So I think we can get ahead of the truck on Route 211. The question is how to get it to stop, short of ramming it off the road. And before you say, 'So what?' that might hurt the animals." Alma had an unfortunate habit of looking back at them while speaking, checking on their reactions. Call really, really wanted to remind her to keep her eyes on the road, but he was afraid of surprising her into jerking the wheel and sending them into a ravine.

"Okay," he said instead.

"How come you couldn't do this yourself, you and the rest of the Order of Disorder?" Alex asked.

Alma sighed, as though the question was very stupid. "Who do you think they're going to suspect first? The Order has been operating in the woods around the Magisterium since we were first allowed to be there, catching, tagging, and sometimes even putting down Chaos-ridden animals. But only when necessary. The Assembly knows we're firmly against these valuable test subjects being slaughtered and so our members must have an ironclad alibi."

"Really warms the heart, how much she cares," Aaron whispered to Call, in a rare moment of snark. Call agreed with him. Havoc wasn't a valuable test subject; he was a pet wolf. Call wished all the animals had somewhere better to go than either death or the Order.

"What about your alibi, then?" Tamara asked.

"Me?" Alma said. "Why, records will show that I was with Anastasia Tarquin, prominent member of the Assembly, tonight. She was kind enough to allow me access to the elementals and we lost track of time, trying some new experiments."

"What about *us*?" Call asked, returning to what he considered the main point.

"That's your lookout," said Alma, careening off the road and onto the highway. They whizzed past the gas station where, the year before, they'd waited for Tamara's butler, Stebbins, to come and get them. The highway opened up in front of them. For a moment Call fantasized that they were going somewhere for no reason, just to have fun. Although maybe not with Alma. That would be weird.

Alma gave a cackling laugh and pulled to a stop. They piled out of the van, grateful for the fresh air. It was cold out, the air nipping at Call's cheeks and chin as he looked around. They were at a fork in the road, where Route 211 and Route 340 split from each other. There was no one on either right now, and the moon hung above them, huge and pale, illuminating the white lines painted down the center of the street.

Alma checked her watch. "They're about five minutes out," she said. "No more than that. We have to figure out how to block their way." She eyed Call, as if wondering if he'd make an adequate human roadblock.

"I'll do it," said Alex. He walked to the patch of grass in front of where the roads split.

"What's he going to do?" Tamara whispered, but Call just shook his head. He had no idea. He watched as Alex raised his hands and made the same piano-playing movements he had before.

Color and light swirled in front of him. Alex leaned back as the lights and colors grew. Call watched with a faint prickle of jealousy. This was what he'd always thought magic might be like, not the deadly darkness that poured from his own hands.

"There they are," Tamara whispered, pointing. Sure enough, in the distance Call could see a large black truck coming toward the intersection from the east. Its headlights looked like bright pinpricks at this distance, but they were coming fast.

"Hurry up, Alexander!" Alma snapped.

Alex gritted his teeth. He was clearly putting everything into this, and Call felt a flash of regret for having been short with him before. The light in front of Alex had darkened, and the color seemed to solidify into shapes — a jumble of yellow-and-orange wooden traffic barricades with the words ROAD CLOSED across them in big black letters. They were huge and looked terrifyingly solid.

"Alex, move!" Tamara called. Looking tired, Alex slumped toward them. Alma pulled them all behind the van just as the truck rolled up, coming to a stop in front of the barricades.

The truck itself was a nondescript eighteen-wheeler, nothing written along the side. When the driver swung down from the semi cab, he looked entirely non-magical. He was even wearing a baseball cap. He went up to the barricade and frowned at it. From the truck came a voice.

"Just move them!" the voice said, clearly irritated and clearly used to being obeyed. "We're on a schedule!"

"What if the road's out?" the first guy asked. "People don't just put up these things for no reason."

Call wasn't sure if Alex's illusion could stand up to physical contact. He had to do something. He looked over at Alma and narrowed his eyes, suddenly totally aware why she'd taught him and Aaron the soul tap.

"We have to knock them out," he whispered.

Aaron gave a quick nod, but he was already looking a bit drawn. They'd both used a lot of chaos magic that day and they weren't going to be able to draw on each other as counterweights if they were both equally exhausted. They were going to have to try not to go too far.

Call's skin prickled. Chaos came easily to his fingers, tired as he was. He had the uncomfortable thought that maybe exhaustion actually made the magic easier and that if he got tired enough, chaos might devour him without him really quite noticing.

The other man got out of the semi cab, climbing down to frown at the driver. He was dressed in olive green, like the other Assembly members. Call remembered seeing him before, but didn't remember where. Tamara drew in a sharp breath. She knew him, of course. He was probably important.

Alex had gone a little wide-eyed, and even Alma looked as though she was ready to call the whole thing off. Call had to act quickly, before panic got ahold of them. They'd come here to free the animals that were trapped in the back of the truck, animals like Havoc, that were in danger. Just thinking about that and looking over at Havoc, crouched down in the ditch, gave Call a fresh burst of resolve.

"On three," he whispered to Aaron. "Soul tap. You take the driver; I'll get the other guy."

Aaron's mouth turned up on one side and Call wondered if he was looking forward to trying the spell for real. Maybe he was thinking about the animals, too.

Reaching out with his magic, he felt around for the soul of the Assembly member. It was different from reaching for Alma's in the safe environment of the Magisterium, where he could take all the time he needed and she was prepared for it. The Assembly member's soul was slippery, hard to latch on to, as if it were darting away from him. He could almost see it — a silvery thing that gave the distinct impression of being twisted around on itself in complicated coils. He reached out, fast, without the time for finesse he'd had before. He felt the chaos magic connect in more of a slap than a tap.

At least it wasn't a squeeze this time.

The man went down. When Call shifted his focus back to his own self, he was lying on his back. Aaron and Tamara were crouched over him.

"Do you know who that was?" Tamara demanded. "Do you know who you just knocked out?"

Call shook his head. Of course he didn't know.

"Jasper's dad," Tamara said.

"Whoa." Call had known Jasper's dad was on the Assembly, had even seen him at the party where Jennifer died. He couldn't believe he'd forgotten. Now he understood the expressions everyone else had been wearing. "I am awesome! Jasper's going to be so mad."

He and Aaron high-fived.

"You are so immature," Tamara said, reaching out a hand to help pull him to his feet. Havoc barked and leaped up to put his paws on Call's chest. Call scratched the wolf's head and looked around. Jasper's dad lay peacefully in the road, his olive-green robes spread out around him on the asphalt. Up close he was a fairly nondescript guy with dark brown hair and a neatly clipped beard.

The passed-out body of the trucker had been laid in a ditch by the side of the road. As Call watched, Alex clambered out of the ditch and walked over to Jasper's dad. He levitated him a little off the ground and began to move him toward the roadside.

Alex looked exhausted, gray and pale, as if he'd drained all his energy. Call glanced around. Where was Alma? Shouldn't she be helping him?

"She's over there," Aaron said, as if reading Call's mind, and pointed. Alma was standing in front of the eighteen-wheeler's door, which was looped with chain and a massive padlock. Her white hair streamed on the wind. She was gesturing with her hands, sparks flying from them — metal magic. The air smelled like hot iron.

"Oh no," Tamara breathed, just as the padlock ripped free and the back of the truck popped open. Alma grabbed the bottom of it and shoved upward, as if she were raising a portcullis.

"They're here," she shouted, and then screamed.

From the truck poured a flood of Chaos-ridden animals. Havoc gave a long yowl as they exploded out of their confinement — wolves, dogs, slinking weasels and darting rats, deer and opossums, and even bears, big lumbering things with multicolored, coruscating eyes.

"I thought they'd be in cages!" Alma cried as they began running in all directions. "Quick! We have to corral them!"

The animals ignored her. She ran after them, levitating a few back to the truck, but it was hard to contain them while adding more.

"We could disappear them," Aaron said quietly. "Into the void."

"No!" said Call. He couldn't do that, even if the animals did look terrifying. Even if some of them were coming toward the place where they were all standing. The three of them, and Havoc, backed up toward their van. Suddenly, it seemed very small to Call.

"Quick." It was Alex, limping over to them. The animals were moving behind him, rushing around the road, chasing one another. They were weirdly soundless, unlike regular animals. Call could hear a low growl, but it was coming from Havoc. "We need to do a looping spell. It's shaping air so that it makes a sort of fence around them."

"Can you do it?" Call asked.

Alex shook his head. "I'm drained." He really did look terrible. Even the whites of his eyes looked gray.

"So are we," said Aaron, indicating himself and Call.

Alex turned to Tamara. "Tamara, I can show you how. It's not that hard."

"I can do it, even if it *is* hard," she told him, her voice steely. "Tell me what to do."

"Whoa," said Aaron. Something had darted by him — something sleek and dark, with blazing eyes. He pressed his back against the van, pulling Call after him. Havoc tried to lunge forward, but Call called him back with a snapped command.

Alex was talking to Tamara in a low voice, and she was nodding as he spoke. Even before he was done talking, she raised her hands and began to move them. She didn't move her fingers like Alex did. It was more like she was plucking harp strings. Call supposed everyone did magic differently.

Call could almost feel the power coming off Tamara. Instead of air, though, it was fire that sprang up in embers, in a wide looping circle around the escaping animals. But even as the fence crackled to life, corralling the great majority, the rest of the animals scattered — some of them toward the woods, and others toward anyone they saw. Now terrified by the fire, their eyes looked maddened and wild. Many of them had their teeth bared.

What does it do to have chaos inside of you? Call wondered. He wanted to reach out and touch one of their souls — to find out what had truly been done to them. But there was no time to do anything but react.

A fox leaped at Alma's throat and she thrust it back. Another went for her legs. A snake whiplashed through the grass under the van and was gone.

"Look out!" Alex wrenched Tamara to the side just as two enormous brown bears barreled toward the van, their massive bodies like tanks. Alex and Tamara hit the dirt as Call threw his hands up to send whatever he could at them — a swath of fire or black chaos, he wasn't sure — but it was like scraping the bottom of a dry well. His hands trembled, but nothing happened.

And then the bear was on him.

He heard Aaron yell as the bear swung its paw, knocking Call to the ground with a single swat. Call rolled to the side, stunned, and the bear reared up above him, roaring. Call saw Aaron thrust out his hand, but the same thing seemed to be happening to him — only dull sparks came from his fingers. There was no magic.

Call reached back over his shoulder to grab Miri just as Havoc sprang. The Chaos-ridden wolf's jaws closed around the bear's neck, sinking into the thick fur. The bear gave a growling wail. Havoc scrabbled to ride its back, claws and teeth sinking in. The bear shook its heavy body, trying to dislodge Havoc, but the wolf hung on. Finally, the bear knocked Havoc free. Havoc tumbled to the ground with a whimper, and the bear lumbered away toward the center of the road.

Miri came out, Call scrambling to his feet. A quick check of Havoc assured him that the wolf was all right. Aaron had found a stick and was using it to try to hold off the other bear. Alex, who had shoved Tamara behind the van, raced back toward them, just as the bear swatted the stick from Aaron's grasp. Alex pushed Aaron out of the way and spun toward the bear, his hands out, air magic spilling from his palms.

But the bear was no ordinary animal. Its eyes spun red-and-orange as it swung claws toward Alex, who yelled and went down on one knee. His sweater shone red and wet in the moonlight, a gory tear in the shoulder.

"Alex!" Tamara exploded from the other side of the van, running toward them. Call could have told Alex she wasn't going to stay put. Aaron had his hands moving, as though he was trying to reach out for chaos magic, but nothing seemed to be happening.

"Aaron!" Call yelled. "Catch!"

He threw Miri. Aaron caught the knife, swinging it toward the bear. Blood flew in a spray as the blade connected with the creature's midsection. The bear roared, its eyes narrowing as Tamara neared them, more fire blooming in her hands.

Faced with fire and blade, the bear spun around and began to lumber quickly away. But the damage was done — Tamara's attention had been diverted, and the fences of fire had begun to fall. The Chaos-ridden animals were spreading out even farther, and some of them were advancing toward the van, their eyes whirling in the night.

Call limped toward his friends, just as Alex crumpled to the grass. There was even more blood on his sweater now. Call could hear Tamara's frantic voice, saw Aaron look down at his hands, empty of magic. They were all drained. There was nothing they could do, and the animals were still coming.

But that isn't exactly true, is it? said a small voice in the back of Call's mind. There wasn't *nothing* he could do. He remembered the Chaos-ridden at the tomb of the Enemy. How they had listened to him. Because his soul had made them.

I have to control them, Call thought. *I have to do something.*

His soul had made these creatures, too.

"Hey, you!" he said, his voice coming out weak and uncertain. "All of you! Stop!"

The animals kept moving. Call swallowed. He couldn't be a coward. They were all in danger. They could die. Even Jasper's dad, who was lying in the ditch, unprotected and hopefully not bearing the footprints of hundreds of Chaos-ridden squirrels.

Call took a deep breath and reached down into his soul, his soul that had inhabited another body before it had inhabited his. A body that had laid its hands on chaos and placed it inside these creatures.

"*Listen to me!*" he shouted. "Chaos-ridden! You know who I am!"

The animals froze. Call froze, too. He could hear his heart beating. Was it working? He raised his voice. "Chaos-ridden! Get back in the truck! Do as I say!"

It felt like the command rang through the air after he'd stopped speaking.

The words echoed in Call's head. Black spots had appeared at the corners of his vision. The animals were all moving — it seemed to him some were turning, starting to join together to surge in the same direction — but Call's eyes had gone blurry. He reached out for Aaron, for his counterweight, but Aaron's magic was so dim that he couldn't find him. He was alone in the dark without Aaron. In despair, he let himself fall backward into nothingness.

CHAPTER FOURTEEN

CALL WOKE SUDDENLY, gasping. He was in the Infirmary. Master Rufus was speaking to someone, probably Master Amaranth. She liked to drape snakes around her shoulders, but she was an excellent healing mage.

"I didn't think the test took so much out of him. Are you sure he's going to be all right?" Rufus asked.

She sounded as though she'd answered this question before. "He's fine, just exhausted. Both boys using their magic at once like that — I'm not so sure you should have allowed them to continue being each other's counterweights. What happens if they both go too far?"

"I will take that under consideration." Call felt Master Rufus's hand go to his shoulder and he kept his eyes shut, pretending to be asleep. "It's our job to keep him safe. We have to keep them all safe or we're doomed to repeat the past."

"Well, at least he's not as foolish as young Alex Strike over there. Managed to fall into a bunch of stalagmites. I swear, the Gold Years get sillier the closer they get to the final gate."

"I heard about his accident," Master Rufus said noncommittally, but there was something in his voice that led Call to think that maybe he knew more than he was letting on.

Master Rufus squeezed Call's shoulder and then departed the Infirmary. Call could hear his footfalls all the way out. He kept his eyes shut. Somewhere across the room, Master Amaranth was humming, doing something that involved clinking glass.

I'll count to thirty, Call thought. *Then I will pretend to wake up. That way she won't know I was faking in front of Master Rufus.*

He began to count . . . but he fell asleep instead.

↑ ≈ △ ○ @

The next time Call woke, Tamara was standing over him. When he tried to speak, she put her hand over his mouth. She smelled like sandalwood.

"Can you stand up?" she whispered. "Nod or shake your head."

He shrugged and she, exasperated, took her hand away. "Don't wake up Alex and don't give Master Amaranth any reason to come in here. It took forever for her to leave."

"I won't," he whispered back and swung down off the bed. His legs held him up. He felt pretty good, actually. Rested. He was still wearing the clothes he'd passed out in on the highway. "What happened?"

"Shhhh. Come on." She led him out of the Infirmary and into the hall. Call gave a last look back before the door closed.

Alex appeared to slumber on, a bandage over his shoulder. Master Amaranth was nowhere in sight.

Aaron and Alma were waiting for them in the hall. Like Tamara, Aaron was in his school uniform. His eyes lit up when he saw Call, and he stepped forward to clap him on the back.

"You okay?" he asked.

"A little sore, but yeah, better," Call said. He glanced at Alma, who was wearing a flowing cotton dress. Her arms were swathed in bandages.

"Are you totally covered in fox bites?" asked Call.

Alma's face darkened. Aaron shook his head and made a throat-slitting gesture at Call behind her back.

"We will not speak of it!" Alma said, glowering.

"Okay." Call wondered if Alma regretted throwing the truck door open. It was pretty much all her fault that he and his friends had almost been killed by bears. "So what are you doing here, then?"

"You fulfilled your part of the bargain," Alma said. "All is prepared for me to fulfill mine."

That meant Jennifer was somewhere nearby. She had to be. Call shuddered at the thought — he wasn't at all sure he was ready to see another dead person talk. It reminded him too much of Verity Torres's head and the riddles. That was serious Evil Overlord business.

Aaron's face looked as if he was having some of the same doubts. But Tamara seemed determined.

"Good," she said. "Let's get this over with."

Alma began to march down the hall. They followed her. Unlike Alex, she didn't seem interested in doing any fancy air magic to conceal them. It must have been late, though, and the corridors were pretty deserted. They stuck close to the walls and took advantage of the shadows.

"Is Alex okay?" Tamara asked.

Call felt his skin prickle. It was normal for her to be concerned about Alex, he told himself, even if she'd never paid attention to him before. It didn't mean anything. "I heard the Masters talking earlier," he reported. "Or at least Rufus talking to Amaranth. He's going to be fine. So you know, you can tell Kimiya that."

Tamara looked puzzled. "She doesn't know he got hurt."

Call gave an airy wave. "Well, you never know what you've missed when you've been passed out, right?"

"Shh," said Alma, gesturing for quiet. They had entered the part of the Magisterium where the Masters' rooms were. They made their way down it in silence to Anastasia's room.

Alma knocked on the door with three rapid taps, paused, and knocked again. A moment later, Anastasia threw the door open. She wore a white crepe dress with a long cape thrown over it, embroidered with black thread. Her silver hair was twisted into an updo. She gestured for them all to come in.

They stepped into her room and Call almost gasped. The whole place was spotless, as it had been before, but on the bare marble table in the middle of the room lay Jennifer.

She looked like she was asleep. Her long black hair puddled around her head. Her feet were bare, and she wore the same bloodstained dress she'd been wearing at the party. Her hands were folded over her chest.

"Her body has been held by the Collegium since the murder," said Alma, locking the door behind them. "They have preserved her against decay, for the time when she might be needed as evidence."

Call wondered if that was how Constantine had preserved Verity Torres's head all those years ago. He felt as though no matter what he did, he veered closer and closer to Constantine's life and Constantine's decisions. It was like being on a collision course with himself.

"Aren't they going to notice her missing?" Aaron asked.

"We will have the body back before anyone at the Collegium is looking for it," Anastasia informed them.

Call thought of how fast elementals traveled and of the Assembly member's particular skill in controlling them. If Anastasia borrowed one of the elementals from the Magisterium, she probably could get Jennifer back to the Collegium pretty quickly. But if Anastasia and Alma could steal a body out of the Collegium, then the spy could have probably managed a lot of sneaky things, too.

After all, he or she was the greatest Makar of their generation.

"I will explain what we must do," Alma said to Call and Aaron. "You're going to have to learn a fairly difficult skill and you're going to have to learn it quickly."

Call remembered Alma trying to teach them about the soul tap. It was hard to learn how to do something from someone who understood the theory and had seen it done but had never done it themselves. It had taken him and Aaron hours to learn. Call wasn't sure they had hours this time.

"And you," Anastasia said to Tamara. "You need to prevent anyone from looking for Callum or Aaron."

"What?" Tamara asked.

"Master Amaranth is likely to check on her charges before we're done. Go back and let her know that Callum has returned to his rooms and that he will visit the Infirmary tomorrow if she likes. We need to be sure that the whole school isn't up in arms, looking for Call while we're in the middle of an illicit magical experiment."

Tamara sighed. "Fine. I'll be back."

"Shouldn't one of us go with you?" Call asked. He wasn't sure he liked the idea of any of them wandering around the Magisterium alone with the spy on the loose. He glanced over at Aaron to see if he was thinking along the same lines, but Aaron was staring at Jen's body on the table, his face white.

"I'll take Havoc. At least I'll be doing something this way, not just standing around watching. I hate not being able to help," Tamara told him, heading for the door. Then she turned back, braids swinging. She was smiling. "Good luck talking to the dead."

Once Tamara left, Call felt very alone. It was just him and Aaron and two crazy old ladies and a corpse.

"Okay," he said. "What do we do?"

"As I understand it," Alma began, reminding Call that she probably wasn't all that sure, "you have to imagine the chaos magic running through the brain of the deceased, like blood. You have to send chaos energy through it, activating the mind."

That sounded hard. And not very specific.

"Activating the mind?" Aaron echoed. He looked as baffled as Call felt.

"Yes," Alma said with more certainty. "The chaos magic approximates the spark of life, allowing the dead to communicate."

Anastasia gestured toward Jen's body on the table. "Call and Aaron. Come closer and look at the girl."

They moved toward the table uncertainly. Jen's eyes were closed but there was a smear of blood on her cheek. Call remembered her laughing at the awards ceremony. It seemed incomprehensible that she would never smile or flick her hair or whisper a message or run through the corridors again.

This was what Constantine had wanted to stop, he thought. This feeling of wrongness. The going away of life and meaning. He tried to imagine if it were someone he really loved lying there, Alastair or Tamara or Aaron. It was hard not to understand where Constantine had been coming from.

He wrenched his mind back to the present. Understanding where Constantine had been coming from was *not* what he was supposed to be doing. Finding the spy was.

"Reach for each other," Alma instructed. "Use each other as counterweights. You carry within you the power of chaos, of ultimate nothingness. What you are reaching for is the soul. Ultimate existence. Use that to reach Jennifer."

That made a little more sense, Call thought. Maybe. He exchanged a quick glance with Aaron before they both closed their eyes.

In the dark, Call balanced himself. It was easier, now that he had practiced, to fall into that inner space. It was like everything rushed away, even the pain in his leg, and everything was black and silent, but in a comforting way, like a familiar blanket. He reached out and felt Aaron there. Aaron's self, his Aaron-ness, cheerful reliability layered over a darker core of determination and anger. Aaron reached back for him, and Call felt strength flow into him. He could see Aaron now, the outline of him, bright against the dark.

Another dim outline seemed to float up toward them. Hair that looked white, like a photo negative, streamed behind her.

Jen.

Call's eyes flew open, and he nearly yelled. Jen hadn't moved on the table, but her eyes were wide-open, their black irises filmed over. Aaron was staring, too, shocked and a little sick.

Jen's mouth didn't move, but a flat voice issued from between her lips. "Who calls me?"

"Um, hi?" Call said. When she'd been alive, Jennifer had always made him nervous. She was one of the older, popular girls. He'd had enough trouble talking to her then. Talking to her now was nerve-racking on a totally other level.

"It's Call and Aaron," he went on. "Remember us? We're wondering if you can tell us who murdered you?"

"I'm dead?" Jennifer asked. "I feel . . . strange."

She sounded strange, too — there was a hollowness in her voice. An emptiness. Call didn't think her soul was present, not really. More like the traces of it, the memory of what was left behind when it departed. Just hearing her talk freaked out Call so much that he was afraid he might start laughing from panic. His heart hammered in his chest and he felt like he couldn't breathe. How was he supposed to break it to her that she wasn't alive anymore?

He reminded himself that it wasn't really *her*. She didn't have feelings to hurt.

"Can you tell us about the party?" Aaron asked, polite as ever. Call gave him a grateful look. "What happened that night?"

Jennifer's mouth twisted into the shadow of a smile. "Yes, the party. I remember. I was having fun with my friends. There was a boy I liked, but he was avoiding me and then — then the lights went out. And my chest hurt. I tried to scream, but I couldn't. *Kimiya! Kimiya! Stay away from him!*"

"What?" Call demanded. "What about Kimiya? What happened? Who's she supposed to stay away from? She's not the one who did this, is she?"

But Jennifer seemed to be lost in the memory, her body thrashing around, her words turning to one long, continuous scream.

Call had to focus on the magic. He closed his eyes and tried to go back to seeing that dim outline of Jen, that photo-negative version. In the dark, he saw her, faded and tattered. If he wanted to, he knew he could make her speak words that were not her own. But he needed her to have her own voice, not his. So he chased those shining leftovers of a soul, glad she was preserved only a short time after the soul's departure. He channeled more chaos magic into her, to shore them up.

When he opened his eyes, her features had gone slack.

"Jennifer, can you hear me?" he asked.

"Yes," she said, her voice flat and affectless. "What do you command?"

"What?" Call looked over at Aaron. He had gone very pale.

"Oh no," Anastasia said. Her hands went to her mouth, one clapped over the other. Alma's eyes had gone wide and she reached out as though she could stop something that was already over. "Call, what have you done?"

Call looked down at Jennifer and she looked up at him, with eyes that were beginning to swirl.

"Call," Anastasia whispered. "Oh no, not again — not again."

"What?" Call was backing away, shock spreading through him. *What?* seemed to be all he could say or think. "I — I didn't — I've never done that before —"

But I have, as Constantine. I've done it a hundred, a thousand times.

Jen sat up on the table. Her black hair flowed down around her bone-white shoulders. Her eyes were swirling fire.

"Command me, Master," she said to Call. "I wish only to serve."

"It *is* you," said Alma, looking at Call with a dawning horror. "Little Makar — why did no one tell me?"

Aaron moved to block Call from the two women's horrified looks, from Jennifer's staring, blazing eyes.

"You should never have suggested we do this," he said angrily. "It's horrible. Stealing her body, that was horrible."

"Go, both of you," Anastasia said. "We'll deal with this."

Call felt Aaron's hand on his shoulder, and a moment later he'd been guided out of the room and was back in the corridor. He pulled the sleeves of his hoodie down over his hands. He was freezing, shivering all over.

"I didn't mean to do that," he said. "I was only trying to hang on to her soul."

Aaron's eyes softened. "I know. It could have happened to either of us."

"It couldn't have," Call hissed. "I'm the only one of us who's the Enemy of Death!"

Aaron squeezed Call's shoulder and let go. "You're not the Enemy," he said. "And the Enemy was just a Makar once, like me. Maybe the first time he did it was by accident. There's a reason," he added, in a lower voice, "that they're all so afraid of us."

Call glanced back at Anastasia's closed door. *Oh no, not again*, she'd said. Did she think Call had done it before, or did she just mean *Oh no, not another Constantine*?

He started to walk back in the direction of their room, limping. Aaron followed him, hands shoved in his uniform pockets.

"I think Anastasia knows," said Call. "Who I really am. Maybe Alma, too."

Aaron opened his mouth as if to say, *You're Call*, and then closed it again. A second later, he said, "She did see you control all those Chaos-ridden animals last night. And you said some weird things before you fainted. I mean, nothing too clear — just some stuff about how the animals should know who you were."

"Hopefully she'll write that off as incredibly strange boasting," said Call. "Did Alex hear?"

"No. He was passed out."

Thinking of Alex reminded Call of Kimiya. He tensed all over again. "We have to find Tamara. We have to tell her that Jennifer said something about her sister."

"Kimiya didn't murder anyone," said Aaron scornfully. "Also, it'd be pretty weird if she was suddenly the greatest Makar of our generation. Way to overlook that, mages."

"No — I don't think she did it," Call said, trying to make sense of the jumble of his thoughts. His head had started pounding. "I mean, if Jennifer was calling for Kimiya or wanted to call for her around the time that she died, then maybe Kimiya knows something. Maybe something she didn't think was important before."

Aaron nodded. "I wish we had *answers*, but at least we've got a clue."

"Aaron?" Call asked. He had another question about that night, one he wasn't sure he wanted to have answered. "Is Jasper's dad okay?"

"See, you do think Jasper's our friend!" Aaron said.

"Not if his dad got hurt because of us, I don't."

"Jasper's father is fine. We made sure he was okay before we tied him up and blindfolded him. I heard him swearing just before we drove away." Aaron was grinning, though, as if he'd won some bet. Call was glad one of them could still smile.

They made their way to the Infirmary, but there was no Tamara there, and no Alex, either. His bed was empty.

Master Amaranth, remaking one of the cots with air magic, gave Call a stern look.

"I wish someone around here would listen to me when I say to stay in bed until I tell you that you're well enough to go," she said.

"What happened to Alex?" Aaron asked.

"I killed him," Master Amaranth replied, and gave a dry chuckle at the looks on their faces. "I actually gave him permission to go — I checked over his wounds and they'd healed. He was just fine when he went. Unlike you."

"Have you seen Tamara Rajavi?" Call asked.

"Yes, she came to tell me that you'd moved back to your own room because you don't like the Infirmary. I don't know what's wrong with you boys. The Infirmary is the safest place in the whole school. The elementals here make sure that's the case."

Call looked around uneasily. He'd never realized there were elementals watching him when he was in the Infirmary. Considering the number of times he'd left it, he guessed that they weren't commanded to prevent people from coming and going. He didn't know what they were watching for — illness, maybe — but he felt better about being unconscious knowing that someone couldn't have just come in and attacked him, at least not without setting off an alarm.

"Did she say where she was going?" Aaron asked.

Master Amaranth gave him a puzzled look. "It's very early in the morning. I assumed she was going back to your rooms so that you all might get some sleep before classes start. Now, Callum, since you've returned, maybe you should consider spending the rest of the night here."

"No," he said, pretending away his headache. "I feel fine. I *am* fine."

"Well, neither of you should be roaming the halls this late at night. Go back to your room. Callum, come see me tomorrow after classes so we can see how you're holding up. And no more chaos magic for a few days, okay?"

Call, thinking of the magic he'd already used that night, nodded guiltily.

They headed back to their rooms. They'd reached the door and Call was moving to open it with his bracelet when they heard pounding feet in the corridor. Both Aaron and Call whirled around to see Alex racing toward them. He looked wild-eyed and had a fresh bruise on his face.

He slowed to a stop, bending over with his hands on his knees as he caught his breath.

"Tamara," he choked out. "He took Tamara!"

Aaron and Call looked at each other in confusion. "What are you talking about?" Aaron demanded.

"The spy," Alex said. "He grabbed Tamara."

Call went rigid. His heart was pounding in his throat suddenly.

"What are you talking about, Alex?" he said.

"Tell us exactly what happened." Aaron looked as upset as Call felt. *"Exactly."*

"I left the Infirmary when I woke up," Alex said. "I saw Tamara heading toward the Mission Gate with Havoc. I went after her because I wanted to thank her for helping me out last night." He straightened up. "I yelled after her, but she didn't hear me. She headed outside, and it was already dark. I thought I saw something moving in the trees so I ran toward her. But I didn't get there in time. Someone grabbed her. I wasn't close enough to see his face, but it was definitely an adult. I sent magic after them, but he sent a huge bolt of something at me. It knocked me back, and by the time I could go after them, I lost their tracks in the woods." Alex's blue T-shirt was stained red where the bandages bunched under it, around his shoulder. He must have reopened the wound.

"I need you two to go after them with me," he said. "Whoever that guy is, he's powerful. I don't think I could fight him on my own."

Aaron and Call exchanged a panicked look.

"We have to tell someone," Aaron said.

"There isn't time." Alex shook his head wildly. "First, we'll have to convince them we're telling the truth and by then, anything could have happened to her."

Call remembered the terrible night when Aaron had been taken by Master Joseph and Drew. He remembered the horrible roiling chaos elemental. There hadn't been time to tell anyone then, either. If they'd waited, Aaron would have died.

"Okay," he said. "Let's go."

They raced after Alex toward the Mission Gate and spilled out into the night. Call was running as fast as he could, his leg screaming in pain.

"That way," Alex panted, pointing toward a path that led through the woods. The moonlight illuminated it brightly. It was, kind of horribly, a beautiful night, full of stars and white light. Even the trees seemed to glow.

They dashed toward it, finally slowing down when the path turned into rocks and tree branches that made running dangerous. Call tried to imagine Tamara being shoved down this path by a terrifying adult mage, someone who was threatening her, maybe hurting her. Then he tried not to imagine it, as anger almost overwhelmed him.

"Havoc," he said suddenly.

Alex, who was charging ahead as quickly as he could, turned slightly. "What?"

"You said she was walking Havoc," said Call. "Did the guy grab Havoc, too?"

Alex shook his head. "Havoc ran off, into the woods."

"Havoc wouldn't do that," Call said. "Havoc wouldn't abandon her."

"Maybe he's following her," Aaron said. "Havoc can be sneaky; he's way smarter than a regular wolf."

"That's probably what's happening," said Alex. "Don't be scared, Call. We're going to get this guy."

Call wasn't scared. He scanned the landscape for Havoc. If his wolf was with Tamara, then surely they'd be able to get away. Tamara and Havoc made for a formidable team.

"You said it was an adult, right?" Call asked, ignoring Alex's condescending remark. He was older than Call and probably thought he knew better. Maybe he did, but he didn't know everything.

Call thought of where they'd come from. They'd left Anastasia and Alma with Chaos-ridden Jennifer, so it couldn't be either of the women. They had a totally separate, totally weird crisis to deal with. Call couldn't think of any other adult who'd been acting weird. Master Lemuel? Call hadn't seen him in a year and it seemed uncharitable to suspect him just because they'd never really gotten along.

"Could it have been one of the Assembly members?" he asked. "But why grab Tamara?"

The answer presented itself to him as soon as he said the words aloud.

To lure me out of the Magisterium.

"Why did you say it was the spy?" Call said. "We still don't know who that is."

"Well, it stands to reason," Alex said. "Who else would it be except someone who's been trying to hurt you?"

"Which means we're walking into a trap," Aaron said. "We're going to have to be very careful and very quiet. Whoever it is knows we're coming. He probably made sure you saw him. Can you do that thing that makes us invisible again?"

"Good idea," Alex said, lifting his hands. Air swirled around them, kicking up leaves.

Call frowned. That made sense — that it was the spy who'd taken Tamara, that he'd done it to get Alex to get them to leave the Magisterium. Kind of. It *kind of* made sense. But how did the spy know that Alex would go and get Aaron and Call instead of the Masters?

How would the spy know Alex was there at all?

That had an answer, though. The spy, or whoever it was,

would know that taking Tamara and Havoc would bring Call and Aaron out of the Magisterium eventually. They'd come looking for their friend.

Though they could have brought all the mages of the Magisterium with them.

Come to think of it, Call didn't remember seeing any evidence of a blast of magic being thrown outside. It was dark, but even in the dark, there was none of the telltale smell of ozone or burning wood.

He looked over at Alex and frowned. They were far from the Magisterium now, and it was increasingly dark. The woods pressed in from the sides and he couldn't see Alex's expression.

"This is the way to the Order of Disorder," Aaron said, interrupting Call's increasingly troubled thoughts. "It's abandoned, though. Alma said they were forced to clear out when the Assembly started rounding up the animals."

"Maybe that's where the spy is holding her." Alex sounded excited, but not like this was a grand adventure and not like he was panicking about Tamara, either. There was an eagerness in his voice that Call didn't like one bit.

The woods were deep and strangely empty without the Chaos-ridden animals, echoing with their absence. Occasionally, a distant owl called out. The wind was at their back, pushing them along. But Call's steps had slowed to a shuffle.

Alex was his friend. When Call had first come to the Magisterium, Alex had been nice to him, even though Call was a surly little kid and Alex was smart and cool, with plenty of friends. And then Alex had talked to Call after Alex had gotten his heart broken by Kimiya. He'd really believed that Alex liked him.

But Alex had access. He was Master Rufus's assistant. He could have gotten Call's canteen and punched a hole in it. He would have had access to whatever Rufus did to make their wristbands open their common room door; he could have used that to hide Skelmis in Call's bedroom. Could Anastasia have let him down into the chamber with the elementals when she went there? Call supposed she might have — after all, he was her stepson. Would she have noticed if he slipped away for a moment? And then, last year — he was the one who'd told Call that the mages had decided to kill Alastair, even though Master Rufus had told Call that had never been true.

But why would Alex do any of that? Call glanced at his impassive face as they moved through the silvery dark. They were almost at the village of the Order. Call could see the big clearing up ahead, the shadows of cottages.

He remembered Jennifer's mouth moving and her last words: *Kimiya, Kimiya, stay away from him.* But who had Kimiya been near at the party? Who would she need to be warned away from?

Just her friends. And her boyfriend.

Alex. It didn't make any sense. And yet. Something was still bothering him, had been bothering him since they'd first seen Alex in front of their door. Out of breath, looking panicked, with blood on his blue shirt.

Blue shirt. Cogs whirled in Call's mind. The image of a ripped photograph, Drew standing with Master Joseph and someone else, someone who was wearing a blue shirt with distinctive black stripes down the shoulder seams.

"I'm cold," Call said, suddenly. "Alex, can I borrow your hoodie?"

Alex looked puzzled. *Aaron* looked puzzled. Call wasn't usually one for borrowing other people's clothes. But Alex shrugged the hoodie off anyway, and handed it to Call.

Call stopped dead in his tracks. Alex's blue shirt was striped with two black lines down the shoulders.

The other two boys stopped and looked back at him. Aaron's expression was worried.

Alex's wasn't.

"Alex," Call said, in as calm a voice as he could manage, "how did you know Drew?"

Alex slowly raised his head. "What do you care?" he said. "You killed him."

Aaron stopped dead in his tracks. The wind howled through the branches of the trees all around them. "Why would you say that?" He looked from Call to Alex. "What's going on?"

"Alex is the one," Call said. He felt numb inside. "He's the spy."

Alex took a step toward Call. Aaron flung a hand out, as if to stop Alex from coming any closer.

"Get away from Call," he warned. "I'm a Makar, Alex. I could really hurt you."

But the older boy ignored him. "Drew was like my brother," Alex said. "Master Joseph recruited me in my Copper Year. He needed a talented air mage. And there was no one more talented than I was. Until you two."

Call sucked in his breath.

"My father was old," Alex said. "Barely even noticed when I got into the Magisterium. Joseph became my father. He taught me and Drew together. Gave us extra lessons. That's why I was good enough to become Rufus's assistant. And boy, did Joseph laugh when I told him that." A grin split Alex's handsome face. "Anastasia was harder to trick. But she fell for it, too, the good-stepson act. She was too busy faking that she cared about my father to pay attention to me." His eyes burned. "Meanwhile, Joseph told me everything. He told me the truth about the Enemy of Death. He told me about *you*."

"So you've known who I was this whole time?" asked Call.

Alex barely seemed to hear him. "Do you know how ungrateful you are?" he said. "Joseph cares about you more than he cares about anything else. Both of you have power, but you, Call, you're special. Do you know what it means to be special? Do you have any idea what you're throwing away?"

"If it means being like you," Call said, "then I don't want it."

Alex's face twisted. Aaron's hand flashed protectively, fire already growing in his palm, but at that moment shadows exploded out of the woods on either side of them. Adults in black clothing, with black masks hiding their faces. Strong hands and arms seized Call and Aaron.

"March them to the village," Alex said.

Call was shoved forward, stumbling. He and Aaron were pushed roughly down the path. He had no idea who was holding him — not a Chaos-ridden; Alex couldn't control one.

Or could he? *The greatest Makar of your generation.*

No, if Alex was a chaos user, he would have bragged about it, Call was sure. It turned out that one didn't have to have anything to do with chaos to have Evil Overlord aspirations.

CHAPTER FIFTEEN

CALL TRIED TO twist out of the grip of the people who held him, but he couldn't. They were too strong. He tried to bring fire to his hands, but as soon as it sparked, someone cuffed him on the back of the head and his concentration fled, extinguishing the flame.

A moment later, he was thrown down in the grass in the center of the abandoned Order of Disorder village, the empty buildings eerie in the moonlight. There were packs and food and a small fire going.

Alex wasn't working alone. The masked figures, whoever they were, must have been waiting here to be summoned by him.

Call rolled to his side, looking for Aaron. Aaron was down in the grass, too. A bulky masked figure had a boot on his back. Call tried to stand but was shoved firmly back down to the ground.

"Let them sit up." It was Alex's voice. Call struggled to his knees to see Alex walking toward them. A massive copper glove was on his right arm, covering his hand, reaching to the elbow.

The Alkahest. The Makar killer.

Call had used it himself to destroy Constantine Madden's body. He couldn't imagine what its power could do to a living person. It would take the chaos inside his soul, or Aaron's, and use it to rip them to pieces from the inside.

"Scared, Makar?" Alex moved the metal fingers of the Alkahest and then laughed at Call's expression. Call exchanged a quick look with Aaron, who was kneeling beside him. There were twigs in Aaron's blond hair, but he didn't look hurt. Thankfully.

Not yet, anyway.

Keep Alex talking, Call thought. *Keep him talking and don't panic and don't let him hurt Aaron.*

"Tamara?" he asked. "Did you hurt her? Is she here?"

That made Alex laugh harder. "You really are an idiot, you know that? I have no idea where Tamara is. I didn't bother kidnapping her. Why go to all that effort when I could just tell you two that I did and you'd believe me? She and your stupid wolf are probably asleep. I guess they'll be pretty sad when they wake up and find out what happened to you two."

"Does Master Joseph know you took the Alkahest?" Aaron asked. "Did he tell you to do this?"

Alex threw his head back, but this time his laugh sounded forced. "He doesn't know anything about my plan — I took the Alkahest and left an illusion in its place. It won't last forever, but it will last long enough," he snarled. "Ever since he started teaching me, I've heard him talk about you. About how the glorious Constantine was returning and how we had to prepare ourselves. The amazing Constantine Madden, who was so important that Drew had to fake his way into the Magisterium, pretending not to even know me. And then it's *you*. What a total disappointment."

"Sorry to hear it," Call said acidly.

"So how come you wanted to kill him? Revenge?" Aaron asked. Call was glad that he was on the *keep him talking* train, because Call was so freaked out that it wasn't easy. "Wouldn't that make Master Joseph angry?"

"He just needs a Makar," Alex said, lifting the Alkahest. "And now I've figured out how to become one. I reconfigured the Alkahest. It won't just rip your chaos magic from you. It will channel that ability into me."

"That's not possible!" Call said, but he recalled how the power had come to him when Constantine Madden's body had been devoured by the Alkahest. Maybe it could be done.

"Says the boy who's been dead for fourteen years," dismissed Alex. "Do you ever think about him? Poor little Callum Hunt, dead before he even got to say his first word. Murdered by you, Constantine, just the way you killed the closest thing I had to a brother. Just the way you killed your own brother. You were never meant to have this power. And now I am going to take it from you and be a better Enemy of Death than you'll ever be."

"Fine," said Call. "Just don't hurt Aaron."

Aaron made a strangled noise. Alex rolled his eyes. "That's right, Aaron, your precious counterweight. Is that what you threw it all away for, Call? Your *friends*?"

"Threw what away?" Call demanded, panicking. He had to believe that someone was going to come from the Magisterium.

Someone was going to find them. Alex was crazy; he was out of his mind. "Being Constantine? I never wanted that."

"You shouldn't hurt Call," said Aaron. "You should take the magic from me."

"All this nobility is really nauseating," said Alex. His gold wristband gleamed as he flicked back a strand of brown hair. He looked spectral in the moonlight. Like an evil spirit. "But if it makes you feel any better, that was my plan. Kill Call, make it look like an accident, and then take your Makar ability, Aaron, killing you in the process. But now that you're both here, in front of me, it's hard to choose."

"Master Joseph will kill you if you hurt Call," Aaron argued. "He jumped in front of Call to protect him in the Enemy's tomb, did you know that? He would have sacrificed his life for him!"

"He always believed Call would come around and want to join him," Alex said. "Want to fight back death, but the truth is, Call, you're too much of a coward. Someone who doesn't want this power shouldn't have it. Really, I'm doing Master Joseph a favor."

He moved toward Call. Aaron started to struggle up but was shoved back down. Black fire started to grow in his hands. "Stay away from Call!"

Alex whirled toward him with the Alkahest. "Don't you get it?" he said witheringly. "If you make a move toward me, I'll kill you, and then I'll kill Call anyway. And I'll make it slow."

Aaron clasped his hands into fists. Call felt his whole body tightening as he prepared to jump up, to try to run —

"Stop!" A voice rang out through the clearing. It was Tamara, Havoc at her heels. Havoc's ears were back flat against his head and he was growling. Tamara had her hand out, and red fire was burning in her palm. "You can't hurt me with that thing, Alex," she said. "I'm not a Makar."

"Tamara!" Call shouted. "How did you find us?"

"Havoc," she called back. "We were in the room and he suddenly started growling and throwing himself at the door, even though I'd already taken him out. I opened the door and he led me right here." She glared at Alex. "And he'll rip out the throat of anyone who comes near me, so don't even think about it." Tamara advanced toward them, and the minions actually took a step back. Fire blazed higher. Call wondered who they were — devotees of Master Joseph, regular non-magic people who'd been enchanted? He had to admit that between Alex's crazy master plan, his minions, and his boasting, he was really racking up the Evil Overlord Points.

Call tried to get up, but he was held tightly in place. He could see Aaron struggling beside him.

"Oh, good," Alex said. "An audience."

Tamara looked furious. Call hoped to see the mages of the Magisterium behind her, but no one was there. This was his fault, he knew. For three years, Tamara and Aaron had been keeping his secrets, hiding important things from everyone, including Master Rufus. Now they didn't look for help from anyone else, even when they could really use it.

Alex leveled the Alkahest toward them and reached out with it. "Maybe the Alkahest should choose. Maybe I'll send it at both of you and see what happens. Maybe it will take *both* your magic. What do you think of that?"

Call reached out and grabbed Aaron's hand. Aaron looked surprised for a second. Then his grip locked with Call's.

Call wanted to tell his best friend how sorry he was, how this was all his fault because he was Constantine Madden. But Aaron spoke before he got a chance.

"At least we're going to die together," Aaron said. Then, unbelievably, he smiled at Call.

We're not, Call wanted to say. *We're going to live.* But as he began to speak, a flash of light blinded him. Tamara had thrown a bolt of fire. Alex ducked away from it, flinging out his own hand, sending air magic to reroute the fire. It shot back toward Call.

The man who was holding Call stumbled back, his grip on Call faltering. The masked man's shirt was on fire and he was screaming. Call shot to his feet, ignoring the pain in his leg. Still holding Aaron's hand, he hauled him upright, too. Everything seemed to be happening at once.

"Havoc, *go!*" Tamara screamed.

Havoc was a dark blur in the air, racing toward Alex. Aaron drew his hand away from Call's, dark chaos blooming in his palm. Alex raised his arm, the Alkahest shimmering with energy. Aaron flung his hand forward, but the dark light that sprang from his hand flew wide, knocking one of the hooded figures aside but missing Alex. The clawed hand of the Alkahest opened, and a blaze of coppery light flew from its fingers.

Time hung suspended. That light was everything that chaos wasn't. It was bright and burning and cold like the edge of a knife, and Call knew without the shadow of a doubt that when it struck him, it would kill him.

He closed his eyes.

Something pushed him from behind. He went sprawling, rolling over in the grass. The bolt of light missed him by inches — he felt something sear his cheek as he tumbled forward and over — and then, fetching up on his side, he raised his head and saw it strike Aaron in the chest.

The force of it lifted Aaron off his feet and sent him flying. He crashed down in the grass several feet away, his eyes wide-open and glassy, staring at the sky.

"No," someone said. "Aaron, no, no, *no!*" Call thought it was his own voice for a second, but it was Tamara's. She was sprawled in the grass next to him.

She'd been what hit him. She'd knocked him out of the way of the Alkahest. She'd saved his life.

But not Aaron's.

Call touched his cheek. It burned. Maybe the Alkahest had only burned Aaron, too. He tried to get to his feet, to go over to Aaron, but his legs wouldn't hold him. Instead, he reached out toward Aaron with all his senses.

He remembered what he had felt before when he'd touched Aaron's soul. The sense of life, of something existing in the world, bright and solid.

But there was nothing there now. Aaron was a shell. His soul was gone, leaving only the shining shadows of Aaron-ness remaining.

Call whirled on Alex, who had torn the Alkahest from his arm. Of course — now it could hurt him, too. Now he had Aaron's power. He almost seemed to be pulsing, like a star about to go supernova. His skin was shimmering and rippling with bands of light and dark.

"*Power,*" Alex gasped. He raised his hand, blackness coiling around it like smoke. "I can feel it. The power of chaos, running through me —"

"Not if I can help it," Call said, flinging out his hand. A bolt of black light shot from his palm toward Alex. He was sure it would kill him, send him screaming into the void.

He was glad.

The spear of magic flew toward Alex. His hand went up, and he caught it. He stared at it wonderingly for a second and Call stared, too, a sick feeling in his stomach. Alex was a Makar now. He could control and manipulate chaos. And he was a better, older, and more experienced magician than Call.

Then he screamed. Out of nowhere, Havoc had slipped out of the dark and sunk his teeth into Alex's leg.

Alex flung chaos, but Havoc was too quick for him, darting away, still growling. He lunged again, and this time Alex didn't have a chance to react: Havoc knocked him to the ground, his teeth ripping at Alex's shirt.

"Get it off me!" Alex screamed. "Get it off me!"

Several of the hooded figures raced up; Havoc released Alex, who staggered to his feet, bleeding from several places. His skin was still rippling, his face twisting. Call remembered how it had been for him in the tomb, when his chaos magic had manifested. How out of control he'd felt, how sick.

Alex flung a hand toward Havoc, but this time the magic that exploded from his hand went haywire. Darkness spilled out in all directions. It poured out in tendrils that rose up into the air and clouds that reached toward the sky. Where it touched, things began to come apart. One of the Order of Disorder houses collapsed as chaos ate away its foundations. Three nearby trees were devoured whole. The ground itself became pocked as pieces of it were lifted away into the void.

Two of the masked figures screamed as they were swallowed up before the chaos dissipated.

Alex looked down at his hands, horrified and yet clearly amazed, too. "Get the Alkahest!" he said hoarsely to one of his remaining minions. "We need to get out of here!" He looked at Call for a moment, then curled his lip.

"I'll deal with you later," Alex hissed, and rushed from the clearing, his surviving followers beside him.

Call barely even cared. He turned back around to see Tamara crouched over Aaron's still body. She was sobbing, her whole body shaking, nearly bent in half. Havoc crept over to her, nuzzling at her shoulder with his black nose, but she kept crying, her face wet with tears.

Call didn't even feel his feet move, but he was there, dropping down next to Aaron, across from Tamara. He touched Aaron's hand, the hand he'd gripped only moments ago. It was cold.

Tamara was still crying softly. She had knocked Call out of the way of the Alkahest. She had saved his life.

"Why did you do it?" he asked suddenly. "How could you do that? Aaron was the one who was supposed to live. Not me. I'm the Enemy of Death, Tamara. I'm not the good one. Aaron was."

She looked at him for a long moment. "I know," she said, tears in her eyes. "But, Call —"

A cry came from above what was left of the village. "There!" someone shouted. Among the trees, Call could see floating spheres. The mages had gone looking for them after all, just like they'd looked for Drew that night. And they'd been too late again. Always too late.

Master North, Master Rufus, Alma, and several other Masters ran into the clearing. North and the others were gaping around at the devastation, at the chunks of earth that were simply gone, the collapsed houses and destroyed trees. But Rufus — Rufus was looking at Aaron. Pushing aside the others, he rushed to Aaron's body, falling to one knee to feel for a pulse.

Call knew he wouldn't find one. There was no Aaron anymore. No counterweight to his own soul. Just this feeling of emptiness, the feeling that something had been ripped away from him that could never be replaced.

He understood now how Constantine Madden could have wanted to tear down the world once his brother was gone.

Rufus closed his eyes. His shoulders slumped. He looked old to Call in that moment, old and broken.

"What happened here?" demanded Master North. "It looks like there was some sort of battle." He frowned at Call. "What did you do?"

Rage exploded inside Call's head. "It wasn't me!" he shouted. "Alex Strike and his — his minions! He has the Alkahest and he killed Aaron. You're letting them get away! Aren't you supposed to be the teachers? Stop them!"

"No!" Alma said, striding toward Call, eyes shining. She pointed one long finger at him. "I didn't see it at first, but now I see you, Constantine. You killed Aaron. You engineered all of this to hide your crimes, including the murder of Jennifer."

Call's eyes went wide. She couldn't be saying what it sounded like she was saying. He didn't even know how to answer her. He couldn't, not with Aaron's body next to him.

"Be quiet," Master Rufus told Alma, surprising Call. "It's obvious there was a battle, but we have no reason to think

Call's lying. And even if he was, Tamara was here as a witness."

"Call's right," Tamara put in. "It was Alex Strike. It must have been Alex all along."

Alma shook her head. "Don't believe either of them! Haven't you wondered how Callum controlled that Chaos-ridden animal beside him? Or how he defeated the Enemy of Death himself? Or why he wasn't a Makar when last year began, but how he became one at the exact moment Constantine was supposed to have been killed? Now we have the answer. Constantine put his soul into Callum Hunt. You are looking at a monster in the shape of a child. I saw him put chaos into a soul and create one of the Chaos-ridden. I know what he is!"

She was raving, Call thought. No one was going to believe her. But no one contradicted her, either.

"Don't worry, Callum," Master North said, but there was something off about his voice. A coaxing tone. "We'll get to the bottom of this. Come with me."

"I can't leave Aaron," Call told him.

"We're all going back to the Magisterium," Master North said.

"No!" Call shouted. He was tired of lying, tired of any of this. "You have to go after Alex! You have to find him! I admit it, okay? Everything Alma's saying is true, except for the part where I killed Aaron. I didn't! Yes, I am the Enemy of Death, but I swear to you that I didn't do it and that Alex did. I swear to you that I would never hurt —"

That was the last thing Call managed to say before he was clapped in chains.

CHAPTER SIXTEEN

CALL'S CELL IN the Panopticon had three white walls and one that was entirely clear, so that he could be seen at all times by the people in the guard tower at the very center of the prison. None of the walls seemed to be affected by magic, so no matter how many times he tried to burn them or devour them, crack them or freeze them, nothing worked. Twice a day, a white box was pushed through a plate of the clear window. Inside was nearly tasteless food and water.

Other than that, nothing changed.

They hadn't given him any books or paper or pens or anything else to do, so Call spent his days sitting on his cot, hating everyone and especially himself.

He'd been there a week. A week of playing through that final battle in the clearing, imagining how it could have gone differently, imagining Aaron alive — and sometimes, in the throes of self-pity, even imagining himself dead. Sometimes he woke up from dreams where Aaron was talking to him, joking around about going to the Gallery or offering to walk Havoc. Sometimes he woke from dreams where Aaron was shouting at him, telling him that he was the one who was supposed to die.

Call wants to live.

Call thought again and again about his own personal addition to the Cinquain. His defining characteristic: a will to survive. That's what he'd thought, anyway. But Call didn't want to be the person who was alive because his best friend was dead. He didn't know if he wanted to live in a world without Aaron in it.

He wanted Aaron back. It was like a roaring in his soul, the sadness of terrible loss. The realization of what Constantine must have felt when he lost Jericho.

Call didn't want to understand how Constantine had felt.

Maybe it was better he was in prison, where he couldn't hurt anyone else, where at least he was being punished for some of his crimes. Maybe it was better that no one came to see him, not even his own dad. Certainly not Tamara, who probably couldn't live with the guilt of making the totally wrong choice. And not Master Rufus, who probably wished Call had never even gone to the Iron Trial.

How could someone have been unlucky enough to have chosen the Enemy of Death as his apprentice, not once but *twice*?

↑ ≈ △ ○ @

Call was lying on the floor, looking up at the ceiling, when steps at an unfamiliar time made him turn his head. Standing outside his cell, dressed in a long white coat, her hair tucked up under a white hat, was Anastasia Tarquin.

She looked at him and raised both her brows in a gesture that reminded him of Master Rufus. It said, *You are amusing me right now, but you won't be amusing me for long.*

Call didn't care. He stayed on the floor. A guard — a woman who banged down Call's food tray with unnecessary vigor — brought the Assemblywoman a chair. Anastasia sat and the guard walked off. Call had guessed that a member of the Assembly would eventually come to take some kind of statement or interrogate him. He should probably be glad it was Anastasia, but he wasn't glad. He didn't want to talk to her. He didn't want to talk to anyone, but someone he knew was even worse than a stranger.

"Come closer," Anastasia told him, folding her hands in her lap.

With a sigh, Call scrambled over to the window and into a sitting position. "Fine, but you have to answer two questions for me."

"Very well," she said. "What are they?"

Call hesitated, because even though he obsessed over these two things in the longest hours of the night, he didn't know what he would do with real answers.

"Is Tamara okay?" he managed, his voice coming out choked. "Is she in a lot of trouble?"

Anastasia gave him a small smile. "Tamara is safe. How much trouble she is in remains to be seen. Are you satisfied?"

"No," Call said. "Havoc? Is he okay? Have they hurt him?"

Anastasia's smile didn't falter. "Your wolf is with the Rajavis and perfectly safe. Enough?"

"I guess," Call said. Knowing that Tamara was all right and that Havoc was alive was the first relief he'd felt in forever.

"Good," Anastasia said. "We don't have a lot of time. There is something I have to tell you. My name is not Anastasia Tarquin."

Call blinked. "What?"

"Long ago I had two sons who went to the Magisterium," she said. "We were not a legacy family. I admit I was uncomfortable with my own magic and took little interest in their schooling. I met none of their teachers, attended no meetings, let my husband take care of it all. It proved a fatal mistake." She took a deep breath. "When I spoke of knowing Constantine and Jericho Madden and owing them a debt, I was telling you only some of the truth. You see, *I was their mother* — which means that I am your mother, in every way that matters."

Whatever Call had been suspecting, it wasn't that. He gaped at her. "But — but how? The Magisterium — they would know —"

"There was no way for them to know," said Anastasia. "It was long ago, and as I said, I barely knew the mages. But when both my sons were . . . dead . . . Master Joseph contacted me. My husband, your father, had killed himself by then." Her voice was emotionless. "Joseph told me what Constantine had done. How he had transferred his soul. I was determined to be there for my son in his new body as I had not been before. I left the country and went back to my homeland. There, I stole the identity of a woman about my age: Anastasia Tarquin. I altered my appearance. I practiced my craft with a newfound devotion. Then, returning as a powerful mage from abroad, I married

Augustus Strike to obtain a seat on the council. No one guessed who I was or my true purpose."

"Your true purpose?" Call's mind was spinning.

"You," she said. "That's why I came to the school. That's why I joined the Assembly. It was all for you. And that has not changed." Anastasia rose, standing and putting her hand against the clear not-glass of the window, as if she wished nothing more than to reach through it and be able to touch Call's hand with her own. Her eyes were sad but determined. "This time I am going to save you, my son. This time I am going to set you free."

ABOUT THE AUTHORS

Holly Black and **Cassandra Clare** first met over ten years ago at Holly's first-ever book signing. They have since become good friends, bonding over (among other things) their shared love of fantasy — from the sweeping vistas of The Lord of the Rings to the gritty tales of Batman in Gotham City to the classic sword-and-sorcery epics to *Star Wars*. With Magisterium, they decided to team up to write their own story about heroes and villains, good and evil, and being chosen for greatness, whether you like it or not.

Holly is the bestselling author and co-creator of The Spiderwick Chronicles series and won a Newbery Honor for her novel *Doll Bones*. Cassie is the author of bestselling YA series, including The Mortal Instruments, The Infernal Devices, and The Dark Artifices. They both live in Western Massachusetts, about ten minutes away from each other. This is the third book in Magisterium, following *The Iron Trial* and *The Copper Gauntlet*.

RETHINK WHAT YOU KNOW ABOUT GOOD AND EVIL . . .

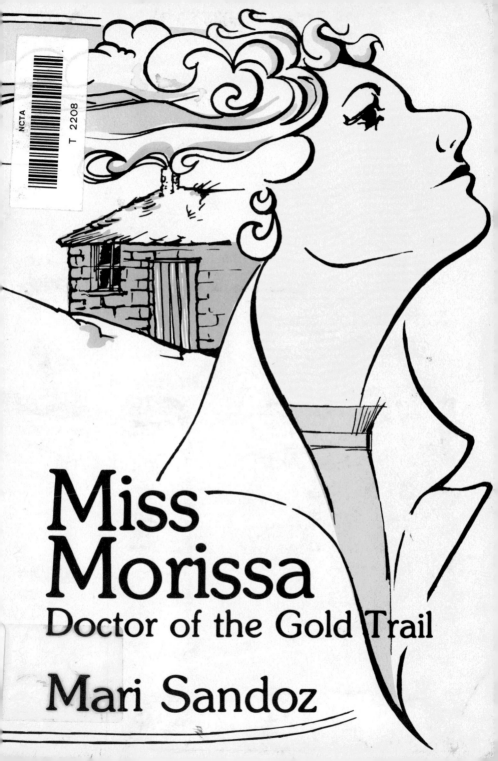

Miss
Morissa
Doctor of the Gold Trail

Mari Sandoz

DATE DUE

Miss MORISSA

DOCTOR OF THE GOLD TRAIL

Desperate Pilgrim,
Ever, ever crossing
O'er the flooding waters
And the fiery sands.

—From Hymn in Homesteader's
Notebook

a novel by MARI SANDOZ

UNIVERSITY OF NEBRASKA PRESS

Lincoln and London

First Bison Book printing: 1980
Most recent printing indicated by first digit below:
1   2   3   4   5   6   7   8   9   10

Publishing by arrangement with Hastings House Publishers, Inc.
Manufactured in the United States of America

Library of Congress Cataloging in Publication Data

Sandoz, Mari, 1896–1966.
  Miss Morissa, doctor of the gold trail.

  Reprint of the ed. published by Hastings House, New York.
  I. Title.
[PZ3.S2174Mi 1980]   [PS3537.A667]   79–23761
ISBN 0–8032–9118–3

DEDICATED TO

DR. MARY E. QUICK, who brought her five young sons into the frontier regions west of the Missouri River in 1867 and carried on a medical practice there for twenty-five years.

DR. PHOEBE A. OLIVER BRIGGS, who went as physician to the Otoe Indians in 1872.

DR. GEORGIA ARBUCKLE FIX, who grew up without a father near Princeton, Missouri, and set up a practice on her homestead along the Black Hills gold trail in 1886.

And a hundred others on our Western frontiers.

I

THE WHEELS OF THE STAGECOACH STIRRED UP A LONG TRAIL OF dust, to sift away eastward like a plume of smoke sprouting from the wide spring prairie. All except one of the passengers were content to be closed in by the heavy side curtains of the coach, even the sunburnt rancher and the naked-faced youth with small dark freckles thick across his cheeks. But the young city woman pulled back the stiff canvas and thrust her head out. She did it with a practicality and foresight that belied the feathered little hat tipped toward her nose. She had asked to change seats so she could look out on the windy side, away from most of the dust. But the wind was strong. The feathers on her hat struggled like agitated yellow birds, and her fashionable bangs that had seemed so duskily black in the shadow were shot with gleaming copper light where the sun ran over them.

With her white skin unprotected by powdering or veil, Morissa Kirk leaned far out to look at the guard carrying a Winchester across his knee, and to watch the driver swing his six fast horses out around the slower travelers. They passed gold seekers, mule freight outfits, and files of canvas-covered wagons drawn by long teams of bulls, the whackers plodding in the dust, their whips snaking out in the afternoon sun, but silently, the wind carrying the sharp, explosive sound away.

As the coach jounced and jolted, a little round-topped trunk tied with other luggage in the rack on top jounced, too, a new pressed-metal trunk that was to have accompanied Morissa Kirk on her wedding journey to Scotland, and was still filled with her trousseau, although her hand was bare of every ring. Beside the small trunk was a doctor's black bag and a chest of surgical instruments, while inside, cradled on Morissa's lap from the rougher bumps, was a case of vials and bottles and other physician's glass.

The coach swung down toward a rugged range of buttes like low, timber-flanked mountains that tapered off to Courthouse and Jail Rocks, standing out together and alone. At their feet the trail turned northwestward, upon the broad North Platte valley of Nebraska, the spreading bottoms grazed so bare that no stock was nearer than the far blue slopes. Morissa could get no glimpse of the river, only a smudging of dust against the ridges beyond, and then gradually a thickening line that reached for miles up and down where the stream must be—a wide, dark gathering like the great buffalo herds that had rested here not ten years ago.

But as the swift coach approached the river, Morissa saw what she had known must be there: at least thirty great circle corrals of covered freight wagons and a far spreading of other vehicles, with tents and bedrolls scattered among them, and knots of men—all jammed together closer and closer toward the new bridge. The crowd was thick as a close-corralled herd, particularly in the one short stretch of trail that was like a street, lined on both sides by tents and low buildings, mostly log and sod, and little taller than the bearded, sunburnt, waiting men.

The crowd milled restless as corralled longhorns, too, all waiting for the bridge to carry them over the roily, flooded stream, release them to hurry toward the Black Hills where gold lay thick at the grass roots. They had seen the real and shining proof of it captured in the tiny bottles of yellow dust that were set in the windows of every depot across the nation—to catch the sun and the eyes of the gold-hungry, and of all those others eager to live on, to prey on them.

It was this rush to the new Eldorado of Deadwood Gulch that had gathered the great wagon trains of mine machinery and equipment here, trains of whisky, too, and mahogany bars and roulette tables, guns and ammunition, and the finery, the mirrors and couches for the fancyhouses. It had drawn all the men waiting here, and the curled and tint-cheeked, impatient women.

While still far off the driver on the box of the stagecoach called out his loud "Yip, yip, yip; yi, yi, yi!"—the signal to get the change of horses ready for the ride to Deadwood if the bridge was opened today, otherwise for the return trip to Sidney. And it would be the return once more, for as they neared the river the passengers could hear the dull thump of the pile driver and knew that none of those so eager to go on would cross this afternoon unless he swam the flood and the quicksand, or took a chance on the French breed, old Joe Lenway, who had his handwritten sign in all the outfitting places back down at Sidney:

I haul you over north river safe
$2.00 dollar a wagon.

2

Horsebackers had met the coach a mile out to make a flying wedge for it past the little rows of shacks and tents to the stage station that sat beside the river. The galloping escort split the packed crowd, afoot and horseback, turning each side back upon itself, like treetops bent both ways by a spearhead of wind that was the thundering stage. The horses stopped with snort and clatter of harness, and the driver carried the lines down in his jump from the high box, the guard with his rifle climbing down, the gun still ready. Inside, the passengers stretched stiffly and one after the other stooped out and down into the curious crowd.

"Hey!—a lady-woman, an' a good looker!" a tipsyish youth shouted above the noise as Morissa Kirk was helped off the high step by a station hand. Then she stood alone in her feathered hat and the traveling suit, dusty but still the dark green of a young cedar on a hillside, with sun-darkened faces turned toward her from all around.

After Morissa, the freckled young man came out. He had peered carefully from both coach windows, his hand on his gun, and now he jumped down and slipped away into the crowd, a man or two speaking of him as he went: "Fly Speck, Fly Speck Billy," but keeping the voice down.

A weary crinkle came to Morissa's hazel eyes. Of course—the dark freckles. But she remembered something else now: This must be the highwayman from up around Dakota Territory, a roadagent as Robin, her stepfather, called him. That smooth boy-face hid a thief, a cold-blooded murderer. And yet, well-recognized, he walked free and unchallenged through this public place.

Uneasily the young woman glanced around the rough crowd eyeing her. There were few women beyond those from the saloons, and most of the dusty, wind-burnt men had guns in their holsters or tucked inside the belly band, as Robin called it. Most of the horsebackers seemed to be cowboys, with big hats, coiled lariats at the saddle horn, guns hanging over their leather chaps, gleaming spurs at the boot heels. Morissa managed to push through to her belongings, wondering how she could ever find Robin in all this throng of people, so far beyond anything she could have imagined. And as she stood there, with nowhere to go, she finally had to doubt the wisdom of her impulsive, unannounced journey into this wilderness. There could be no place here for her, not even a spot to spread a blanket for a night. Truly none was so bold as the blind mare who would not see.

When the crowd began to drift back to the whisky stores and to watch the thumping pile driver, Morissa Kirk found the station keeper.

"Yeh," he admitted, replenishing his cud now that he had the opportunity, "Yeh, I know Robin Thomas." But Robin was off across the river there, boss of the graders refilling the new approach to the bridge.

Washed out yesterday. Water came roaring down the old Platte so they couldn't even set pilings.

"Across there's where he's working." The keeper pointed off over his shoulder with the plug of tobacco he had gnawed, off to the weathering bridge that stood like some long, low, many-legged creature, the pile driver at the far end like a lifted head, looking.

As Morissa followed her trunk to the log station building, a shouting came from the riverbank, followed by a surge of the crowd down that way. On the far side of the wide rolling Platte, a wagon broke from the mass of people waiting there also. It swung around far out, and then headed in toward the river, turned expertly a little upstream, coming at a good pace—the momentum to carry it through the quarter mile of flood and quicksand.

At the shouting the bridge workers all stopped to look, the piling hammer silent as they relayed a message across. "It's old Joe Lenway!" the palm-shielded voices called out. "Hold the Sidney coach. Lenway's bringin' a sick man over!"

A murmuring and a movement stirred around Morissa, with words of uneasiness and protest. The river was too high, after the sudden thaw in the western mountains and a May blizzard that had buried the Fort Laramie region last week. Too dangerous, but Joe Lenway would try anything for two dollars.

"Why'n't the man wait a little, so's they can lay planks over the missing spans a the bridge when they gets closer—?" someone demanded.

"Hell, he's probably bad sick—an' the stage don't wait," another answered.

Morissa was being carried along toward the river by the push of the crowd, the yellow feathers of her hat squeezed in between trail-soiled shoulders and dusty beards, but she could see the moving wagon and a man rise up to whip his team into the gray stream. The horses tried to rear sideways at the flood edge, but with firm line and whip old Joe got them in, throwing water high as they went off into the river, still struggling to turn back. Under the fury of the driver's lashes, they settled to the pull, the current boiling up around their bellies, then at their breasts. The wagon swayed and lifted, the end swung downward by the current's force. But the man fought and cursed to hold the horses steady to their upstream turn until they began floundering as in quicksand, and tried to rear above it, leap its pull. The sudden jerk threw the driver to the dashboard, then, as he recovered himself, the team and the wagon lurched forward together once more and went off into deep water as over a bank, sunk clear under. Joe grabbed the tail of a swimming horse, and behind him a bedroll, no, a man, was washed up on the flood. For a moment the appalled crowd watched a feeble splashing and then the man was gone.

"Save him!" Morissa Kirk cried out, commanding them as though

4

none could see that this must be done, even before the man came up, free of the blankets now and still struggling a little, trying to help himself. But the current was too swift, boiling, turning, rolling, and he was drawn back under almost at once.

By now two riders had broken from the watchers at the far side and spurred downstream. Where the current swept in toward the bank, they sent their horses into the water. When the man reappeared, like a chunk of dark waterlogged piling, and rolling low, their ropes shot out —once, twice, and again. Suddenly a loop caught, the man stopped, swung in an arc against the angry water, and then one of the horses was struggling back against a taut rope, drawing the man in like a bawling calf to the branding fire. At the bank the cowboys carried him out, laid him on dry ground, still and unmoving, while they stood around him, helpless.

Now Morissa Kirk could not restrain herself. Grabbing up her wide skirts she pushed back to the stage station and with her little doctor's bag hanging from her arm she swung herself up on one of the horses at the hitchracks before anyone could stop her. With a knee crooked around the horn like the knob of a lady's sidesaddle, she was off on the rearing, fighting, white-stockinged black, through the crowd and then over the bank into the cold snow water in one splashing leap, the shouts of anger and warning lost behind her.

The horse snorted and began to plunge as he felt the sand moving and alive under his feet, but a sharp cut of the saddle quirt sent him forward in a wild, angry thrusting against the water, and when they hit the edge of the worst quicksand, the most treacherous shift and suck of it, he quieted and forged ahead, a well-trained animal long experienced in such streams. Free in deep water at last, he swam the current with strong, steady strokes, but the flood swirling about Morissa's thighs caught at her skirts, swept them out to balloon in the weight and force of the current, to drag at the horse. Hampered by the pounding bag on her arm she grabbed at the heavy garments, kept drawing them up as she could. But gradually the laboring horse was forced downstream, slowing in his wild push across the current, sinking lower into the water for all her quirting until only his nose was out and it seemed she must kick her skirts off and swim for it herself. Shouts rose all along the banks and anxious riders plunged in from both sides but suddenly Morissa's horse began to paw for footing again—in quicksand. Yet with the feel of something like bottom, he strengthened and finally they were out on the other side, the crowd pressing close around.

Morissa was soaked, even her yellow feathers hanging wet, but the doctor's bag was still on her arm and as someone grabbed the bit of the horse she slipped off and ran in her pounding skirts. The watchers parted for her, opening the circle around the man still so quiet and remote there on the ground. She stooped over him, felt for his heart under the wet clothing and laid an ear to his breast, but there was no beat, no warmth, nothing of life. Quickly she motioned for space, drew the tongue free, and showed a cowboy how to turn the man, grasp him about the middle and lift up, bringing a gush of dirty water bursting from his mouth and nose. Then, with the man's head turned up sideways on his arm, Morissa knelt over him, lifting, pressing, forcing herself to calm her breath to the slow rhythm as someone brought a buffalo robe and started a little fire. When she tired she shook back the hair stringing over her face and gave her place to one of the men while she opened her bag, hoping for something that might help, something to save this man, drowning and sick with a disease of which she knew nothing at all.

By now most of those waiting on the north bank had gathered in close, curious, watching, barely shifting for a man who came pushing through, elbowing his way. The young woman did not notice him or his exclamation when he saw her, but the one word "Morissa!" from Robin Thomas started a wave of low voices that spread clear back. Morissa?— then this must be his stepdaughter, who was a lady doc.

While the young woman fingered her vials and powders, she glanced anxiously at the man on the ground, and the cowboy bending up and down over him. Still no color came, and gradually the watchers began to murmur among themselves. "He's a goner," some were saying. "Sick man dumped in the cold water like that—"

"Yeh, probably same as dead anyway, hurrying him off to Sidney like they was."

"Well, he won't die for nobody tryin'—the poor little bastard!"

The words brought Morissa's head up sharply, her face suddenly dark and flushed. But the speaker was not observing her at all, only the man, and so she hid her foolish anger. Yet she was less confident now, more fearful that in her hurry and her inexperience she might have forgotten something, something that could have been done. The man had no life to swallow anything, no signs of any living that she could see, and so without hope she took over from the cowboy again, knowing that one moment lost could be the fatal one, or one second of faltering in the rhythm.

The young doctor worked until the studied breathing made her dizzy and her arms ached to breaking. But when it seemed that she must give up, a change came, an almost imperceptible change, without a movement or any other indication that she could identify, yet she knew they were winning. Against the excitement of this, she held herself to the steady pressures and finally a tiny bubble rose to linger at the man's gray lips. Tears stung the young woman's eyes but she shook them away, and when there was breathing, shallow and weak, but breathing, she turned the man up and groped for her bag. Somebody pushed a bottle into her hand. Without glancing around she looked at the Old Crow label, licked a test drop spilled on the back of her hand, and nodded. Carefully she gave the man a little swallow and then another, and finally she got him out of his wet clothing and rolled into the warmed buffalo robe beside the fire.

"I been sick couple weeks, I guess, bad sick," the man murmured to the doctor's questions. "I been havin' a gnawin' a long time, inside the belly there, like it had a hole—"

That, and his name, Tom Reeder, was all Morissa discovered before his voice trailed off into exhaustion and sleep. So she had him carried away toward a tent and when she had time to thank the man who offered the shelter, she realized that it was Robin, still waiting in his long patience. He let her sob out her relief against his bearded cheek while he stroked her shoulder and held back his rush of questions for a more appropriate time.

But in a moment Morissa remembered her patient and gathered up her awkward, bedraggled skirts to run after him, barely seeing a man who had stopped his horse in her path. The fine bay he was riding was wet to the mane, the rider soaked too from a Platte crossing—a tall, sunburnt man of the region there to stop her, stern, his gray eyes very angry.

"Don't ever do that again, ma'am," he warned. "That Cimarron horse isn't broke for ladies. A wonder you wasn't killed—"

At first Morissa was angry, too, but her manners came back swiftly enough. "Did I take your horse? I'm sorry, but I don't think I've hurt him, Mr.—"

"Polk. Tris Polk."

"Thank you, Mr. Polk. You have a good right to be proud of that splendid animal, so ready for an emergency."

But the man did not rein aside. Instead he stood his stirrups, his palms crossed easily on the saddle horn. "Well, let me tell you something, ma'am," he said. "In these parts taking the poorest crowbait without the owner's permission's a hanging matter—"

"Oh, really?" Morissa inquired, her anger back. "I am sure in these parts, as in all others, letting a man die without attempting succor would be a matter of murder to an enlightened conscience, Mr. Polk."

With this she went around him and his horse, leaving the man free to look after this soft-voiced girl who could muster such fire to go with her courage, and poise too—muddy and bedraggled as she was, with a hat as silly as any that the women of the roadranches or the Black Hills dance halls might be wearing. But now it clung very unfashionably and slaunchwise to the heavy hair that drooped over the shoulders of the once-handsome green suit.

"I'll try to make arrangements for a plankway to get you back by the

7

bridge—" the man called after the girl, his horse slipping daintily through the crowd behind her.

"Thank you, sir," Morissa Kirk replied, only half turning, hiding the wry smile. "My father is Robin Thomas, boss grader here. He'll see that I am cared for."

Then she hurried on to her patient, the handsome smoky eyes that followed her almost forgotten.

When the full moon rose to silver the boiling flood waters, the pile driver was still working, but in the yellower glow of the lanterns strung up along the tower, as though to guide the hammer that fell with such urgency. Beyond, up toward the ridges against the north, a bonfire lit the sandpits where teams worked at plow and buck scrapers to drag earth down to the new abutment. Understandably Clarke, the builder, wanted to open his toll bridge as soon as possible, before the high water eased off and the more daring and impatient tried to ford the stream. Many of the hungrier gold seekers had planned to risk a crossing in the morning but they hesitated now that they had seen a man come so close to drowning. Even old Joe Lenway, with all his experience, had lost one of Reeder's horses for him—just laid down and died after he got the wagon out half a mile down the river. True, a white woman with feathers on her hat had made it across, but she was on Tris Polk's best saddler, one that had swum the flood waters of every stream from the Red River of Texas past the Yellowstone up north. Besides, this young woman for all her city fripperies seemed to have the daring of an Indian squaw running from the military.

By night Morissa Kirk was settled in Robin's one-room soddy, set beside his wagon corral south of the river. Undismayed by the bare earthen walls inside, almost as though she didn't see them, or the dirt floor and the nail-keg chairs, she had changed her drying suit and brought out her diploma and arranged her medical books and essentials in a big box, pegged up on the sod wall for shelving and cupboard. She hung her clothing and the white hospital jacket behind a blanket above the cot; she unpacked a few of her pretty things from the trunk, too, and set her silver toilet articles and the crystal scent bottles on the bare window sill. She even shook out her China silk and the reception gown of rose and gold brocade, making a steady fussing of it all, giving herself no free moment to think of what lay under the thin ice of her energy all the last week, covered over, shut away.

The rising moon had brought a chill creeping up from the river, carrying the raw smell of cold flood waters with it. Far down the valley and up past the haze-veiled Chimney Rock, and on west, scattered lights were blinking long past the supper cooking—mostly the fires of those

8

who had little interest or money for the inviting doorways near the bridge. Coyotes howled off in the breaks, answered by the dogs in the camp and perhaps a wolf or two, drawn toward this gathering of men and yet afraid; drawn also by the bawling of the beef herds being held along the river, and the occasional low of the quieter work bulls.

In the camp near the bridge there was the thin sawing of the breed fiddlers, the thunder of cowboys galloping in through the moonlight, with their "Yahoos!" and pistol shots. Their horses scattered the cursing crowd from their path, and the dust they raised shimmered in the lantern light from swinging doors and lifted tent flaps.

Although his graders must work through to morning, Robin Thomas felt that no matter how worn by the trip and the day, Morissa should not be left all alone tonight. He asked no questions of her, no explanation, just washed the dust from his long graying hair and beard, buckled on his gun, and took down the lantern. Then, with Morissa neat in a scotch-plaid walking suit only moderately bustled, and a sailor tilted over her bangs, he took her to see the camp, from Clarke's supply and whisky store at one end to the roadranch of Ettier, the Canadian Frenchman, at the other. They followed the light thrown by the lantern around to Etty's place first—a string of weathered sod and log shacks surrounded by a thick sod wall with strategic gun slits for defense. "Old Etty's been around here, on and off, more than twenty years. Stood off outlaw gangs and a few Sioux bucks full of whisky too, although he's married to a Sioux breed—nice woman," Robin said.

Inside the smoke hung thick around the kerosene wall lamps, the low rooms packed, particularly around the bar and the fiddlers. In one Morissa stared at stacks of gold coin glinting in the smoky light, so open and handy for any holdup's taking.

"Yes, it does look easy," Robin admitted, "but I saw a couple in here one night, trying to take it away from Etty. Instead they got that sawed-off shotgun he keeps under the bar, sticking up over it and aimed at the belly. I helped bury one of the robbers."

Between Etty's place and Clarke's were shacks, tents, and open-front shelters with counters rough-sawed from pine in the Wild Cat Mountains. These counters were all that separated the crowd from the whisky and the card sharps or perhaps a beckoning woman, her crib no more than a cot or bunk on stakes sunk into the ground behind a piece of hanging canvas. There were even covered wagons offering the evening's entertainment and necessities, the price a little less because it was three steps up, with the need to duck the head under the wagon bows.

All were busy tonight, particularly where there was gambling, with so many doubly hopeful now that a belt of gold nuggets had been found on Tom Reeder after he was pulled out of the water today, and more yellow dust in the little plank box in his wagon, fortunately chained

9

tight to the wagon bed. Morissa saw the leather pouches of gold it contained—enough to keep the man for life, it seemed. How he got it all, or where, she did not ask, but because the box was carried into the stage station by two men with armed guards riding alongside, all the camp knew what it must contain, and that it was a great deal.

The news of the gold and the nearness of it, the actual sight of such a treasure accumulated somehow by this one puny little man was like the swift warming fire of a placer strike in their midst. Within an hour some had traded their wagons and outfits for saddle horses, tame enough, if possible, to carry a pick and shovel and gold pan. Only half of those who started across the river made it, and one who was washed up on the north bank left his horse to drown in the quicksand. The rest were turned back by the refusal of their horses or their own courage. Some hurried west along the old Overland trail to the rock ford up the river, but that route was a couple days longer, and led up through wild and rugged country full of Indians and outlaws. Besides, tomorrow the native planking of Clarke's bridge would surely thunder to the thousands of impatient hoofs, and so for this one night many spent as though the hot drag of fortune already weighted down their jeans. Some even dropped coins into the hat of the sky pilot outside a whisky saloon, a tall, gaunt, bearded man with the anger of God on his tongue and the fire of another Eldorado burning in his eyes.

The girl held the hem of her skirts out of the dust as Robin Thomas guided her skillfully around the thickest press, past the lurching drunks, the loud-mouthed trouble-seekers whose guns should be taken away before they found it, and the urgently woman-hungry. Several times he stopped to introduce Morissa: "My daughter, Doctor Kirk—" saying it proudly to the handsome, bearded and warm-eyed Henry Clarke of the bridge, and to some Army officers.

"Yes, we're heading for Red Cloud Agency up the trail there," the young lieutenant said. "Reports are that the Sioux warriors have been slipping away north to Crazy Horse—gathering against our troops headed into the Yellowstone country."

"Plenty of them red devils're workin' up around the Black Hills," a freighter standing nearby complained. He had some mules driven off his last trip to Deadwood, and had bullet holes in his wagons to prove the attack. "There's thousands of them hungry bucks no more than a day's ride from here. Claim the bridge's on their land. Probably be burning it some cloudy night."

"Won't be an Indian loose by frost time," the officers promised as they moved jauntily away into the crowd, kept close together by the glowering faces all around them—men who remembered that the miners, even the women, were thrown out of the Black Hills by the

10

troops last year. One word from them could shut out every man here, close up the gold trail and its bridge tight as a jailhouse door.

Robin offered no softening words to all of this. Instead he showed Morissa her first ranch foreman, a man working for Bosler, the rancher and beef contractor charged with defrauding the Indians on government beef deliveries. Bosler had one of the biggest cattle outfits of the West. Claimed a hundred fifty miles of water here, and had the guns to hold it. "But that's the north bank, across the river—"

Morissa glanced over that way in the pale moonlight, but there was no time to consider these things tonight. She met several owners of the big freight outfits and an advance man for an English troupe of singers. They planned to put on some Gilbert and Sullivan for the miners at Deadwood Gulch, if a hall could be found, or some natural outdoor amphitheater. "Anywhere out under God's gentle sky," he said fervently, and received a roar of boisterous laughter, particularly from men who had faced blizzard and dust storm and hail.

Tris Polk came up, too, courteous this time, impersonally complimenting Morissa's riding and her skill with the sick. "—I hear the man is sleeping for the first time in days," he said.

"But it may not mean much. We can only hope," Morissa replied, matching the man's impersonality before the hundreds of people who stopped to watch this second encounter, to listen.

There were only a few women out tonight, mostly around the dances, particularly Etty's big one where the breed fiddlers sawed and stomped, and with Huff Johnson, who had a handsome Junoesque blonde standing beside him at the faro table. She couldn't be lured away even by Tris Polk, it seemed. "But Huff'll have trouble keeping Gilda Ross if Polk really wants her—" Robin predicted.

He pointed out a dozen men who were known as outlaws: holdup men, roadagents, murderers. Fly Speck Billy was still there, but when the young man lifted his hat gravely to Morissa, so recently his fellow traveler, Robin looked at the girl in surprised concern.

She managed to laugh a little. "Oh, water finds its own level very quickly. Or, as you recall Mother saying, 'Short grace for hungry folk.'"

"Or rubbin' your nose in a hog trough don't even make friends of the hogs," Robin answered sourly. Fly Speck was just out of the Ogallala jail because everybody was afraid to testify against a cold-blooded killer. And tonight many others of his kind were here, with the nearest sheriff clear down at Sidney and probably as anxious to stay alive as the next man. Robin had seen too many like Fly Speck since the days he helped grade the Union Pacific to Utah. He wondered what fat cow was drawing these buzzards here tonight. Clarke and the others hired good protection for their property. Sure, such protection was by

11

gunmen too, professional killers picked for their wide reputation, swift as striking rattlers, ready to shoot for the highest bidder. If that happened to be the law, it was lucky.

"—I got my fill of their breed years ago, but Jackie's excited as a kid by them," Robin said with deep concern. "I try to keep him up with my horse herd, helping the guard against Indians and horse thieves. Hard on him but keeps him away from the show-offs around the bridge here."

"Oh, Jackie's only sixteen," Morissa started to comfort. "He'll be all right—he's of your good stock—" but she caught herself, always having to stop her stupid tongue.

Robin seemed not to notice the girl's confusion. "Most of the outlaws here probably seemed good boys at sixteen to their mothers or older sisters," he said, "although I hear Fly Speck and many of the others were already hitting it for the frontier only a jump ahead of the sheriff by then."

Morissa stirred from her sudden weariness to look around again. Over half of those moving through the patches of light and shadow wore heavy cartridge belts, as Robin himself did. Some of the others, the gamblers at least, were certainly armed, too, if less conspicuously. It was a silencing thought, and after a while Robin decided that the girl was finally wearied to sleeping, so he took her back through the pool of light his lantern cast for their feet.

They stopped at the grading corral to look in on Tom Reeder in one of the bowed wagons, sleeping heavily although his small dose of morphia should have done no more than quiet him. As Morissa replenished the fire in the little wagon heater and smoothed the buffalo robe over the man, she wondered how much of this was disease and how much exhaustion and anxiety from guarding his treasure through the long dangers of Deadwood Gulch and the robber-infested trail. But it might be pneumonia developing after the snow water, or only a drug-given respite from a bad conscience.

Robin still seemed uneasy. "Reeder's gold could be what tolled in so many outlaws who're usually more comfortable operating over in Wyoming," he said. "Still, there can't be that much dust in that ditty box of his. If it got out that a haul was coming down, why wasn't that little string of wagons he traveled with held up? It must be something else. I better get back to my outfit—"

But in the little soddy beside the corral gate the father delayed his going and finally settled down on a nail keg for his evening pipe. Morissa sat hunched forward on the cot, worn and pale now for all her sunburn, her hat still on, staring straight before her. For a moment Robin thought of a grouse or a dove, wounded and huddled close as possible to the ground, looking straight ahead, as a man does with blood

12

in his mouth, his staring eyes slowly whitening. But this girl who had pulled herself up from her days as a woods colt on a poor-farm was no dove or even a grouse, no matter what the wounding, nor how surely she had fled to crouch here on the cot beside a wilderness river, here where none except her stepfather knew her, or few were sufficiently whole to see her pain.

"Morissa," Robin said softly, "Morissa, do you want to tell me why you came? Last I knew the wedding was next week—"

A long time the girl made no reply, so still the old cot did not creak. "No—I guess there's nothing to tell," she said at last.

"It wasn't just a lovers' quarrel?"

Morissa shook her head, her eyes bleak in the lantern light. "He asked for his ring back," she said. "Couldn't take me into the family, not after what his sister found out—" The girl stopped, her full soft lips quivering for the first time.

"Found out?—about your mother? Oh, I could kill the fool!" Robin exploded, his voice loud as though shouting against a northwest blizzard wind. "No," he added, more moderately, "that wouldn't help. But you know you are welcome here with me, Morissa, to all these poor accommodations. Now get a little sleep. We'll need you tomorrow. There will be man and animal hurt in the tearing hurry tomorrow."

He started out, but turned at the door and slowly unbuckled his gun. "I better leave this with you. There's no law here for anybody, you know, except what you make."

Reluctantly the girl reached out and took the heavy cartridge belt, holding it away from her as she laid it on the end of the cot, not touching the grip of the revolver that fit so snugly into its worn leather nest.

II

MORISSA AWOKE INTO THE EMPTINESS OF A GREAT SORROW AND loss. She kept her eyes closed and held herself quiet, waiting for what seemed a nightmare to pass. But the sense of it remained, and finally she had to acknowledge that she was not asleep, that the foolish goose-mush of dead tears in her eyes was real, and to admit once more that her grief and desolation were of the daytime, of the waking hours. "Allston—Allston," she found herself repeating monotonously, over and over, the dull sound of it like some far, hard-heeled foot on stone. But there was another drumming, the memory of one of her grandmother's

13

sayings: "It's nae lack o' tongue that keeps the kine from speech—"
Nor lack of the beloved that keeps a woman from her work.

So, while still hiding in her own darkness, Morissa swung her long, gown-covered legs over the side of the bed and was astonished that they dropped so soon, the bed so narrow, only a creaking cot. Her sleep-blurred eyes flew open to the bare sod walls and the early sun stretched over the packed dirt floor from the bare dusty window. Horsebackers were riding by on the trail that passed just outside, the campers beyond it out and shouting, rattling harness, getting under way. Then she remembered. She was at the North Platte bridge and she had a patient in one of Robin's wagons, a man who almost died yesterday.

Amazed that she could have slept so deeply when there seemed so little rest all the last week, she dressed quickly, slipping into her gray street brilliantine with the mustard-colored braiding, although calico would have been more suitable to a wilderness. But this was warmer, and would shed the dust of today. Then, with her hair still in the thick braid down her back, she went out, stopping to look under her palm toward the sun just up over the long, low bridge that waited in silence now, the hammer down, the last of the pilings set, work teams moving to draw the tower away.

But a very sick patient was waiting, so the young doctor hurried across the dewy ground. The man was awake, attempting to sit up, his gaunt, gray-stubbled face bleak with fear at the approach. When he saw who it was stooping under the wagon bows, he let himself back, yet still uneasy, alarmed.

"My outfit—was it all lost?" he whispered.

"Oh, no, Mr. Reeder, only one of the horses. Your box is safe at the stage station, your gold belt too," Morissa Kirk assured him cheerfully as she turned out the swinging lantern, refolded the soogan that served as a pillow, and turned the heavy buffalo robe back. She smiled down into the whitened, suspicious eyes and nodded in approval that his tin cup of soup was empty. Then she took the man's temperature and pulse, washed his gaunt-face and prepared him for the examination she had postponed when there was still the shock and exhaustion and the danger of pneumonia from the flood. Yesterday he was a man to be kept alive; today he was one to be cured.

After a while he began to talk, slowly, weakly at first, but with urgent snatches about some trouble last night. "All that yellin' an' shootin'," he complained in a vague, futile anger. "Mebby they was stickin' up the stage station, my gold all gone—"

"Oh, I don't think so. Mr. Clarke has a good guard set," Morissa comforted. "But there are a lot of wild, lawless people around a place like this. I know a little about such things. My father is boss grader here."

14

The man's pale eyes considered the young woman, still suspicious, guarded. "They was a powerful lot a that noise last night," he argued stubbornly. "An' they hung a man."

Morissa looked up at this, and put the thermometer back between the gray lips. He mumbled around it, and she shook her head, but when she squinted in satisfaction at the tube he started his rambling talk about the night again.

"Well, at least your dreams aren't dull," the young doctor soothed as she started to go over the man methodically, particularly the hollow belly and the bony chest that was only yellowish skin over bones as bare as the wagon bows. "It's there, the hole that's gnawin'," the man said as she probed below the ribs for a possible growth or sign of infection, congestion—anything that might cause this emaciation, and was pleased that there was only a general tenderness, and also that the man seemed able to forget that she was a woman. But suddenly, in the midst of his aimless rambling about the hanging, Tom Reeder stopped and grabbed for the buffalo robe. "I ain't gonna be shamed this way by no she-doc!" he shouted hoarsely, sweat popping out milky on his face.

Morissa tucked in the corners of her mouth and wiped the man's forehead. "Would you object to your nakedness if I was a prostitute?"

That brought a swift flush of weakness to the hollow eye sockets. "No—" the man admitted, looking away from the face of the handsome girl. "No, I guess not. Mebby the body's an evil thing, an' that's shamin' to decent eyes."

"Nonsense. Have you never heard that the body is God's temple? It can be desecrated but never made shameful. Here, turn this way."

And at the matter-of-factness of the young woman, Tom Reeder became silent, apparently in weakness, although his wasted muscles were tense, ungiving as ropes of chicken wire. So Morissa turned the talk to his dream again. "—Maybe it was after you awoke this morning, and then dozed off. That's when you remember the dreams so clearly."

"No, I hearn him, yellin'—"

"Who?"

"I don' know—some poor bastard," he said, closing his eyes. He did not see the pain his words brought to the young face bent above him. Quickly the doctor spread the buffalo robe over the man as over a child and went out. Later she brought him beef broth that Clarke's cook sent over and the egg she whipped up in a little hot whisky and sugar. The man helped lift himself obediently to the cup, but was palsied with weakness, and then lay back, belching and exhausted, his fading eyes closed.

Her head stooped to the wagon bows, Morissa considered her patient, a frown of perplexity under her soft bangs. Such weakness and emaciation without real pain, only that feeling of a hole through the middle—

15

it might be an ulcer. Not yet perforated, judging by the low temperature, but a serious ulcer nevertheless. Surely the man had a very bad stomach. Yet the West, with its game eaten before the juices broke down into carrion fit only for the iron stomach of a buzzard, had relieved many such ailments. "Fresh meat and the healthy weariness of the outdoors," Dr. Aiken of the medical school had told Morissa's class. "We used to send our chronic stomach cases out to the Indian country to die, get them off our doorstep, but they had a way of returning robust and cured. Many developed a taste for game with the animal heat—"

From the step of the wagon, Morissa looked toward the bridge, with its railings that were like the rickrack edgings of an apron string. The last span of planks was being put down and the scrapers glistened as their smooth undersides were flipped over to the sun. The queue of those waiting to cross reached far back along the trail, as far as the turn at Courthouse Rock. Up close horsebackers and lighter wagon outfits, the actual gold seekers, were trying to push into the space saved for Clarke's pony express rider and the stagecoaches, the nearer ones maneuvering and shouting, ready to jam the narrow bridge the moment the long toll arm went up. But mounted men with rifles across their saddles stood against them.

There was another group of watchers, a smaller one and mostly afoot, down at the water's edge. They looked toward the bridge too, but were motioning to a span where something hung from a point of the railing, something that resembled a suspended man.

Shielding the sun from her eyes, Morissa went over that way planning to laugh a little, if she could, as one did at the dummies hung to telegraph poles along the tracks at Sidney to shock the gullible Eastern passengers. But she slowed her step when one of the group called to her. "That's number one on this bridge, Doc, an' room for a lot more!"

The form was unmistakably a man, a man with a tortured, an awful tilt to the head, his chin turned up and a little to the side, as though in pained disdain of the noose about his neck, the horror only in the staring eyes, and in the body's acceptance of defeat in all the downhanging lines, the hands turned palm out in pitiful supplication. To Morissa it seemed a willful, a deliberate and dreadful violence; a sacrilege put upon the most beautifully balanced and artistic instrument, the human body; a defilement upon the finest, the noblest creation, the mind of man.

In a cold fury at this tolerance, this public approval of such violence, such murder, the young doctor could endure no further sight of these people here, not one glimpse. Forgetting her hair still in the braid, she gathered up her skirts as from contamination and hurried over to the

16